HIS TO CHERISH

TITANS QUARTER, BOOK 3

SIERRA CARTWRIGHT

HIS TO CHERISH

Copyright @ 2021 Sierra Cartwright

First E-book Publication: March 2021

Editing by Nicki Richards, What's Your Story Editorial Services

Line Editing by Jennifer Barker

Proofing by Bev Albin and Cassie Hess-Dean

Layout Design by Once Upon an Alpha

Cover Design by Rachel Connolly

Photo provided by Depositphotos.com

Promotion by Once Upon An Alpha, Shannon Hunt

All rights reserved. Except for use in a review, no part of this publication may be reproduced, distributed, or transmitted in any form, or by any means, electronic or mechanical, including photocopying, recording, or by any information storage and retrieval system, without prior written permission of the author.

This is a work of fiction. Names, characters, places, brands, media, and incidents are either the products of the author's imagination or are used fictitiously, and any resemblance to any actual persons, living or dead, is entirely coincidental.

The author acknowledges the trademarked status and trademark owners of various products referenced in this work of fiction. The publication/use of these trademarks is not authorized, associated with, or sponsored by the trademark owners.

Adult Reading Material

Disclaimer: This work of fiction is for mature (18+) audiences only and contains strong sexual content and situations.

It is a standalone with my guarantee of satisfying happily ever after.

All rights reserved.

DEDICATION

For everyone who has ever taken a chance on love.

CHAPTER 1

"Which floor?"
"Twelve, thanks." Emma exhaled her relief. The gentleman in the elevator had patiently held the door open while she hurried across the lobby of the New Orleans office building. She'd been at lunch too long—the quarterly gathering with her college girlfriends had been too scandalous and delicious to leave. As the waiter had brought a second glass of wine for each of them, they'd shared stories of their sex lives—the thrills and droughts—and now she was in danger of running late for a meeting with a client.

The man pushed the button for the twelfth floor and then fifteen—presumably his—as the compartment closed.

"How's the book?"

"Umm. This?" Self-consciously she moved the bestselling paperback behind her. "I just borrowed it from a friend." Borrowed it? Pried it from Kathleen's unwilling fingers was more like it. Everywhere Emma went, people were talking about the novel, and after some of her friends' confessions over lunch, Emma had been desperate to read it. Though she had a couple of friends who were into BDSM, she knew little about it. What she did know intrigued her. But where would she find a man into that kind of kink? Her last boyfriend, Aaron, had called her a freak when she'd bought a couple of scarves and asked him to tie her up with them. Later, she found out that was only the beginning of their problems.

"Do you know anything about the novel?"

She took a second look at the man next to her. He was taller than her, by at least a couple of inches, and that said something. In heels, she wasn't used to looking up at many people.

He appeared to be in his mid-thirties, and his thick dark hair had a hint of gray at the temples, which added to his dangerous and distinguished good looks.

Even though she knew she was staring, she couldn't look away. His eyes were a startling shade of green, dark and intense. She had an odd, feminine sense that he saw through her tough exterior into her innermost secrets.

"So, do you?"

Stalling for time, she pretended to misunderstand. "Do I what?"

"Do you know anything about the book?"

He captured her gaze. Instinct told her to look away, but she couldn't. Unnerved, she tightened her grip on her purse strap. "It's hard not to. It's being talked about everywhere." Realizing she was in danger of babbling, something she did *not* do, she changed the direction of the conversation. "Have you read it?"

"I haven't read it, no. There's no need."

"No need?"

His scent seemed to brand the air—something crisp and outdoorsy, a stamp of primal male power and intrigue.

He reached inside his suit jacket.

Emma made a decent living as a financial adviser, and she recognized quality. The suit that had been exquisitely tailored to fit his toned body cost at least a month of her salary.

"I live the lifestyle."

"The lifestyle? Meaning?" A bell dinged, indicating that she'd reached her floor.

"I'm a Dominant." He extracted his wallet, then offered her his business card. "Look me up if you're curious."

Without looking at it, she accepted his offering and tucked it into her purse.

The doors slid open. As if hypnotized, she remained rooted in place.

Because she hadn't moved, he reached out to press a button to prevent the car from closing. As he did, a wink of gold flashed from his cufflink. What kind of man still wore those to work?

"I look forward to hearing from you. Ms.…?"

Automatically, maybe foolishly, she provided it. "Monroe. Emma Monroe."

He smiled, and something warm passed through her. "Very soon." This man, tall and broad, had an air of easy command, as if he was accustomed to issuing orders and having others obey. She had an insane urge to treat him with respect he'd yet to earn. Her entire body warmed beneath his attention.

He stepped aside, and she exited the elevator. Wondering what had happened, Emma just stood there.

"Oh my Lord! You were on the elevator with Philip Dettmer? Hello…? Earth to Emma…"

She looked at Lori, the firm's receptionist. Lori had been with Larson Financial almost as long as Emma had been. "That was Philip Dettmer?" Though it was fruitless, she looked over her shoulder.

"Yeah. The one. The only." Lori sighed. "The unbearably sexy."

Emma knew his name—who in Louisiana didn't? He was legendary when it came to buying businesses, whether or not they wanted to be bought. He owned stakes in the local football team and was rumored to be a billionaire. From his air of confidence, she certainly believed it. Of course she knew the name, but she didn't follow the local media enough to have recognized him.

Lori was making an elaborate show of fanning herself with a file folder. "Every time I see him, he makes me want to do things that are immoral."

Tingles still raced through Emma's body. "Does he come here often?"

"He has a business associate in this building. Gavin McLeod."

Another name she recognized.

"Anyway, you know Marjorie who works in the lobby? She sends a text to a few of us when Mr. Dettmer walks in. I do my best to catch a glimpse of him. Maybe I should just start riding the elevator when she messages me."

"He saw my book." Emma held up the paperback.

"Whoa. Seriously?"

"And, uhm, he asked if I'd read it."

"Holy shit. You talked about *sex* with Philip Dettmer?" The manila folder swished to the floor. "Get *out*!"

"Not about sex exactly."

"Just about kink?"

She didn't tell Lori that he'd passed along his business card and invited her to look him up.

"I'd get naked and do the nasty with him in under a second. The jealousy monster has colored me green."

The phone rang, and Lori moved to answer it, chirruping a professional greeting, even though she gave Emma a wide smile and a big thumbs-up.

Emma continued to her office and shut the door. For a

moment, she leaned her shoulders against the wood. Her heart was racing, and she couldn't seem to banish the scent of him.

Good God, she had this kind of reaction, and he hadn't even touched her.

She took a deep breath, then smoothed her skirt as she walked to her desk to hide the book. As she closed it in a drawer, she told herself to focus. Her client was due to arrive in less than five minutes. Her voicemail notification was blinking madly, and she still had investments to research before going home. She didn't have time to think about Philip Dettmer, or having him do delicious, naughty things to her.

Despite her determination, she struggled to keep thoughts of their interaction at bay. Her concentration repeatedly wandered off, and as a result, she had to stay at the office longer than anticipated to finish her projects.

Once she arrived home, she kicked off her pumps, then changed into leggings and an oversize T-shirt bearing a map of the French Quarter. After grabbing a glass of wine, she hurried into her office to power up her computer to learn everything she could about Philip Dettmer.

Page after page of information appeared, covering everything from his business dealings to his charitable endeavors. But then she couldn't resist opening *Scandalicious*, her favorite online gossip magazine, to read stories about his failed marriage. His ex—Anna Lively—had made a number of vague but awful allegations of marital misconduct. She'd never given any details, saying a gag order prevented her from discussing the proceedings. But she'd painted her husband as the villain among villains.

For the next year or so, there were no mentions of Philip. But then articles about him began to pop up, along with rumors of romances, a few of them with actresses or models, and even an heiress. Emma leaned forward to study the dates on his recent pictures. Since his divorce, it seemed as if none of his relationships had lasted more than a single date.

He looked heart-stoppingly hot in a tuxedo on the red carpet. He was fuck-me gorgeous in jeans and a brown leather bomber jacket. And, oh God, the one of him emerging from the Caribbean-blue surf? As she'd already guessed, Philip Dettmer worked out. The picture was grainy —probably a *Scandalicious* paparazzi shot—but she noticed a small amount of tantalizing chest hair that arrowed downward, disappearing into the waistband of his swim trunks.

And he wants me to contact him?

Dare she?

She shook her head. *What's wrong with me?* She shouldn't be contemplating a hook-up with a billionaire. A hook-up? More like a scene where he tied her up and spanked her.

He was out of her league, and she knew next to nothing about the kinky lifestyle he professed to live.

Before she could change her mind, she closed her web browser and powered down the computer.

With a sigh, she returned to the living room to pick up the paperback before heading to the master bathroom to turn on the bathwater. Tonight a shower wouldn't do. She needed a long, leisurely soak with bubbles, wine, and her book.

An hour later, she'd read a hundred scorching pages that had left her feeling restless. She'd finished the glass of wine, and she'd reheated the bathwater twice.

Emma slammed the book closed, dropped it on the floor, leaned back against the bath pillow, and closed her eyes. Part of her wished she'd never started down this path.

Until now, every one of her sexual experiences had been ho-hum and boring. Her last relationship had ended more than six months ago, and clearly the drought was getting to her. How else could she explain the fact she was fantasizing about Philip Dettmer tying her hands behind her back and bending her over the bed? He'd use one of the scarves she'd bought, or maybe handcuffs… He'd tell her, in detail, what he was going to do to her before slapping her ass hard.

She opened her eyes. It was almost as if she could feel the pressure of his open-handed strike on her buttocks.

What the hell was going on? Emma had always been practical and realistic, never given to flights of fancy. She'd studied hard, graduated with honors, and secured a great job. But now…?

She climbed from the bathtub and wrapped herself in a fluffy towel. Maybe it was because she'd read the book, or from the risqué lunch conversation, but she was more turned on than she remembered being. She grabbed a vibrator from the nightstand drawer and lay down on the bed.

After turning on the switch, Emma parted her thighs and placed the egg-shaped toy against her pussy. She finally admitted the truth to herself. Her arousal wasn't from the novel or from the discussion with her friends. It was the chance meeting with Mr. Dettmer. The scent of him, combined with his aura of authority and bold words, had made it impossible for her to have a single rational thought.

The vibrator's humming, pulsing sensation pushed her to the edge. Even though she dug her heels into the mattress and continued to move the egg against her swollen clit, the orgasm loomed out of reach.

Frustrated, she turned the toy to its highest setting and pinched her right nipple. The pain was exquisite. Would Mr. Dettmer do the same if she scened with him? Or would he use clamps on her? In her fantasy, he tormented her ruthlessly, showing no mercy even though she begged for it.

Would he be like the hero in the book, using bondage

gear to tie her up while he ripped orgasm after orgasm from her poor body?

In her fevered imagination, she submitted to him. Emma had no idea what that really meant, but she wanted to find out. She wanted to kneel for him, to follow his orders, to get rid of her inhibitions with a man who wasn't afraid of her sexuality. For her, that was what it was really about. Even when she was in a committed relationship, her sex drive was never satiated.

Her pussy got wetter and wetter as she imagined Philip Dettmer's hands on her body. His touch wouldn't be gentle, but it would be what she needed.

Enough to actually call him?

Before today, she might have said no.

But the lunch with her friends had been liberating. Talking about the book had allowed Emma and her friends to share their innermost desires.

One of her best friends, Shelby, was in a lifestyle BDSM relationship with her fiancé, Trevor. According to Shelby, he'd helped her get past her awful hang-ups about commitment, and she seemed even more confident now than she ever had. Emma knew her friend occasionally visited a club in the French Quarter with Trevor.

The idea of being with a Dominant in public made Emma tighten her grip on her nipple. As she squirmed, she pictured Mr. Dettmer slapping her pussy *hard*.

The combination of her thoughts and the slight pain was enough to make her cry out. Then she imagined him naked, his cock erect, digging his hand into her hair before forcing that big dick inside her needy pussy. The thought of him relentlessly fucking her pushed her to the edge.

Wave after wave assailed her. She'd never had an orgasm this sustained. Shock waves of sensation flooded her pussy. This was what she'd always wanted, dreamed of.

Soon the intensity from the vibrator became too much, and she dropped it, leaving it humming on the mattress while she drank in gulps of air.

It took a full minute for her to breathe normally again. Finally, she sat up and switched off the small egg. Her legs were wobbly as she stood to pull on a nightshirt.

The climax had been good, and yet the odd restlessness persisted. She usually fell asleep after an orgasm, but tonight she tossed and turned as scenes from the book teased her. In her imagination, she was the heroine of the story, and Philip Dettmer tied her, spanked her, tormented, and clamped her. He administered the pain she craved, until she screamed her pleasure and begged for the relief that he repeatedly denied her.

It was well after midnight when she drifted off, and she was awake again before her alarm clock rang. Her heart beat quickly, and her blood hummed as if she'd already had a pot of coffee.

Sometime during the night, she'd reached a decision to get in contact with Mr. Dettmer.

She wanted the experience he offered, at least once. He might be disappointed in her, but she'd have the memory to last a lifetime.

Before she could change her mind, she grabbed his business card from her purse, then picked up her phone. Needing fortification before taking the leap, she shuffled into the kitchen and made a cup of coffee from her single-cup brewer. After a long sip, she opened her email program and typed in his name.

For minutes, she struggled with what to write before settling on something mundane. *"It's Emma Monroe. I met you in the elevator yesterday. I'm curious."*

Her hand shook as she hit Send.

Over the next hour as she got ready for work, she

agonized, alternately wishing she'd never sent the email and obsessively checking for a response.

Emma was on the way out of the door when her cell phone signaled an incoming email. Curiosity wouldn't allow her to leave it unread. What if it was from *him?*

She juggled her to-go cup of coffee, her purse, and her tote onto the hallway table. Her heart momentarily stopped, then raced on madly when she saw he'd answered.

Call me.

He'd offered a phone number, and nothing else. Emma collapsed against the wall and stared at the screen.

After much internal debate, she took a deep breath and touched the number. The phone gave her the option to confirm her choice. This time she didn't hesitate. Her mind was made up. She wanted to be with a man—at least once—who didn't think her sexual desires were abnormal.

The first ring hadn't even finished when he answered. "Dettmer."

Oh God. She'd forgotten how rich his voice was, how compelling. With a single word, he'd made her damp. "Hello…" She paused, uncertain how to address him. Sir? Philip? Mr. Dettmer?

He waited. Even through the phone lines, she sensed his patience. "It's Emma Monroe." She hesitated. This was more difficult than she'd imagined. "We met yesterday in the elevator."

"How's the book?"

"It's, uhm…"

"Did you masturbate last night?"

Her knees weakened. "You don't waste time on small talk, do you?"

"Do you want me to?"

Awkwardly, she laughed. "It might make it a bit easier."

"Is that what you really want, Emma? For me to make

things easier for you? Or do you want to confess to me that you played with yourself last night while you thought about me and what I might do to you if you begged prettily enough?"

His words, a whispered, sexy purr, made her gasp.

Before she could formulate an answer, he went on. "How many times did you come, Emma?"

The dialogue in the novel had been one of the things that had turned her on most, but now that Philip Dettmer, *the* Philip Dettmer, was being so blunt, she found herself flustered. "Just once," she said.

"Did you use a toy, or just your hand?"

"Uhm... A toy." The word *Sir* was on the tip of her tongue, and she almost, almost, used it. She'd never had that kind of inclination with any man before, but then she'd never met a man this powerful, this direct.

"Tell me more. Where were you? What were you thinking of?"

Thank God she hadn't returned his call from the office. "Last night I took a bath." She hesitated, but he didn't fill the silence. She sensed he'd wait her out, no matter how long it took. Nervously she continued. "I had a glass of wine, and I read for about an hour in the tub. You know, the book I had in the elevator."

Again he said nothing.

"Then I went to bed with my vibrator."

"Continue."

With her free hand she pushed hair back from her face. "I was thinking about scenes I'd just read, but my imagination took over." Admitting all this was embarrassing. Part of her wondered what she was doing. Emma reminded herself that she'd sought him out. "I was tied up." Before courage completely deserted her, she went on. "I imagined a sharp slap between my legs."

"On your pussy?"

"Yes."

"If that's what you mean, then say it."

No man had ever demanded she use dirty language. It was unnerving. Liberating. "I imagined being slapped on my pussy."

"Ah. Was that when you came?"

She whispered her confession. "Yes."

"Has that ever been done to you?"

"No. Never."

"Is it merely a fantasy? Or would you like to have your pussy spanked, Emma?"

Oh. God. She could barely breathe. The tone of his voice—seductive *and* firm—sent a bolt of electricity through her body.

"Answer the question."

"Yes."

"Speak a little louder, please."

This man would never let her hide. It took all her courage to be honest with him. "Yes." She cleared her throat. "I would like that."

"Good girl."

His words were a purr of approval, making her heart race.

"How much experience do you have with BDSM?"

"Actually, to tell the truth? None. And when I suggested it to my boyfriend—"

"Current or prior?"

"Oh! Prior." She was flustered, and a little offended. "I'm not a cheater, Mr. Dettmer."

"Glad to hear. Please, go on."

The fact that they were on the phone made this discussion easier. "Anyway, Aaron called me a freak, and he used that as an excuse to start dating another woman—someone who was less demanding."

"While he was still seeing you?"

It had been worse than that. "I was living with him." Admitting this brought back the pain as well as the humiliation. "We'd been looking at rings…" *Talking about having babies.* "Anyway, he said no self-respecting man would want to be married to a woman who had those kind of perversions."

"He was a fool, Emma. Complete and total. Everything you want—and more—is perfectly normal. If you want my opinion…?"

She was curious. "Yes."

"Aaron was a coward who had likely checked out of the relationship long before this. Couples who are committed to one another workout the issues that they have by talking about them, not by walking away."

She nodded, even though he couldn't see her.

"You're as beautiful as you are bold. Any man would be lucky to claim you as his. Something was wrong with him, Emma, not with you. I promise you that."

His reassurance chased goose bumps up her arms.

"And let me tell you this. Plenty of women love having their pussies spanked." That husky growl of sexiness was back in his voice. "And frankly, I enjoy doing it." He waited a moment, allowing the time to stretch while her pulse rocketed into overdrive. "If you'd like to have your gorgeous little cunt tormented, *by me,* all you have to do is ask."

Her knees wobbled, and terror tightened her vocal cords.

With that seemingly infinite patience, he waited.

Finally she cleared her throat. Hoping she was using the correct words, she asked, "Will you please spank my pussy?"

"I'd be honored to, as hard as you want. When?"

She almost repeated the question before realizing how inane that would sound. "Whenever you're available."

"We have a few options. You can come to my home. We can go to my club. Or I can come to you."

Emma hadn't thought through the practicalities. If she went to him, she had the option of leaving if things spiraled out of control. At her place, she would feel more secure. She wasn't sure about the idea of playing in public, but that was probably the safest option, at least until she knew him better. "Maybe a club would be best." Absently she wondered if it was the same one that Shelby went to. If so, maybe she knew Mr. Dettmer.

"Agreed. I'll be traveling extensively in the next ten days. How about we meet two weeks from now? Are Tuesdays good for you?"

She wasn't sure if the time was too long or far, far too short for her to work up the nerve to go through with this.

"Emma?"

Determinedly she shook herself out of her reverie. "That will be fine, Mr. Dettmer."

"My club is in the French Quarter."

Parking was notoriously difficult there, and she didn't like to go alone.

"I'm happy to send a car so you don't have to worry about anything."

There were constant reminders of who she was dealing with. She was pretty sure he didn't mean he'd send a taxi or rideshare service.

"I will always ensure your safety and comfort, Emma."

"Thank you. That would be nice."

"Wear a skirt and heels. Your shirt should be button-down. I'll leave the choice of undergarments up to you. If things go the way I hope, they won't stay on long. In the meantime, I'll be in touch with a list of reading materials. Of course I'll be available to answer any questions." He paused. "I look forward to getting to know you much, much better. By the time I'm done with you, you'll have no secrets to hide."

Her hand was shaking as he ended the call. She pressed the device nervously against her chest. *What have I agreed to?*

CHAPTER 2

"My God, Emma. You're so very stunning when you suffer for me."

Although he was in San Francisco, and they hadn't yet played together in person, Philip Dettmer's approval slid through her, feeding her determination. She could do this.

Right now, they were connected via video conference call, and she was lying naked on her back, with her legs spread and her nipples clamped with terrible Japanese clovers.

"Now, place the chain between your teeth."

Which would make the pressure even more unbearable. Why had she admitted she wanted to play with these little monsters to begin with?

Ever since that fateful elevator ride more than a week prior, he'd stayed in contact with her. In addition to calling her each evening, he sent her articles to read, and he'd even sent her a few BDSM instruction manuals. Additionally, he'd recommended she join an online group where she could network with other submissives and learn more about the lifestyle.

After a few conversations, he'd begun to give her instructions. The first—and most important one—was the most difficult. Not to orgasm without permission.

Last weekend, he'd had fancy Bonds electronic equipment—a camera, new computer, monitor, microphone—delivered and set up, and it hadn't taken her long to realize that he enjoyed watching her play with herself.

"You're hesitating."

She sighed. Because of the way the camera and computer monitor were positioned, she couldn't see him, but he could see every part of her exposed body.

"Emma?"

His voice was both calm and patient, as she'd come to expect. "It will hurt."

"I imagine it will." Humor laced his words. "By not doing as you're told, you're adding more time to the clock."

Her nipples were already a little sore, but she knew he wouldn't relent. Nor did she want him to.

They talked every day, and he wanted to know everything about her. He'd shared plenty in return, including the fact his divorce had left him determined to avoid committed relationships. Since she wasn't looking for that either, this temporary arrangement suited her fine.

As part of their ongoing discussions, they'd agreed on a safe word that was easy to remember. She decided on *transfer* since it was a term she used often at work. If she uttered it, whatever they were doing would immediately stop. And he'd given her the option of saying yellow to slow down or talk about things.

After she'd read the books he'd sent over and done a lot of research, she'd sent him a limits list—toys or scenarios that were hard nos. He'd also insisted on her sharing things she wanted to explore. Stupidly, she'd said she was curious about clamps. Since she didn't have any of her own, he'd sent her several different choices. Neither the lightweight tweezers nor the mandible-style ones had provided her with enough pleasure, which was how she found herself in her current predicament.

"You're at two minutes."

Damn him. He was relentless, and this was awful. Paradoxically, she loved both.

"You're welcome to use a safe word. Or I can just add another fifteen seconds."

"Let's just stay at the two minutes. Sir."

"I'm not sure where you got the idea that this was a negotiation, my delightful submissive. You're now at two minutes and thirty seconds."

She closed her eyes.

"And heading to forty-five."

This was never going to get any easier. On the other hand, the sooner she got on with it, the sooner it would be done. Maybe if she didn't stall, he'd allow her to play with her vibrator for ten minutes before bed. "Yes, Sir." Her voice trembled with misery, and he chuckled softly. *Sadist.*

With a sigh, she grabbed the chain and placed it between her teeth, which elongated her nipples.

"Now tip your head back."

That was impossible. No way she could endure that kind of agony.

"It wasn't a request, Emma. Please do as you're told."

Whimpering as each excruciating moment passed, she complied with his order.

"Fuck." His whisper wrapped around the room, giving her strength. "I wish you could see yourself, the way your face expresses your pain, the way your body vibrates from the tension."

As he'd previously instructed, she concentrated on his words and on her breathing.

"I'm watching the timer. I'll let you know when you're getting close. For now, surrender to the moment."

Emma did her best to relax, not that it was easy. But imagining the way she looked to him made this more bearable.

During their numerous conversations, he'd been clear about the need for honest discussion, and he'd been transparent in return. He'd expressed that he'd always had an interest in BDSM and that he wasn't involved in a relationship. He fulfilled his need to Dominate with a willing submissive at the club. After a scene or two, he returned to his regular life, free of entanglements.

He admitted that giving women what they wanted sexually was the ultimate aphrodisiac for him. She absolutely believed him. His rare smiles were reserved for when she sighed with satisfaction after an orgasm.

Philip lapsed into silence, and the only sounds were of her tiny moans and her breathing.

As the seconds ticked on, her experience began to transform.

She allowed her shoulders to soften, using a technique she'd learned in an introductory yoga class.

"That's it, Emma." His words were as soft as they were approving. "That's it."

Then she decided not to think about how much longer she had to get through, and instead surrendered to the moment.

Shockingly, she began to get aroused. Then, desperate for an orgasm, she moved one hand between her legs.

"I know you're needy, but please keep your arms at your sides. And spread your thighs farther apart. I want a good view of your pussy."

His demands were impossible.

"You can do it."

"Oomph." Her temporary Dominant had no interest in her protests. In fact, he seemed to thrive on her misery.

Her torment went on forever. Now that he wouldn't let her touch herself, she was ready to climb the walls. Everything was too much. The pain, the longing, the sexual frustration.

"Time. You may remove one of the clamps."

One?

"And you may thank me for my generosity."

Of course she should have thought about that right away. He'd repeatedly prompted her to express her gratitude when he was kind or thoughtful.

Since she was still holding the chain in her mouth, her words of thanks were garbled. She released one nipple and cried out when the blood surged into it, creating a fresh wave of agony as well as a greater demand for an orgasm.

"You'll be more than ready to meet me at the Quarter on Tuesday evening."

"I'm ready *now*."

Somehow he must have understood her garbled words, because he chuckled, and it wrapped around her with diabolical amusement.

When her nipple returned to its regular size and shape, he allowed her to release the second from its constraint.

Trying to escape all the sensations rushing through her body, she arched her back.

"The way you're feeling? The endorphins? They can be addictive."

No doubt he was right. The more she played with him, the more she wanted.

"Would you like to say something to me now that I've allowed you to remove both?"

"Thank you." And she meant it. "Thank you, Sir."

"Please get dressed."

She blinked as she sat up. Was he serious? "You're really not going to let me come?"

"Did I say anything confusing to you?"

"But—" Emma stopped herself from saying anything else.

"Smart girl."

"Call me back on the telephone." With that, he signed off.

As she slipped into a silk robe, she was so very tempted to touch herself. After all, he would never know. But she would.

From the research she'd done, she knew that a power exchange—and turning over control—was part of having a Dominant. Most of it was a wild thrill, but the way he withheld climaxes was frustrating as hell. She sighed. And if he let her do as she wished, he wouldn't be what she wanted at all. God. The contradiction was so confusing.

Emma poured herself a glass of wine, then went outside onto the patio. The fall air was unbelievably warm and heavy with humidity. This evening, that suited her. After what she'd just gone through, her muscles were tight, and being outside soothed them.

Once she was seated on a comfortable chair, she pressed Philip's speed dial number.

It hadn't taken her long to be accustomed to spending her evenings with him, no matter where he was in the country.

She looked forward to talking about her explorations as well as catching tidbits of information about his life. It was intimate, reminding her of what she was missing by not being in a relationship.

When he answered, he skipped the normal greetings. "That was very good, Emma. You pleased me."

She would endure a lot just to hear the warm note of approval in his voice. "Thank you, Sir."

"Perfect response as well. You're learning."

"Sir is an excellent instructor."

"Tell me about the experience."

Emma enjoyed the way he deconstructed everything they shared. "The reality wasn't as bad as I'd expected."

He remained silent while she looked for the right words. She took a sip of her white zinfandel before continuing. "It hurt, but not like I thought it would. And the pain vanished almost immediately." But the urge to masturbate remained, and it was every bit as powerful as it had been ten minutes ago.

"I'm looking forward to being the one to put clamps on your nipples."

The idea of his powerful hands cupping her breasts rocked a blast of pleasure down her spine. "Are we allowed to do that at the club?" A couple of days ago, she'd talked to her friend Shelby, who—as Emma had guessed—was also a member of the same club that he was. Evidently, the owner, Mistress Aviana, had rules to protect submissives and others to ensure privacy. In all the years that she'd been in business, there'd never been a single scandal.

"Yes and no."

"Oh?" Shelby hadn't told Emma very many details about the place, and even her searches had revealed frustratingly little information about the building, and there were no pictures online. There were occasional Explore days, where the space was open to nonmembers, but details were only revealed to people who signed up and signed a nondisclosure agreement. Otherwise, it was impossible to get an invitation.

"There are no exposed nipples allowed in the club, so you'll see a lot of pasties and tape to cover up. But there are private rooms available, and if we're in one of them, then we can do anything we want. Mistress Aviana's Safe, Sane, and Consensual policy reigns, and scenes are checked on by her dungeon monitors."

"Are you saying that's what you want to do? Be alone, I mean."

"Not at all. What happens is entirely your call. We decided to meet at a club for safety concerns."

Back then she hadn't known him as well as she did now. Last week, Mr. Dettmer had spoken to Shelby and Trevor. Philip had given them permission to talk about him, and he gave her the name of a submissive to contact for a recommendation.

All the things Emma heard contained a similar thread. He was honorable. Even though he attended the club's special events and often dined there, he rarely scened. And he wasn't looking for a relationship.

"You don't need to make a decision now. I can always clamp you through your clothing."

Which wouldn't be the same. On the other hand, she wasn't sure she wanted others watching her BDSM introduction. "I'm willing to consider it." That her friends spoke highly of him, combined with their hours of deep conversation, had helped her to develop a level of trust.

"When we're at the Quarter, would you like to use a scene name?"

"I'm not sure what that means or why I'd need one."

"We have members you might recognize. Politicians, movie stars."

"Billionaires?"

"One or two of them as well." Even though she couldn't see him, the smile in his voice reached her. "For obvious reasons, some may want to protect their identities, so they use a nom de plume at lifestyle events. A lot of people use their initials or a nickname. You can even select the same handle as you use in the online group you're in."

Emma grinned. She wasn't sure she ever wanted to be called Miss Kitty out loud. "What name do you use?"

"I go by Master Philip."

The honorific was delicious enough to make her toes curl. "That's sexy."

"Hmm. Glad you approve."

"And is that what you want me to call you?" After reading a few books, she'd automatically added a Sir on to most things she said, and he'd never corrected her.

"The way you say Mr. Dettmer is charming. The right amount of deference."

That was the way she meant it. She had tremendous respect for his business accomplishments, and he deserved respect as a Dominant.

"I'll leave it to you. Either Mr. Dettmer or Master Philip is fine."

Enjoying the suburban night sounds—children playing amid the high-pitched background of a cicada's song—she took another sip of wine as she contemplated an alternate identity. The idea was liberating. At work, she could be Emma, the account executive. Then at night she could be someone else entirely. "Is it okay if I think about the scene name?"

"Of course."

"Is there anything else I need to know?"

"You'll be perfectly safe at the Quarter. Mistress Aviana will ensure it."

"She's the owner, right?"

"Yes. I'm confident you'll meet her on Tuesday. She approves all memberships and guest passes. I'll send over some forms in advance for you to fill out." She found it fascinating how his tone was now a little more brusque, businesslike. "But you'll need to sign them in front of her."

"That makes sense."

"I'm looking forward to seeing you."

Right now, if he suggested meeting tomorrow, she'd be

there. As it was, she still had time to talk to Shelby, maybe go shopping together, ahead of her trip to the Quarter.

"Have you read more of the book from that first day?"

"I finished it."

"You enjoyed it?"

"It was enlightening."

"Have you started another?"

"Of course." She grinned. In this one, a swashbuckling pirate abducted the sleeping heroine from her bed, spiriting her away in the middle of the night while she was wearing nothing more than a thin cotton shift. After taking her to his ship, he'd locked her in his cabin and demanded marriage in addition to her sexual obedience. Each time, the heroine refused her enemy's demands, even though her internal resistance to him was crumbling around her. The way he tied her up and relentlessly tormented her—bending her to his will—lived in every one of Emma's dreams. Emma couldn't wait to devour the next chapter in an hour or so.

"Is there anything in particular you want to discuss? About the new story?"

"Right now? No." Even after what they'd shared, she wasn't prepared to invite him that deep into her psyche.

"I'll be ready to listen when you're ready to share."

Which might be never.

"In the meantime…"

Emma's breath caught. That tone, sharp yet sexy, made her sit up. He'd slipped into Dominant mode, and she'd responded instantly, from her submissive instincts.

"You were very good this evening. I'll allow you to masturbate, as long as you clamp your nipples."

"They're so sore, though." She swallowed. "I'm not sure how much more I can take."

"Well, you certainly are not required to get yourself off."

His sexy words made the night air even hotter.

"But it's the last chance you'll have before I see you."

"Wait… You mean…?" He wasn't going to let her come at all until they were at the club?

"You understand perfectly." His words were final, with no room for compromise. "How much are you willing to endure to receive pleasure?" He allowed his question to hang, unanswered. "Send me a text message letting me know what you decided." With that, he ended the call.

Damn you, Sir. Glass of wine clutched in her hand, she stood to pace the patio. He'd trapped her, well and truly. If she wanted the climax that her body demanded, she'd have to pay for it.

How much am *I willing to endure?*

Emma shivered. No doubt she hadn't even begun to figure out the answer to that question.

Philip exited his office building on Common Street, strode past the ornate clock out front, then continued to the curb where a sedan awaited him. Cressida, his driver for the day, stood ready, her hat perfectly perched and her tailored suit as crisp as it had been when she first picked him up at five this morning. As she opened the back door, a light breeze ruffled the blonde hair that hung halfway down her back. "Mr. Dettmer."

"Thanks for waiting."

"Anything for one of my favorite clients." With a professional nod, she closed him inside.

Even though he owned two vehicles, he sometimes preferred to use a service. He enjoyed the luxury of being able to make calls and work instead of dealing with the stress of rush hour traffic.

But today was special, and Cressida was doing him a

personal favor. She was the owner of the car company. Instead of working from the office, she'd agreed to act as his personal chauffeur. When he considered the logistics of attending the Quarter this evening, he'd decided he'd pay anything to have Cressida on duty to care for his lovely submissive. When he promised Emma he would always ensure her comfort and security, he meant it. "Shaughnessy Community Law Offices, please."

"Yes, sir."

He settled back, forcing himself to concentrate on the business at hand rather than what would happen after hours. As always, since the day he met Emma, harnessing his thoughts hadn't been easy.

For years, he'd been wrapped up in his divorce, fighting through countless ugly details and untold lies, and he wasn't anxious to embroil himself in that type of quagmire ever again. At one time, he'd believed in the almighty power of love, and he'd been obsessed with having a child of his own. Now he was resolved to pass along his estate to his nephews. The current count stood at three, but that was assuming his sister didn't add any more to the brood.

He'd been perfectly content to leave happily ever after to others, and his actions had reinforced that determination. He rarely dated, and he never took out the same woman more than twice. Not only was life less complicated that way, but he preferred being alone to the messiness of an actual relationship.

Or so he believed until the wide-eyed and innocent Emma had awkwardly attempted to hide that bestseller behind her back.

Now?

He was captivated. The more they talked and played on video, the hungrier he became, and he looked forward to talking with her in the evenings. He loved her confessions, about what she wanted and the things she was learning. Introducing her to BDSM was its own reward, one he couldn't get enough of.

His phone signaled an incoming message. He smiled when the notification icon showed it was from Emma.

I sent my paperwork to the Quarter.

She was perfect for him in every way. *Well done, Emma. Did you decide on a scene name?*

Rose.

Nice. It was a beautiful choice for her. And of course, because its stem had thorns, the blooms needed to be treated with care. Like the woman herself. Innocent, yet self-protective. Seemed perfect. *Your driver will pick you up at six o'clock. I'll be waiting for you at the reception area.*

Minutes passed without a response. Finally he sent her another text, one that she couldn't respond to with a simple yes or no.

Tell me how you're feeling and what you're thinking.

She'd admitted to being nervous. Excited too. But no doubt her emotions were tumultuous. It was one thing to explore their relationship over the phone and video, perhaps another to walk into an unfamiliar place and face him in person.

Determined.

Which was about as noncommittal as possible.

Is there anything I can do to make this easier for you?

Can you figure out how to slow time down for a little while?

Was she having second thoughts? *Call me if you need to talk.*

For a moment he considered offering her a way out. Maybe a more honorable man would, but he was afraid she'd seize it.

She replied with a smiley face emoji.

He took that as an encouraging sign.

Cressida eased to a stop at the curb in front of the building his friend and business associate, Mason Sullivan, was rehabbing. "I'll be less than an hour." Though he didn't have any idea why he'd been invited to the meeting, nothing should take longer than that.

"That'll give me time to put out some fires at the office."

She was every bit as busy as he was, and he knew the demands on her time. "I'll let myself out."

Even the massive double doors in front of him had been polished, lovingly restored to their nineteenth century beauty.

Everything about the interior spoke of refinement.

After checking the list of occupants in the marble lobby, he took the stairs to the second floor.

As he reached the landing, Philip extended his hand toward Mason. "Hell of a job. The place is stunning."

"She's a work in progress. Hoping to finish the third floor in the coming weeks."

Sullivan had made a name for himself renovating New Orleans. He and his beautiful wife-to-be even had their own television show on a home improvement network. This project, fixing up the once derelict home of the Shaughnessy Community Law Offices, was worthy of celebration.

"I want to have a discussion with you about the 1212 Building."

Philip was certainly open to that. He'd gotten so pissed off by the constant rent increases and unaddressed issues that he'd bought out the landlord, which left him as the new owner. And he'd discovered there were always a million complaints from the tenants. The property management service he'd hired was doing a less than stellar job. Every time he entered the historic building, someone stopped him to discuss their unhappiness. "Something needs to happen."

Suddenly the door in front of them opened. "You should sell the monstrosity and move in here." The voice of John Thoroughgood boomed off the walls of the entire second floor. "Get rid of the albatross around your neck. Dealing with complaints all day isn't your strong suit, man."

"I'm guessing that's the point of this meeting?" Philip was swept into the former football player's bear hug.

"You're nobody's fool."

This time, Philip got off lucky. Thoroughgood only broke one of his ribs.

Greetings exchanged, they followed Thoroughgood into the remarkably expansive anteroom.

Mounds of paperwork and dozens of files littered the top of an unoccupied desk. Drawers of a nearby file cabinet stood open. No doubt it would tip over if it hadn't been wedged between the wall and a stack of boxes. "Excuse the mess. I need an assistant."

"What happened to the last one?"

"Quit." He shrugged his massive shoulders, straining the seams of his rumpled and battered blazer. "I don't know why I can't keep anyone employed."

Philip cleared his throat while Mason murmured something as polite as it was noncommittal.

Thoroughgood swept his arm wide when they reached his office. "Have a seat."

At least in his private office, there was a semblance of organization. Flanking the massive window were signed football jerseys, one bearing his name and number from the years he played at LSU, the other from his short NFL career.

The back wall contained a built-in shelving unit, and it was filled with photos of Thoroughgood meeting stars and dignitaries. In addition to numerous trophies and awards, there were team pictures and moments of his glory framed for everyone to see. A football—obviously from a winning season—was protected in a glass case.

As he sat, Philip nodded toward the memorabilia. "Impressive."

"You could have your own museum," Mason added as he took a chair.

"Where I was is nothing compared to where I'm going."

Philip knew Thoroughgood meant it. His charitable efforts kept his name in the news. He was a legend who used his fame for the good of the community.

"Which brings me to the reason I invited you both here today."

Intrigued, Philip sat back and steepled his fingers. "Go on."

"I'm planning to put together an investment consortium. But all of us together are better than any of us alone."

Mason nodded. "I'm listening."

"We all have different strengths." Thoroughgood glanced at Mason. "You have an eye toward renovation. The work you did with Lawton on this building has renewed interest in the area. So I suggest we form a group. We invest money locally. Buildings." He shot Philip a cold stare. "Businesses. Revitalization. Expanding the arts. And we give fifteen percent of all our profits to charitable organizations. Hoping we can paint and repair homes for seniors or folks who are struggling. Maybe do yard clean-up. That sort of thing. The companies we work with all have to have a similar mission as ours, and because we'll be so big, we'll have leverage."

Winning the same types of favorable deals that international firms enjoyed. And if things were managed well, their individual portfolios would thrive as well. Philip nodded. So far, he was interested.

"I'm hoping you'll bring the cash."

"Of course." Philip's words were dry. "I was hoping for once you'd invited me for my exquisite taste in decorating or innovative approaches to hiring and bid procurement."

The other two men looked at each other, and Thoroughgood cleared his throat. "All very valuable skills."

Then Mason grinned. "How about you just stick to the money?"

"I'm wounded." Philip placed a hand over his heart. "Fatally perhaps."

"When we hire a director and lease an office, go ahead and submit ideas for artwork or furniture. I'm sure your opinions will be welcome."

Aware of his own shortcomings, Philip tapped his index

fingers together and responded to Thoroughgood. "Smart-ass."

"Who else are you considering?" Mason asked.

"I figured the three of us could make those decisions together. Thinking about Gavin McLeod."

The tycoon was known for his almost scarily accurate ways of predicting market trends. Not in terms of actual numbers, but the things that would impact each index's performance. More than once, he'd been called a clairvoyant. He insisted he just looked at all available information and drew natural conclusions. Other mere mortals scoffed at that idea.

"Linc Murdoch is also on my short list. He's been thinking about doing some real estate investing. Hoping to sell him some real estate in the next six months."

Another good suggestion. The man could be an ass, but he was a smart one. "Agreed. Who else?"

Thoroughgood took a breath and drew out the moment. "Aidan Holcomb."

Philip arched an eyebrow in surprise. "The Cutthroat?"

Thoroughgood linked his fingers on top of his desk and leaned forward. "Rather have him with us than against us."

"Or nowhere within a three-state region."

Mason shifted in his seat, scraping the legs against the floor. "And you're supposing he's ever done anything with an interest other than increasing the Holcomb holdings?"

"He can always refuse." Thoroughgood's tone was easy, a bit of a contradiction to his much sterner body language.

And if truth be known, there were some unsavory allegations floating around about the man's company. "You sure we want to be associated with him?"

"There's a shitpile of legal work to be done to be sure the consortium is protected." Thoroughgood's response was more of a dodge than an answer.

"How about talking to David Shaughnessy?" Mason's suggestion proved that he was at least considering Thoroughgood's suggestion. "He recently joined Barney and Scheck. We can lean on them for a reduced rate. Or free, if they want to join the consortium."

Ten minutes later, Philip gave a tentative yes to the plan. Getting things organized and turned into reality would take months, if not a year.

"Until we have an official meeting, let's keep this confidential." Thoroughgood pushed a piece of paper toward each of them.

A nondisclosure agreement. Made sense.

When they were both done signing, Mason suggested dinner. "Hannah is out setting up the baby registry with Fiona."

Philip and Thoroughgood exchanged glances and shrugs. "Baby registry?"

"Meaning she's selecting the gifts she'd like to receive at the upcoming shower that you'll be attending."

Philip tucked his pen in his jacket pocket. "Uh…"

"I'd prefer to face a defensive line." Thoroughgood made a show of pushing the paperwork into a drawer. "We are available for a bachelor party."

"Not getting an invite if you don't show solidarity with this whole *putting a diaper on a doll* thing."

As if weighing something, Philip held up his palms. "Bachelor party." He lifted his right hand. "Baby shower."

"Vegas." Mason responded so quickly that he must have been prepared for the argument. "Atlantic City. Lake Charles. The Bahamas. Monte Carlo."

Now Philip was intrigued. "Monte Carlo?"

"Haven't decided yet."

"She's registered at Nixie's." Mason looked at Philip. "Tell your admin to send a gift. A nice one." Then he addressed

Thoroughgood. "You'll have to go shopping yourself since you can't keep anyone employed."

"Cheap shot. I'm throwing a penalty flag on that play."

The two men grinned.

"Back to my original question. How about dinner?"

Thoroughgood pushed back his chair a few inches to pat his belly. "I'm in."

"Dettmer?" Mason asked.

Philip checked his watch. Right on time. "Otherwise engaged."

"Oh?"

"Meeting someone at the Quarter."

"Danielle?"

She was one of his favorite submissives. After she'd sworn off dating two years ago, she started spending more time at the club. She only played with Tops who were not looking for attachment. Despite her rule, at least two men had offered their hearts, only to have them broken.

"No." Philip kept his private life to himself, so why he answered, he wasn't sure. "Someone else."

Neither of his colleagues immediately responded. Too shocked, he supposed.

After a second or two, Thoroughgood smiled. "Enjoy yourself."

No doubt he would.

"The baby shower is a couples event. You're welcome to bring a date."

"Fishing for information, Sullivan?"

Mason shook his head.

Tonight was a one-time happening to help Emma's fantasies come true.

But is it?

At first he told himself that it was because he wanted to educate her about the various aspects of the lifestyle. If he sent her interesting materials, he could guide her. If they talked, she could ask questions, and he would learn which things turned her on, ensuring he was a better Top.

But that didn't explain why he'd rearranged his schedule so he was available every night. And it sure as fuck didn't explain the amount of money he'd spent on Bonds technology equipment so he could watch her torture herself at his behest.

Fuck, she was sexy. So responsive, eager to learn.

"Dettmer?"

He shook his head, realizing Thoroughgood had said his name. From the frown on the man's face, it may have been more than once.

"Asking if you're going to be at the Quarter for Aviana's fifth anniversary party."

The owner was planning ahead. Her Putting on the Ritz bash would be held in January, just after the New Year. "Received the invite today. I plan to attend." For a moment Philip pictured himself attending the upscale event with a lovely submissive on his arm—Emma specifically.

Then he shoved the notion aside.

After tonight, she would go back to her regular orderly life, and he'd return to the chaos of his. Funny, until now, he hadn't realized how closed off he'd become. His interactions with Emma had shown him how much he'd isolated himself, sidestepping all emotional entanglements. And now that he saw Sullivan's ridiculous smile every time he talked about Hannah, Philip wondered if he wasn't paying too high a price to protect his heart.

CHAPTER 3

I'm losing my mind. Of course I am. Aren't I?

Trying to stop the unnerving dialogue inside her head, Emma paced the length of her kitchen—again. For the third time in less than an hour, she placed a call to her friend Shelby. "Pick up. Pick up." She was desperate to talk to someone other than herself. If Shelby didn't answer, no doubt Emma would wear a hole in the hardwood floor.

She'd taken half a day off work to do a little shopping—including buying new clothes—and to soak in a hot bath in preparation for meeting with Master Philip. Now she was questioning her decisions. An afternoon without distractions had given her far too much time to think, to question her decisions, and to work herself into a frenzy.

"Hey, Emma."

Emma blew out a relieved breath. "Am I crazy?"

"Of course not." As always, Shelby was loyal. "Are you having second thoughts?"

"Yes. No. I mean not really." Emma stopped pacing to stare out the window above the sink. A moment later, she sighed. "I don't know."

"Nerves are normal. I still get them when we go to the club."

"You can't be serious. Isn't that where you met Trevor?"

"It is. But that doesn't mean I don't get butterflies when I walk through the door, and that's part of the reason I like to go—never knowing exactly what to expect. It's a rush, a thrill. And a lot of the people in my circle are also members." She thought for a second. "It's a community of sorts. Family."

"Well, except I won't know anyone there."

"Right now, that might be true. But you'll make lots of friends if you keep attending." Shelby paused. "You don't have to go with Master Philip, you know. The club has Explore days. I'll get you a guest pass sometime. There's an anniversary party coming up, and the special events are always the best. Trevor and I played together at Western Night. When I saw him in jeans and spurs...I mean..." She sighed. "Yum."

Emma laughed at her exaggerated sound.

"Anyway, I digress... The theme will be Putting on the Ritz. So we'll dress up in our skimpiest finery. A bunch of us will probably have dinner together before going, and you're more than welcome to join us."

Being one of numerous people, some she didn't know, might make her feel like an outsider. Maybe going with Master Philip, where she had his complete attention on a quiet night, would be best.

"I just don't want you to think tonight is your one and only opportunity. If you have doubts or second thoughts, don't do it. Call him or send him a text. You're under no obligation to meet him tonight or ever for that matter. He'll understand."

The possibility of leaving her fantasies unfulfilled terrified her more than the idea of showing up. "It's not that."

"Okay." Shelby waited, then, when Emma didn't go on, spoke again. "So what is it?"

"Maybe I'm scared because I don't know what to expect." And she didn't do well with that, which was part of the reason she lived in the same area where she'd grown up and had been at the same company since she graduated from college.

"That's natural. But it's important to know that Mistress Aviana is very serious about the Quarter's rules. Everyone there—including dungeon monitors—will be looking out for you. You've said that Master Philip has been very patient with you."

"He has." And the experience had been sublime so far.

"Everything you're going through is normal. You'll be fine. Just do what's right for you. You can cancel, reschedule, or go with the intention of enjoying yourself, even if you're a little freaked out."

"Sounds reasonable." Much calmer, in control of her racing heart, Emma nodded.

"And I'm going to want all the details. Why don't you and I arrive a few minutes early for happy hour tomorrow so we can catch up?"

Everyone in Shelby's bridal party was planning to gather after work at the Maison Sterling in the French Quarter. Supposedly, they'd discuss wedding plans, but the last time they met, the fivesome had ended up having so much fun that they'd never gotten around to even looking at bridesmaid dresses. "That would be perfect."

"Can you get there half an hour early?"

Which meant quitting work by four. "I should be able to."

"When I say I want all the details, I mean *all* of them."

"After putting up with me, you deserve them."

"Go." Shelby laughed. "Quit being your own worst enemy."

After hanging up, Emma determinedly strode to her bedroom and pulled out the new clothing she'd bought.

Self critically she decided it wasn't terrible. The skirt hugged her curves, and maybe the shirt was a little tighter than she remembered, making her look bustier than she really was.

Her bra and panties were lacy and opaque. At the lingerie store that she'd visited over the weekend, there'd been a huge selection of beautiful garments that were meant for people much braver than she was. Master Philip would no doubt prefer something more daring, but tonight he was playing with someone who didn't even like to wear bathing suits in public.

By the time her phone chimed, signaling that her car had arrived, she was a mess of nerves.

"Good evening, ma'am." The driver smiled as she opened the back door. "I'm Cressida."

Having a female driver calmed her, and Emma was grateful for Master Philip's thoughtfulness.

She slid onto the leather seat and was engulfed in luxury for the first time in her life. Her parents were divorced, and her mother worked two jobs to support them. Emma had worked her way through college, and though she'd earned a few promotions at work, her mortgage payment took a huge bite out of her paychecks. Since she wanted to be more secure than she'd been growing up, she rarely treated herself to the finer things in life.

Once Cressida exited the neighborhood, she glanced in the rearview mirror. "There are chilled beverages, if you'd care for one."

"I think I might be able to get used to this." Emma selected a bottle of sparkling mineral water.

"First private car?"

Emma wrinkled her nose. "It's that obvious, isn't it?"

She'd been fortunate enough to have an amazing mentor, and she managed a number of high-profile portfolios, so she should have been able to pretend this was an ordinary circumstance.

"I'm glad you're enjoying it. The first time I saw a limousine, I was about ten or eleven. We didn't really have a lot of money, but back then, I didn't know we were poor. We didn't take expensive vacations. But every couple of years, we'd go camping for a weekend in the Hill Country. To escape the heat, we'd take little excursions to Austin, and I remember seeing this monstrosity of an SUV. It was bright yellow, and the windows were up, so I couldn't see inside. But as it rolled down the street, some guy popped up through the sunroof and he was whooping and hollering as he opened a bottle of champagne. He shook it first so it went everywhere. It was an image I never forgot. And I wanted to be in one every day." She grinned. "So I started my own company."

Emma leaned forward. "Are you kidding me? As in you own a whole fleet of vehicles?"

"Well, more than a few. Yes." In the rearview mirror, she smiled. "Including a bright-yellow monstrosity. I don't drive very often anymore, so having an appreciative customer makes it even more worthwhile."

Because she was always interested in business, Emma was intrigued. "Has the rise of rideshare companies harmed your service?" Then she realized how nosy the question sounded. "Sorry, I shouldn't have asked."

"Not at all. I'm sure it's impacted some, but we are growing. There's always a market for special events, and we have a steady base of customers who like to have a driver at their disposal for a day or more."

Made sense. "So how did I manage to get you as a driver?"

"Mr. Dettmer requested me."

"Really?"

"He tends to get what he wants."

Emma took that as a warning. Just then, her phone rang. Master Philip. *Of course.* After excusing herself to Cressida, Emma answered his call.

"I trust you're comfortable?"

"It's fabulous."

"Good. I'm tracking your arrival, and I'll meet you outside."

"Tracking?"

"On the car service app. You're about seventeen minutes away."

"You leave nothing to chance, do you?"

"Not when it comes to you and your safety. See you soon."

After dropping her phone into her purse, she sat back and uncapped her drink. Her hand shook a little, almost causing her to spill the water.

Though the trip slowed significantly once they reached the crowded and narrow streets of the French Quarter—which was filled with cars, bicycles, pedestrians, and even motorized scooters—she arrived on time.

Much sooner than Emma was ready, Cressida drew alongside the curb. "I'll be on standby. Mr. Dettmer will let me know when to return for you."

"Thank you." Before she could say anything further, Master Dettmer himself opened the door and offered her a hand.

She accepted, and lightning arced through her. This was the first time they'd actually touched, and nothing could have prepared her for the experience. His grip was as firm as it was reassuring.

When she was on the sidewalk in front of him and the car pulled back into traffic, time ground to a halt. All the chaos around her vanished, and nothing in her world existed but him. She'd never experienced anything like it.

"Emma. Or should I say Rose?"

His question was like champagne, light and heady, leaving her giddy.

"I'm so very glad you're here."

He swept his gaze over her, seeming to take in every detail. How had she not remembered that his dark-green eyes were so intense?

"You're very beautiful, you know."

His voice held such sincerity that she didn't dare protest. Instead, her response was immediate and unfettered. "So are you."

He smiled, soft and slow, transforming his expression from smoldering to appreciative. "No one's ever said that before. Thank you."

If she had hesitated for even a moment, she would have kept her mouth shut. Yet she meant it. Of course she'd seen him on camera since their first meeting, but nothing matched the power of being in his presence, drinking in his lethal charisma.

This evening he wore slim-fitting black trousers and a snow-white shirt with the top two buttons parted—tantalizingly.

The sun played off the strands of silver in his hair, adding to his devastating good looks.

She wanted to pinch herself to be sure that she was planning to have a BDSM scene with one of the city's most handsome and compelling billionaire Doms.

"Shall we?"

Even though his words triggered an instant flight instinct, she forced herself to nod. She was grateful that he continued to hold on to her as he guided her toward a nondescript green door that she otherwise wouldn't have noticed since it was tucked between a restaurant and a to-go bar advertising rum-laden hurricanes in massive plastic glasses.

"Stay close." He let her go long enough to press the bell located on the wall and turn his face toward a tiny camera.

A tiny *snick* echoed, and he opened the unlocked door. "Go ahead." He placed his palm on her lower back, once again steadying her, offering the reassurance she needed. "I'll follow you."

Knowing her life would never be the same after she crossed the threshold, she took a deep breath and entered.

She curved her fingers around the polished rail as she climbed the time-worn stairs to the second floor.

Once they reached what appeared to be the reception area, she was unsure what exactly to do, so she stepped to the side. The area was vast and wide open. A gorgeous crystal chandelier hung overhead, with its pendants refracting the light into a million moonbeams. The hardwood floors gleamed, and wainscoting covered the bottom half of the walls. A table against the far wall was adorned with the tallest fuchsia-colored orchid she'd ever seen. Additionally there were a number of elegant carved wood cubbies, along with a cloakroom. Most striking was the frosted-glass door with a fleur-de-lis etched into it.

This was not what she expected a dungeon to look like. But of course it made sense that the private areas wouldn't be immediately on display.

"Welcome back, Sir." The woman who greeted them from behind a podium wore her bright-pink hair in a sleek bob that framed her face.

"Trinity, I'd like to present my guest…" He trailed off.

Realizing he was deferring to her, she gave her legal name. "Emma Monroe."

Trinity smiled invitingly. "Welcome to the Quarter. You'll be known as Rose going forward, unless you choose to let others know your name."

"Thank you."

"I've notified Mistress Aviana that you're here. She'll be right with you."

Before Trinity had finished speaking, a woman breezed in, all smiles and warmth.

"Rose, I believe?"

In shock, Emma glanced at Master Philip, who nodded.

This was Mistress Aviana? Maybe she'd spent too much time watching online videos over the past two weeks, but she'd pictured Mistress Aviana in black leather and carrying some instrument of torture.

Instead, the woman was at least as tall as Emma, and towered over her in her thigh-high platform boots. Her short silver dress hugged her body. She was willowy, with long platinum hair hanging to her waist. Everything about her shouted royalty, and she was exactly what Emma had not been expecting.

"Milady." Master Philip gave a slight bow.

While he'd covered most things, he hadn't told Emma how to act in front of the club's owner, and she'd never been more uncomfortable in her life. Should she bow as well? Curtsy? Offer her hand?

As if unconcerned by her lack of response, Mistress Aviana went on. "Trinity tells me we've received your paperwork."

Along with a pen, Trinity offered a file folder to Aviana.

"Thank you. Now, Rose, let's step aside, shall we? Philip, if you don't mind waiting where you are?"

Though he tilted his head questioningly to the side, his response was filled with respect. "Of course, Milady."

After exchanging glances with Master Philip, Emma gulped back her sudden apprehension and followed the Quarter's owner to the table against the far wall.

"Welcome to our world." Mistress Aviana turned her back to the others and kept her voice low. "Since it's your first visit—of many, we hope—I wanted to go over a few things with you." She placed the folder and pen next to the orchid. "Your online profile indicates you're just starting to explore BDSM."

"That's correct." She'd had no idea that Mistress Aviana would do research on her. But again, it made sense. "I'm curious."

"Of course. All of us were new to this at one time." Her voice held notes of kindness and patience, not something Emma necessarily associated with a confident businesswoman who was clearly a Domme. "While I'm confident that you're in good hands with Master Philip, it's not unusual for newcomers to be somewhat overwhelmed. If that happens to you, you're welcome to talk to me. Trinity will be at the reception station and will know how to reach me at all times. Dungeon monitors are available as well. If questions come up for you later, you're welcome to phone the club."

Emma couldn't imagine casually calling Mistress Aviana for an afternoon chat. She was powerful, oozing charisma and confidence, and no doubt she had plenty of important things to attend to.

"Your safety and well-being are our biggest priorities. The Quarter's safe word is *red*. If you use it, one of our dungeon monitors will intervene in whatever is happening. You'll recognize them by their black vests adorned with a gold fleur-de-lis. As you no doubt saw on our list of rules, there is no nudity permitted outside of the private rooms. Our bar is open until three a.m., but no one is allowed to drink and scene. If you order an alcoholic beverage, we will mark your hand with an X. Since Master Philip is your sponsor tonight, he can lose his membership if you break the rules. Likewise, you'll receive a lifetime ban."

Emma nodded as Aviana went on. "No beverages are permitted outside the bar area, with the exception of bottled water. Very importantly, please watch any scene from a respectful distance and do not interfere in any way. If you have doubts as to whether something is okay, please ask someone—me, a dungeon monitor, or Master Philip. Any questions so far?"

"No…" *Ma'am? Milady? Mistress?*

Proving why she was so successful, Mistress Aviana answered Emma's unspoken question. "Any honorific is fine, and none is required. We are not a high-protocol club. So in your case, you and Master Philip may want to decide how you proceed."

Even though she said that, Emma noticed that Aviana and Trinity both addressed Master Philip with respect, and likewise, he had formally greeted Mistress Aviana. "Thank you. That makes sense…" But in this setting, her sentence felt unfinished. "Milady."

"Then I'll wrap up with the reminder that our privacy clause precludes anyone from acknowledging another member or guest outside of the Quarter, unless both parties agree."

Again, Emma nodded.

"In that case…" Mistress Aviana opened the file folder and fished out the papers that Emma had filled out. She placed the last page on top of the pile, then offered a pen. Helpfully a bright-orange sticky note indicated the line she should sign on.

Once she had, she exhaled.

Then Mistress Aviana summoned Master Philip.

When he arrived, he placed a hand on Emma's shoulder. Instinctively she leaned into him, and he rewarded her with a comforting squeeze before letting her go.

Maybe Shelby had been correct. So far, everything was okay.

Aviana extracted a second piece of paper from the folder

and then offered the pen to Master Philip. "This will acknowledge your sponsorship of Rose this evening. As you know, you're responsible for her when she attends with you."

He didn't hesitate before affixing his signature, the P and the D large and distinct. He crossed the double Ts in Dettmer with a broad, sharp stroke.

"As I'm sure you know, Rose, you'll be able to petition for your own membership after three visits. And you're able to attend with other people in the interim. I do recommend you take advantage of the Explore days. You'll meet other newcomers and begin to form friendships. And you'll have the opportunity to mingle with other Tops."

A low rumble, much like a feral growl, emanated from Master Philip.

Pretending as if she'd heard nothing, Mistress Aviana pushed all the forms inside the folder. "Enjoy your evening."

Then suddenly Emma was alone with her one-night Dominant.

"I thought we might start with a tour of the dungeon, and then we can decide how we'd like to proceed."

"Really?"

"What did you expect? That I'd order you to strip and kneel for me right here?"

The gruffness sandpapering his words crashed an odd mixture of desire and terror through her, forcing her to lock her knees to remain upright.

"Or perhaps you'd like that?" He lowered his voice, making it more intimate. "Would you, Rose? Does the idea of being bared to me, kneeling for me, excite you?"

"I…" It scared her how much the thought appealed to her. She would have never guessed she was the kind of woman who'd get on camera and do the things that he requested of her. The thrill of it had become slightly addictive, making her wonder what would happen once their evening was over,

HIS TO CHERISH

and they went their separate ways. How would she fill this new need? Find another Dominant to play with? The idea made her tummy clench.

Fighting for control, unprepared to pull off her clothes right here, right now, she pulled her shoulders back. "I'd prefer to have a look around before we begin, as you suggested."

He nodded. "The coat check is open, if you'd like to leave your purse here."

Within seconds, they had a claim ticket. And it was then she realized he didn't have anything with him. Maybe he meant to only use his hands on her?

The thought made her toes curl. She couldn't wait for that.

Master Philip led the way through the frosted-glass door. "Welcome to the dungeon."

In here, the light was much dimmer than it had been in the reception area, and music thumped out a primal beat. The few people she saw shattered even more of her misconceptions. Not everyone had a perfect body or was of a particular age. With each passing moment, she relaxed more and more.

Across the room, she noticed a throne on a raised dais. She pointed. "Is that what it appears to be?"

"Mistress Aviana's place of honor? It is. It was a gift, I understand, from one of her submissives. He was obviously a talented carpenter."

"That's impressive. Like it belongs in a real-life castle." Which fit her earlier impression of the owner. More princess than Dominant.

"You'll have to get a closer look later. The detail work is exquisite. Let's start at the bar, so you can orient yourself. It's to your right."

The space was enclosed with thick glass, which cut down

the dungeon noise. It was decorated in Mardi Gras, Louisiana-proud style. Neon signs from local breweries were attached to the walls and ceiling. Memorabilia from local colleges adorned the glass shelving. Photos and paintings of New Orleans sites hung on the walls. It was a casual, inviting place.

A person sat at the wooden bar, a tall beer in front of him. At one table, two businessmen were engaged in a conversation. In the far corner, a man knelt next to the table while a woman fed him some French fries. It wasn't very far removed from what Master Philip suggested she do a few minutes ago. Now she realized no one but she thought it odd.

"Mistress Aviana outlined the drinking rules, I assume?"

"She did."

"Are you ready to continue?"

The Quarter was a safe place to explore her fantasies, and she wanted to do exactly that. "I'd like to see more."

She followed him from the bar.

"As I mentioned, this is the main dungeon." He stopped. "You'll recognize the Saint Andrew's crosses."

"Yes." There were rows of the wooden structures in a couple of different areas. A woman was attached to one of them, and two men were striping her with floggers, in alternating turns. Emma could only imagine the exquisiteness of the pain the woman must be experiencing.

"And spanking benches."

She nodded. None of them were occupied, but in her research, she'd seen how versatile the equipment could be.

"What do you think of them?"

Was he asking for a particular reason? Her mouth dried as she pictured herself on top of one, waiting for his commands.

"Ready to try one out?"

With her tight skirt, that would be impossible. "Not quite yet."

"Of course." He smiled, then changed the subject. "Do you see that door over there?"

Since it was painted black to match the rest of the area, it was a little difficult to discern. "Yes."

"It leads to *Rue Sensuelle.*"

She translated from the French. "Sensual Street?"

"Or as it's known by members, Kinky Avenue. You'll see numerous staged scenes, and the club changes them out periodically. They cater to role-play."

On a couple of their calls, they'd talked about it at length. For some reason, a kidnapping fantasy appealed to her. And she imagined Master Philip spiriting her away, tying her to a bed, and keeping her there while he had his wicked way with her.

"The club is more or less built in a U shape, meaning *Rue Sensuelle* wraps around the main dungeon. There are stairs that lead to the private rooms. There's a landing that serves as an observation deck where you can watch scenes happening in all the public areas. So it's your choice. If you'd like to walk through the role-play area, we can. Or we can head straight for the private rooms."

Nerves made her want to postpone the inevitable as long as possible. "I'd enjoy seeing everything."

"Of course. That will help you get a better idea of the Quarter's layout." He led the way to the door and opened it for her.

The music was a little quieter back here, more like it had been in the bar area. They stopped in front of a mock schoolroom, complete with desks, books, a globe, a map on the wall, and a chalkboard. Someone had written on it, in cursive, multiple times, *I WILL NOT CALL MY DOMINANT A HARD-ASS.*

She laughed. "Aren't most Dominants hard-asses?"

"That depends on the nature of the relationship."

Emma turned to face him. "Oh?"

"As you've already ascertained, there are as many ways to practice BDSM as there are people involved in the lifestyle… from living it 24/7 to confining scenes to the bedroom."

"Still… Aren't those canes in the corner? In that brass container that looks like an umbrella holder?"

"They are indeed. And it can be part of the role-play. The Dominant may not be a hard-ass outside of the fantasy."

"I see."

"It's all about each person getting what they need."

"So…?" She appreciated that he allowed her the space to formulate her question. "What if one person likes something and the other doesn't?"

"Remember the conversations we've had? BDSM requires a deep level of trust and honesty…the more the better. Negotiation is crucial. So, to specifically answer your question… let's say you have a certain fantasy that I don't share. The next step is to discuss it. Are there elements I find acceptable? Are there things you're willing to let go of but would still make the whole thing intriguing? In other words, we figure out a way to make it work for both of us. Or, if it crosses a nonnegotiable line, I can refuse to participate."

"Are there things you wouldn't do?"

"There are." He traced his forefinger down the side of her cheek.

It was the most intimate thing he'd ever done. Unable to help herself, she turned her face toward him in offering.

"Cutting your beautiful skin for example. Adorning you with permanent marks. Damaging you mentally or physically." His eyes blazed with intensity. "I told you in one of our first discussions that pleasing my submissives brings me joy. If you share what you want, from those deepest, most secret places in your heart, I will do my best to make them come true."

Even stealing me away, tying me to a bed, and ravishing me? Since she didn't have the courage to ask, she settled for a noncommittal nod.

Though he lowered his hand from her face, the emotional grip he held over her only deepened.

They continued on past a principal's office. It didn't take her long to understand that each area for role-play was separated by partitions. Next was an office setting, complete with a desk and a credenza. They continued to something that resembled a Victorian parlor, including a settee and ornate furnishings like a Tiffany-inspired table lamp. A feather duster took center stage on a set of library shelves.

A stark area with a dais and a pair of stocks spiraled nervous energy through her, causing her to breathe faster. "This one is a no from me."

"Is it?" He stopped. "Why?"

His question forced her to examine her instant reaction. "I'm not a big fan of being on display like that."

"Understood."

"Like…" She struggled to understand her visceral reaction. "They were actually used for punishment and humiliation. And I'm not sure I could deal with that."

His reassurance was quick and unhesitant. "I promise you I'd never ask it of you."

"Is it…?" *God.* She prayed it wasn't. "A thing for you?"

"The humiliation angle?" He shook his head. "Not at all. I promised I wouldn't harm you in any way—that includes emotionally."

"I had no idea an inanimate object would make me so upset."

"There are times that you may find yourself objecting to things you've enjoyed or that haven't bothered you in the past. A word, a phrase, a touch, a particular scent, anything can trigger an uncomfortable memory or feeling. It's important to talk about them. Use your safe word. Don't try to push through."

Over the time that she'd been researching BDSM, she'd read about triggers, but until that chill chased through her, it had been abstract. Now it was very real, and she appreciated the discussion. "I'm curious…" She gulped. "There's a part of this scene that appeals to you?"

"There is."

A shiver—maybe more from interest than fear—whispered through her.

"The contraption is adjustable height-wise, so a submissive can be positioned with her bottom sticking out. For example, bend at the waist."

It was his first command of the evening, and it made her heart race. "Now?" The word emerged squeaky.

"Please."

Focus on Master Philip.

"There's no one else near us."

Not that it would matter if there were.

"Do it now, Emma."

He used that same tone when they played over video. Their conversations began with warmth, cordial chitchat. But then he'd issue a command, and his voice was sharper, honed by flint. He was unlike any other man she'd met—and no other could compare.

Determinedly she shoved aside her embarrassment and did as he said. The material of her skirt tightened around her buttocks.

His footfall echoed with purpose as he moved in front of her. "Extend your arms."

She did as he asked. The position was more awkward than uncomfortable.

HIS TO CHERISH

Master Philip captured her wrists and held them firmly. Though she could have pulled away, she wasn't even a little bit tempted. Instead she appreciated his strength and aura of command.

"Very nice. Obedient."

Liquid warmth flooded her. She loved his purr of approval and would do almost anything to earn it.

"Now look up and meet my eyes."

Emma tilted her head back. Approval was written there, and the headiness made her weak.

"Imagine me securing you in this position. You could squirm all you wanted, but you wouldn't be able to escape the torment I have in mind for you."

When she murmured, he stroked his right thumb across her pulse.

"I wish there was a mirror so you could see the way you look to me."

Though she hated the humiliation aspect, she glanced sideways at the apparatus. Viewing it from his perspective. "It looks uncomfortable." But it was no longer terrifying.

"Mistress Aviana is thoughtful. It's padded."

He gently released his grip and offered assistance while she stood and found her balance.

"There are many, many other options when it comes to having your body on display for me." Leisurely he swept his gaze over her. "The camera is a poor second to seeing you in person."

Desire banked in his eyes, and in that moment she would have given him anything he asked for.

"As we've discussed, I will not push you past your limits. Role-play never has to be something we indulge in if it doesn't appeal to you."

After she nodded, they walked on, following the outside of the U shape until they reached a medical examination room. A woman had her feet in the stirrups moaning with pleasure, begging for more, while a man was lightly slapping the insides of her thighs with a star-shaped crop.

Master Philip leaned in closer and whispered in Emma's ear. "Not everything involves pain."

Turned on in ways she'd never even imagined possible, she took in a tiny breath, grateful that he'd brought her on a night that wasn't crowded and that she was able to become familiar with the Quarter at a pace that suited her. As the moments passed, she was becoming more relaxed, and the evening in front of her no longer seemed quite as intimidating.

The last partitioned-off space made her breath catch.

A lone metal-framed bed occupied the middle of the room. Thick leather buckles were attached to the headboard and footboard. A rustic wooden chair stood sentry near it. Rounding out the scene were a sturdy table and a lamp with no cover. It was as if someone had crawled inside her fantasies and brought them to life.

"Emma?"

Due to the way his eyebrows were knitted together, it was clear he'd been trying to get her attention. "I'm sorry?"

"You like this? Hate it?"

"I uhm…" Ever since Aaron had used her kinkiness as an excuse to cheat on her, she'd avoided dating and kept her desires to herself, even though she knew Master Philip not only expected it, but demanded it.

"We can go back to the schoolroom, and you can write out that you won't hide from your Dominant. I think a hundred times seems about right."

She gasped as she tipped her head back to look at him. *Are you serious?* And what if he was? The dynamic they were exploring was frightening and appealing at the same time.

When she didn't answer, he increased the stakes. "Two

hundred?" His jaw was set, and there was no doubt he'd see through a falsehood.

"Actually? I like it." The admission wasn't all that painful.

"Tell me more." His words were phrased as an invitation, but a note of command was woven through them.

"The night you were in San Francisco…you asked me about the book I was reading."

"I remember. You weren't ready to talk about it."

Admitting this still wasn't easy. "It's a historical. And the hero's a pirate who kidnaps the heroine from her bed."

"Does he take her to his ship?"

"Of course. And she confesses she's a virgin, and her father has promised her to the local vicar. So she can't have sex until marriage." Did he think she was crazy for being captivated by the storyline? If so, he didn't show it. On the contrary, Master Philip remained where he was, giving her his complete attention. "Anyway, since the pirate is secretly planning to never let her go, he's content to wait on that, but he's determined to ruin her for any other man." Much like Philip was doing with her. "So he finds ways to…uhm… torture her and make her fall for him."

"Such as?"

It shouldn't surprise her that he'd ask. "Unless he's with her, he keeps her imprisoned." Emma glanced toward the bed, envisioning her Dominant fastening those buckles around her wrists even as she screamed, fighting against him and the inevitable.

"So he has her tied up?"

She nodded as her mouth dried.

"What does he do to her, specifically?"

This was becoming more and more difficult for her.

"Push aside any sense of embarrassment." He tucked a lock of her hair behind her ear, then feathered his fingertip down her jaw. "Where is the hero standing?"

His touch was hypnotic, and his soft command was compelling. He made this whole thing so easy for her. "He sits next to her on the bed." Which brought them close together and terrified the heroine as much as excited her. "He places a hand on her stomach."

"And then lower?"

He lowered his hand but didn't move away.

"Yes. To bunch up her dress and move his hand between her legs." She frowned as she tried to remember a specific detail. "I think she must have been wearing some sort of undergarments."

"Hardly a consideration for a pirate. If she had on something, presumably it had a drawstring. As a man of the sea, he'd know a thing or two about knots. At any rate, men have been figuring out ways to separate a woman from her clothing since the dawn of civilization."

She laughed. "I'm sure you're right."

"Even today...it's exhilarating to work a hand beneath a woman's skirt while at dinner...and it's so much better if it's a business lunch. Trying to unobtrusively ease a finger beneath the gusset of her panties to find her clit while she's trying to carry on a polite conversation."

Emma squirmed.

"Fantasies are sublime, aren't they? About your pirate and his abductee... What turns you on?"

Since he'd shared his own without embarrassment, she continued talking about hers. "There's something about being helpless and forced to do something against my will. Because deep down I really want to, but being tied up would let me escape from the forbidden or the guilt and just surrender to the moment. And of course, it's only with a man I really want."

"It's a very common fantasy."

"Is it?"

His grin was easy. "It wouldn't be one of the most popular places on Kinky Avenue if it wasn't."

"Really?"

"There's a wait time on the weekends. Sometimes as long as a couple of hours."

"In reality, though, I can't imagine anything worse than being abducted." So in her mind, it was always with someone she knew, and she controlled all the events.

"A club provides a safe outlet for that kind of play."

"Of course."

"In the future, perhaps I can make that happen for you."

Her heart leaped. Was he imagining that they'd continue after tonight? A future had never been part of their arrangement.

When she hadn't responded a full minute later, he suggested they head for the second story.

The railing was crafted from wrought iron—very old-world New Orleans style—with fleur-de-lis artistically linking the bars. Mardi Gras beads hung from strategic places, adding a festive note.

When they reached a balcony-type landing, Philip led her toward the front where she was able to take in the entire dungeon, including Rue Sensuelle. "The place is huge. And I guess I hadn't noticed all the couches before." Not surprising. She'd been wide-eyed, cataloging all the equipment she'd only seen online.

"They're mostly for cuddling. After care."

After care. "Is that the reason you tell me to call you back after we've..." She never could find the right words. When would it become more natural? "When you've given me instructions over video?"

"Yes. I always want to make sure you're okay, that you don't have any questions."

So it had nothing to do with wanting to talk to her and

enjoying some sort of connection. Instead, he'd simply been fulfilling his duties as a Dominant. She exhaled her disappointment, stung, even though it shouldn't.

What?

She started to fall for him? Despite their agreement? More than ever, she couldn't allow that to happen.

Determinedly setting her jaw, she turned her attention away from him—and her own naivete—to continue watching the couple in the medical examination room.

The doctor was now helping his patient to remove her shirt. Beneath it, her nipples were covered with tape.

While the woman sat there, wringing her hands, her partner walked behind her to cup her breasts. He squeezed, then kneaded, pressed them together, made a show of weighing each in his hand.

Emma exhaled a shaky breath.

"Shall we continue upstairs?" Master Philip's voice jolted her. "Or would you prefer to watch for a few more minutes?"

"Honestly?" She turned her head in his direction. "I could stay here forever."

He grinned. "So be it."

The doctor pinched each of the submissive's nipples in turn, then with a satisfied nod, said something to her, offering his hand as she lay back.

The woman curled her hands into fists when he walked away for a moment only to return with a crop. Unlike the one with a puffy star, the leather piece at the end was much smaller.

"That looks as if it might be a little more painful."

"The keeper?"

"Is that what it's called? The little piece on the end?"

"It is, and you're correct. It stings. How much depends on the force behind it."

The Top balanced the shaft on the gentle swell of her

belly, then spent the next couple of minutes securing her to the examination table with pink rope.

Emma's breathing became more and more constricted as the submissive writhed around, her feet still captured in the stirrups.

"Are you okay?" He touched her shoulder.

"Fascinated."

"It's part of your fantasies. Being bound."

She nodded. Master Philip had taken in her every word.

Once the submissive make-believe patient was secure, the doctor forced the shaft between her teeth. As she bit down on it, holding it steady, he picked up the other crop and used it again on her inner thighs.

"Keeping her engaged in the scene." Philip whispered his words against Emma's ear, sending warm shivers through her. "Perhaps he's hinting at what's to come or building anticipation. Maybe confusing her or creating fear."

This time, dread flooded her.

The doctor cropped the patient's pussy, then slid a finger beneath the gusset of her panties, as if checking for a reaction.

He nodded with apparent satisfaction.

Again he spoke, and the woman thrashed her head back and forth.

"She can't speak with the crop in her mouth. How does that work with a safe word?"

"She can drop it, or they no doubt have a safe signal."

Somewhat reassured, she returned her attention to the couple.

He tucked the implement he was using beneath the table before taking the one from between her teeth and kissing her in a way that was intimate and spoke of deep affection. Then he spent at least a minute toying with her breasts once again before lightly dancing the small end of the crop across her nipples, making them hard.

"Potentially he's warming her up. So that she can take more than she did earlier. The endorphins are higher for her now."

"Is that what you do?"

"I always warm up my submissive."

Another part of his Dominant duty?

The doctor made a show of elongating one of the woman's nipples and used the keeper on the underneath of her breasts.

Emma squeezed her eyes shut for a moment, and when she opened them, the submissive tied to the table was thrashing as she begged him to allow her to come. All the while he spoke to her, though Emma couldn't make out the words.

The woman sat up as much as her restrictive bonds would allow, screaming his name.

He dropped the crop onto her belly, then pressed his thumb to her clit. She thrashed harder, and tears spilled from her eyes before she settled back into place.

Her Dominant fisted her hair and held her while he kissed her.

I want to be her.

Once he released her, he picked up the crop again and made slow circles on her tummy before reaching for her other nipple.

"How are you doing?" Master Philip whispered against Emma's ear.

Dare she admit it? "I'm…" *Turned on. Aroused.* "Intrigued."

"With the way you responded to nipple stimulation when we scened over video, I was guessing you might be."

She turned toward him.

"It will be much different for you when I'm the one

tormenting you, when you have no idea how hard I'll squeeze or how long the pressure will go on."

Would she beg like the woman in the medical role-play? Cry?

The scene they'd been watching ended with the Dominant smoothing his hand across the woman's forehead and releasing her from bondage.

"Shall we?"

It was the moment she wanted and alternately dreaded, and she had no reason to delay any longer.

He extended a hand to indicate she should precede him up the stairs.

A podium, a replica of the one in the reception area, with a plaque of the club's fleur-di-lis adorning the front, blocked the entrance to a hallway. Not that it was needed. A bearded blond-haired man, larger than any person she'd ever seen, stood there, arms folded across his chest. He stared at her through piercing blue eyes, taking in everything about her. He was as broad as a massive oak, and his biceps rippled and bulged. If Master Philip hadn't been behind her, she'd have been intimidated enough to take a step back.

"Tore. I'd like to introduce my guest for the evening, Rose. Rose, say hello to Tore, Mistress Aviana's most trusted adviser and dungeon master."

Which explained his vest. "Nice to meet you." Again the honorific tripped her up. "Uhm… Sir?"

"Tore is fine." His voice boomed, and she imagined the walls shook.

"I'd like to show Rose a private room, if that's acceptable. Room six, if possible."

How often did Master Philip attend that he knew the exact room he wanted? Another reminder that she was nothing more than a plaything to him.

The dungeon monitor picked up the electronic tablet in

front of him. In his hands, it appeared to be a child's toy. How could he even use it? Then he grabbed a stylus to navigate—which was the only thing that made sense.

"It is. Check back in if you want to use it."

"Of course."

Before allowing them to pass, Tore reminded her of the club's safe word and informed them both that he would personally check on any scene they engaged in.

Emma nodded.

Master Philip placed his palm reassuringly in the middle of her back and guided her down the hallway. When they arrived at number six, he reached around her to turn the handle.

She entered. Then, maybe because it was just part of the tour, he left the door ajar when he followed her inside.

A black vinyl spanking bench took her breath away. This close, it seemed much larger than the ones downstairs, and it had numerous O-rings strategically placed, all glistening with threat and promise.

The space was well thought-out, and even included a stainless steel counter and sink with a cabinet beneath it. Soap and sanitizer had thoughtfully been provided.

A pulley system attached to a side wall ran to an overhead beam. The only other things in the room were a metal rolling cart and a chair.

"What do you think?"

After a moment's hesitation, she admitted the truth. "It's not as overwhelming as I made it out to be in my head."

"Your breaths aren't as frantic as they were a minute ago."

She turned to him. He stood with his legs shoulder-width apart, arms folded across his chest. For a moment, with his dark hair and snow-white shirt, he reminded her of a pirate, both tempting and frightening. "That's ridiculously observant."

"As I've mentioned, everything about you and your pleasure matters to me.

Not for the first time, his magnificence took her breath away.

"Why don't you get up on the bench?"

She smoothed her palm down the front of her skirt. "I'm not sure that's possible."

He grinned. "You can pull it up a little bit while still preserving your modesty."

How ridiculous am I being? It wasn't like he hadn't seen all her secrets on video.

Obviously filled with the confidence of experience and his knowledge of her, he took two steps closer to her. His scent—that of confident masculine success—overwhelmed her, dominating her awareness.

Under his watchful eye, she wiggled the skirt up her thighs. Since that wasn't enough to give her the freedom of movement that she needed, she continued to raise it, until the hem was at her waist.

"Beautiful panties." He smiled, and there was no trace of teasing in it. His words were simple, and honesty echoed in them.

Emboldened, she accepted his hand. Within seconds, she was on top of the bench with her knees on the rails, and she adjusted her position so that her weight was evenly distributed.

"You look lovely."

He hadn't taken his eyes off her.

"I'd like you to straighten your spine and raise up so that your pussy isn't touching the bench."

It took her a couple of seconds to find the position that he asked for.

"Perfect." He stood in front of her and traced her collarbone, pausing at the hollow of her throat.

Then, keeping his gaze on hers, he outlined the V of her shirt's neckline. "Link your hands at the small of your back, and then pull back your shoulders and arch a little, as if you're offering yourself to me."

Well and truly, he was getting inside her mind, hypnotizing her with his soft commands.

She did as he said, and the change of position instantly made her feel more sensuous.

"That's it." He glanced away to unfasten her top button. Her breath caught as he dipped a finger between her breasts; then he drew a slow tiny circle on one of them.

Once again, he captured her gaze. "Is this what you want?"

She nodded.

"I need to hear it."

"Yes." Her voice was faint, so she tried again. "Yes, Sir."

His smile was slow, transforming his features, showing his pleasure. And it undid her.

"Exactly what I was hoping for. I will confirm our use of the room. I have a bag in the cloakroom."

"I'd wondered about that."

"I made sure to pack all the implements I thought would please you."

Even...?

"Even nipple clamps."

How did he know her thoughts before she did?

"Will you be all right if I leave you long enough to fetch it? I'll be back in five minutes, maybe less."

She cocked her head to one side. "Is this some sort of a test?"

"Not at all." He took hold of her shoulders, his touch as gentle as it was reassuring. "You're welcome to come with me."

The idea sounded ridiculous once he said it aloud. "I'm a big girl."

"All this—everything tonight—is a new experience for you." He lowered his hand, and her breast was warm where he touched. "Being uncertain is normal."

"I'll be fine." When he didn't respond to her, she added, "Promise."

Evidently satisfied, he nodded. "Five minutes." He turned and strode to the door.

Once he reached it, she began to maneuver her body so she could dismount from the bench.

He paused and faced her. "It's my preference that you would stay where you are. But I won't require it of you."

He might not consider this a test, but to her, it was. Here, alone, uncertain and uncomfortable, the minutes might stretch into a lifetime. And he wanted her half-exposed, waiting patiently with nothing to distract her from her galloping thoughts.

"Center yourself. Think about what lies ahead and how much having you waiting for me like this will please me."

Arms folded and with infinite patience, he waited for her answer.

"Yes, Sir." The air conditioner kicked on. Then the door closed with a sharp *click,* and she wondered if it was possible for her to put his desires before her own.

CHAPTER 4

Unbidden, the words Master Philip had used the first time they'd scened over video returned to her. *"You're so very beautiful when you suffer for me."*

Is that what I'm doing? Suffering for you?

And did he always want that?

The position he'd left her in—her arms folded still behind her, her pelvis a couple of inches off the vinyl—was becoming more and more taxing. And the more that realization crawled through her mind, the bigger it became until her discomfort consumed her thoughts.

With a sigh, she shifted, seeking to rebalance her weight or relieve some of the pressure from her knee joints. Allowing her shoulders to roll forward would help, and so would sitting down flat. For a moment, she considered climbing off the contraption and walking around for a minute or two. A small amount of exercise might help restore her energy. And if she was fast enough, he would never know.

The door opened, and she stifled a gasp, sitting up a little straighter.

Tore filled the space, his broad shoulders all but touching the casing on either side. Embarrassment at her submissive position raced through her, but she reassured herself that this was normal for him.

"Master Philip will be back in a moment."

She was supposed to carry on a conversation while she was like this? Skirt around her waist, breasts thrust forward? "Thank you."

Without another word, he turned and vanished, leaving her alone once again with her inhibitions wrapped in doubt.

Had her temporary Dominant asked Tore to check on her? Would he report that she'd been slouching? Or was the dungeon master simply conveying a message?

She sighed and tried to harness her thoughts—shoving away her questions about Tore's motivation.

Instead, she reconsidered what Master Philip had said. Leaving her alone, asking her to stay in position, was not a test of her dedication. But she couldn't help that she'd made it into one and, as usual, was overthinking the entire situation.

It should be easy enough to do what he asked, especially since the request was so simple, and it was all part of providing her with an unforgettable evening.

After today she would need to continue her exploration with other people, or she could just take the experience and file each scintillating detail among her memories—something to look back on fondly, maybe even wistfully.

She made her decision—to surrender, wringing every drop of joy possible from this experience. With determination, she closed her eyes and pulled her shoulders back, returning to the position he'd ordered her into earlier. Then she schooled her breathing, concentrating on pleasing him, rather than herself.

A *snick* startled her, and she opened her eyes and gasped.

"You're absolutely radiant." He placed his bag on the floor, then pushed the door closed before crossing the room to stand in front of her. "No matter what, you could never disappoint me. But this—seeing you like this, as I left you? Knowing you had to find it within yourself to transcend your doubts and cramped muscles?" Slowly he walked around the bench, and with each of his steps, she imagined the approval in his eyes. "It's sublime, Emma. *You* are sublime."

His approval sent waves of warmth through her. Climbing off the bench earlier would never have been as rewarding as this moment right now. But she had to be honest. "I didn't make it the entire time."

"Thank you for the confession. As I said, you can't disappoint me." He placed a gentle kiss on her forehead.

It was all she could do not to lean into him and beg for more. A real kiss, a caress… Things she had no right to expect.

"Now let's give you a break. You may relax."

With a huge, grateful exhalation, she sank onto the top of the bench and unlinked her hands. He was there, rubbing her wrists and lacing his fingers between hers.

She had never been cared for like this before, and she luxuriated in it.

Against her ear, he spoke. "When your Dominant is kind or considerate, it's customary to express your appreciation."

The gentle words, part reminder, part rebuke, made her open her mouth wide. *Oh my God. I knew that.* They'd discussed that a dozen times. How could she have forgotten? Except for the fact that she was lost in him, his touch, the scent of his power. "I'm sorry."

"Don't be. I'll make you pay."

She shuddered.

"Perhaps it'll serve as a reminder."

"I..."

He pulled away and looked at her. His eyes danced, but darkness lurked there, at odds with something she might otherwise read as teasing. "You still haven't said thank you."

How could she, now that her mouth was dry, and terror chilled her veins?

They'd scened over video, and she'd followed his directions, but this—being so close to him—wondering how serious he was about a punishment, was totally different. Not that she ever would, but on a chat, she could hang up and walk away. Today, that option didn't exist. "You're making me a little nervous."

"Am I?"

Since his voice held no inflection, she ascertained nothing from it. Emma forced herself to resist the impulse to wrap her arms around herself.

"Do you believe your fear is warranted?"

"Uhm..." How should she answer? "Maybe."

He leaned in, close enough that they breathed the same air. "But not enough for you to actually say thank you, even if it's expressed a little late."

"I am sorry. You're right. I do know better. What I mean is..." In the stories she devoured and the videos she binge watched, being a submissive was much easier, more instinctive. But her nerves had scrambled her thought processes. "Thank you."

Master Philip remained where he was, legs shoulder-width apart, broad and strong. Oddly, the fact that he hadn't moved reassured her. He didn't radiate anger, but instead a measured curiosity. "For?"

She blinked. For...? "Letting me rest?" It was more of a guess than a statement.

Confounding her, he didn't respond, so she filled the silence. "And for massaging away the stiffness."

If her words moved him at all, it wasn't obvious from his implacable stance. Emma dug deeper. "For your never-ending patience."

"Never-ending patience?" At that, he grinned. "Do you take me for a saint?"

"Okay, so, uhm, that part was a little over the top?"

He held his thumb and forefinger about an inch apart.

"I thought maybe it was." The tension vanished from her shoulders. "And are you still planning to"—*punish me?*—"make me pay?"

"Of course." He drew his eyebrows together. "In a scene, or anytime we're interacting as Dominant and submissive, I don't joke about things like that."

"Maybe I was hoping you had a short memory."

"Keep hoping."

He fetched his black bag, its leather worn from age. Emma turned her head to follow his movements as he carried it to the shelf near the sink area.

As he placed the satchel down, she noticed an unusual emblem on the back—a golden-colored owl, appearing to be cradled in laurel leaves. Above it was Greek lettering. Maybe from the college he'd attended?

Before she could ask about it, he unfastened the bag's two buckles, then lifted the flap.

No matter how much she moved around, she couldn't see inside.

Instead of removing any contents, he returned to her. "Like your pirate, I'm ready to be inside your clothing."

Her brain turned sluggish, and her responses slowed, but she nodded.

Master Philip offered a hand and helped her down from the bench. She was glad when he continued to hold her for a moment, because her legs suddenly didn't want to support her. "Thank you."

"You're a quick study."

His warm approval made her smile. It was shocking how important it was to her.

"In case you were thinking of asking, no. It won't make me forget your earlier transgression."

This whole BDSM thing with him was like being on a seesaw. She went from a thrilling high, back to the bottom, all in the space of mere seconds.

"Do you mind if I undress you?"

She shook her head. A man had never asked that of her. Of course, she'd had clumsy encounters where a lover had pulled off her shirt or fumbled with her bra before she'd taken pity on him and done it herself. But this was different.

Each of Master Philip's movements were strategically calculated and executed. Even the idea of just standing there for his pleasure while he removed her clothing, an item at a time, thrilled her.

Her Dominant took his sweet, sweet time. He started with her shirt, pushing the top two buttons through their tiny holes. But instead of continuing, he whispered his fingertips across her delicate skin, arousing her and leaving behind trails of goose bumps.

She was still fully dressed, yet her breaths were becoming more shallow.

Emma expected him to finish what he'd started, but he chose to tug the hem of her blouse from beneath her waistband. Once he had done that, he lowered his head, feasting his gaze as he revealed her to him, an inch at a time.

Then he finished, arrowing his touch downward to settle on the slight swell of her belly. God she ached to have her clothing out of the way so that they were skin to skin.

"Roll your shoulders forward."

She did, helping him as he removed her shirt. Rather than

letting it fall to the floor, he placed it on the bench behind her.

"Turn around for me."

The rasp of her zipper sounded unnaturally loud, mixed with her tiny murmurs.

Because the skirt was so formfitting, he had to draw it up over her head, his fingertips grazing her skin, sending wildfire through her.

"This is a look I definitely like."

He cupped her buttocks, then squeezed, making her gasp. He was so damn strong, and the way he pressed into her flesh spoke of restrained power. "Face me. I want to look at you."

After he released her, she did as instructed.

"I've seen your sexy body on camera, but you're even more beautiful in person." He took her in, sweeping his approving gaze down her body, ending with her stilettos. "Excellent choice on the lingerie. The lace is enticing and feminine. Provocative while protecting your modesty."

If only he knew how she had agonized over the decision of what to wear. Now she wished she'd had the courage to be a bit more daring.

"It's classy, Emma. Like you. I love it. Never second-guess yourself. Your instincts are perfect."

"Thank you." Her words were forced. She wasn't accustomed to accepting compliments, but she knew he expected her to respond to what he'd said.

"So pleasing."

He reached behind her to unfasten her bra, then lowered the straps before tossing the lingerie onto the bench. "Jesus. Your breasts are gorgeous." He cradled them in his palms, making her whimper.

She wanted more…more pressure, perhaps even a slight bit of pain.

"Raise your arms and cross them above your head."

Not knowing what to expect next was throwing her into a delirium that was as maddening as it was seductive.

After she had done so, he gripped her wrists and asked her to slowly spin a circle for him. As she did, the cool air from the air-conditioning whispered over her nipples, making them harder.

"Now... I'm sure it will be uncomfortable after a couple of minutes, which is an added bonus, but I'd like you to keep yours arms where they are."

Each time they played, she understood a little more how serious he'd been when he'd mentioned he loved it when she suffered for him.

"And if so, I'm happy to secure you to the hook in the ceiling." He glanced up, and she couldn't help but to follow the direction of his gaze.

When she first entered the room, she'd noticed it, but hadn't understood its significance.

"The choice is entirely yours. You can follow my order by your own free will, or I can ensure your compliance. And you're welcome to change your mind."

"I'll keep them in place, Sir."

"Very well."

Mesmerized, she watched while he lifted her breasts. And then he was totally in control, his fingers firm as he squeezed and kneaded.

Overwhelmed by sensation, she pitched forward, grabbing his shoulders for support so she didn't fall over.

For a moment, he held her while she found her footing. Then he grinned. "It seems you might need a little help after all."

"Actually I'm fine. I was just... I mean, that won't be necessary, Sir." If her protest had any affect on him, he didn't show it.

After releasing her and instructing her to get back in position, he walked toward the wall, where he worked the control that lowered the hook from the ceiling. He stopped when it was an inch or two higher than her fingertips. It took all her mental fortitude to stay where she was rather than instinctively lowering her arms.

Then he crossed to his bag and returned with a pair of soft cuffs that he wrapped around her wrists.

He checked the fit. "You'll need to stretch out your body in order to reach the hook."

Seconds later, she was well and truly helpless.

Smelling of power and ruthlessness, he leaned toward her. "Tell me your safe word."

Unable to look away from the steel in his eyes, she gulped. "Transfer."

"And if you need a break or to slow down?"

Emma appreciated this. She'd been swept up in the moment, forgetting that she was responsible for going along with what happened. "Yellow."

"Use them anytime. Of course, I'll watch for signs of distress, but I don't want you to go anywhere emotionally uncomfortable."

This time, unable to find her voice, she settled for nodding.

"How does it feel?"

"Sir?" She frowned.

"To be at my mercy? Knowing I can do anything I want to your body."

Oh God. Oh God. This was her absolute fantasy come true. He'd paid attention to every word and detail when they'd been talking downstairs. The moment—her helplessness—was overwhelming.

"This, for example." He captured her right breast and lifted it as she tried to step back. But the restraint, combined with the way he'd placed his other hand behind her, on her buttocks, prevented any escape.

He curled his fingers into her flesh, and her mouth parted. "You're mine, Emma."

Instantly her mind raced to protest his statement. She wasn't his. This was temporary. A game. Nothing more. Tomorrow she'd be Emma Monroe again, a single woman who went to work, then returned home to an empty house and lonely bed.

"Say it."

She shook her head.

Then he lowered his head and sucked her nipple into his mouth. Her knees weakened, but this time her bondage prevented her from going anywhere, and she could do nothing but cry out. For what, she wasn't exactly sure. For him to stop? Or for him to take her to heights she'd never experienced before.

Her clit throbbed, and her body demanded an orgasm.

He removed his mouth but didn't loosen his grip. Then he looked at her. "Say it."

"But…"

Sharply, he smacked her ass. There was nothing playful about it. It stung with his demand.

"Last chance."

She might not want to admit it, because the ramifications frightened her, but she nodded. "Yes. I'm yours." For now, this instant, she was. There had been no one before him. But what terrified her was that there might not be anyone after him.

"Again." He released her breast, then possessively wrapped her up, then brought her into sharp contact with his body. He was hard everywhere, his muscles powerful and his cock rigid. "This time with more meaning."

His words, his force, made her tremble. "I'm yours."

"Not enough." He released her breast to slide his hand between her legs. Then he cradled her sex, making her whimper.

His eyes never left her face as he slid a finger inside the gusset of her panties. Heaven save her. She wanted this every bit as much as she did in her wildest imaginings, and she was also every bit as nervous as she anticipated she'd be. Of course, she had control here; he'd reminded her of that before they started. But the truth was, she'd abdicated it—and herself—to him.

He moved his finger near her clit. "I can smell your heat, my Emma."

She'd never been more aroused in her entire life.

"Do you want to come in my hand?"

Closing her eyes, she nodded.

"You know I want your words. Demand them."

"Yes." She opened her eyes, and if possible his gaze held even more determination now. "Yes, Sir. I want to come."

Gently, fleetingly, he touched her clit. Then he moved away at her first gasp.

"Damn you."

He grinned, and she knew—with deep, feminine certainty—what he was doing. Owning her. Proving his point.

"Then tell me."

"I..." She was lost, to the way he pressed against her tiny bundle of nerves, then sliding the same finger into her pussy. "Master Philip!"

On and on he went, never changing his pace, teasing her, slipping in and out of her, making her wetter each moment.

Her climax remained just out of reach, and she did her best to thrust her pelvis against his hand in silent entreaty.

"It's mine to give when I want. *If* I want."

Inside her head, the world exploded into a kaleidoscope of colors.

This time, when he entered her again, he added a second finger, prying her apart. She was no longer capable of rational thought. Everything was lost to the need for his possession.

"You want it? Then say it."

She cracked and the walls she'd built around her heart, and emotions tumbled away, demolished by his dominance. "Yours." A sob caught in her throat, and tears stung her eyes. "I'm yours. *I'm yours.*"

"Fuck. Yes."

Then he gave her what she'd been silently begging for.

He dropped to his knees in front of her, pulling her panties down. "Spread your legs."

Because of her bondage, she had to rise onto her tiptoes to obey him. He had one hand on her lower back, and he used the other to spread her labia.

He devoured her, circling her clit with frantic little licks, finger-fucking her, pulling away for a moment so he could deliver sharp taps to her swollen, wet pussy. "Now. You've earned it. Come."

Unceasingly he continued as wave after wave hit her. She climaxed with a scream only to be swept into another and then a third.

He bombarded her with sensation, making her weak. Her head lolled to the side, and if she had been able to move, she'd have collapsed to the floor in a nerveless puddle. It wasn't possible to endure anything more than she'd already experienced.

And yet Master Philip wasn't done with her. He brought a wet finger back and pressed it against her anus.

Shocked, she brought her head back to center. She'd never tried it, but the sensation sent her arousal skyrocketing.

"Virgin there?"

"Yes."

His smile was filled with wicked satisfaction. "Good."

For a moment he left her, and before she could wonder where he was, he was back in front of her, and this time his finger was slick and chilled. "Relax. Bear down. I'm going to take you."

Where had fantasy ended and reality begun?

Even as he eased his finger inside, he ate her pussy. It wasn't as easy as she expected, but the ache of the stretching discomfort added to the millions of explosions ricocheting through her. "Sir…"

Rather than replying, he seated his finger all the way inside her.

"Fuck! I can't do this. I can't."

He didn't pull out, but he gave her a momentary reprieve. "I don't hear a safe word."

His words, soft and calm, crashed into her. Did she want a break? Taking her rear filled her in ways she'd never experienced before. It was uncomfortable, and more, it was overwhelming. The orgasm that was building was different, more intense than the others had been.

"Emma?"

Then she was honest, first with herself, then with him. "I think I just need to come."

"Tell me what you want."

"What you're doing is fine." *Great. Amazing, even.*

"That's not good enough. Use words. Be explicit. *Be dirty.*"

His request left her momentarily paralyzed.

He pressed the tip of his tongue into her pussy.

As best she could, she spread herself, putting more of her weight into the cuffs above her.

She thought he'd continue to use his mouth, but he didn't. Even though he didn't pull away, he kept still. How could she possibly ask him to continue the torment? Because they'd played together several times over video, she'd thought she had some idea of what to expect from scening with him. But nothing could have prepared her for the force that Master Philip exerted. "I…"

This was more difficult than she imagined. The memory of the hurt of Aaron's betrayal taunted her. But to get what she wanted now, she'd have to shove that pain aside.

The need to orgasm hadn't gone away. It was still there, gnawing at her body and snapping with impatience. Dirty wasn't her forte. But he gave her the courage to do anything.

After taking a breath, she tried again. "Fuck my ass with your finger, Sir." Then with a whisper, a plea, she added her entreaty. "Please."

"And what else?"

"Eat my pussy." He'd liberated her from her inhibitions. "Eat my pussy. Make me come hard. I want to scream your name."

If he responded, she didn't hear him.

He gave her everything she asked for, and more.

And when she climaxed, it was with a force she'd never experienced before. His tongue was inside her. His finger filled her. But her splintering emotions spiraled her into another dimension, where nothing existed except pleasure.

She was gone, and she didn't even realize he'd stood and somehow managed to unfasten her from the hook.

When her breathing returned to normal, she was on his lap in the chair, and he was massaging her shoulders.

"That was… I mean…" After blinking, she pressed herself away from his chest, then shook her head. "How did I get here?"

"Perhaps subspace?"

"I read about that. But I wasn't sure it was real."

"Oh it is." He tucked her wayward behind her ear. "Absolutely."

"I just know that was…" *What?* "Something." As if she'd waited her entire life for the orgasm. "You were wonderful."

"Thank you."

Horrified, she looked at him. "Oh no! I'm supposed to say that, aren't I?"

"I'm keeping score." His eyebrows were set sternly, but a smile hovered around his mouth, making him appear much less intimidating, but not quite approachable.

Anticipation traced up her spine. If his idea of punishment was anything like that… "Thank you for the orgasm." *Or ten. Maybe a dozen.*

"The pleasure is mine. I've wanted to do that from the moment you stepped on the elevator."

Still woozy, she placed her head on his chest again. And he allowed her to stay there until she roused herself.

"Well, then, the scene can begin when you're ready."

She blinked. "You mean that wasn't it?"

"That was the preamble. And there's the matter of your punishment."

"I'm not sure I can take anything more."

"Your call entirely. If you'd like to end it now, that's understandable. I'll help you get dressed, and I'll either call Cressida, or we can find a couch or go to the bar to decompress."

Spending time together appealed to her, but she wasn't quite ready to end the evening. "I'm intrigued by what else you have planned."

He nodded. "Tell me when you're ready."

A few minutes later, she caught her breath enough to ease herself away from him. It shocked her that she was naked, and had been entirely comfortable, despite the fact that he was still dressed.

Her discarded panties were on the floor, and she scooped them up.

"Since I want you back on the bench, you might want to put your belongings on the shelf."

She scooped up her garments and carried them to where he was standing, in front of the sink, washing his hands. Since she was so close, she was hoping to peek into his bag, but frustratingly, he'd closed the flap.

He uncapped a bottle of water and waited while she took a couple of sips. "You're steady?"

"I am."

"Wait for me next to the bench, please."

His voice was lower than it had been moments ago, turning her blood sluggish. Seconds ago, she'd been wrapped in his arms, and now, she was his to command again.

"Now, Emma."

She crossed the floor, her heels echoing off the hardwood floor.

"Stand with your back to me."

Which meant he didn't want her to see what he was doing.

From his side of the room, metal clanged, and she couldn't resist looking over her shoulder...to find him watching her every action.

Damn him.

"Third infraction, if I'm counting correctly."

Confounded Dominant. Of course he'd cataloged every misstep, and he wouldn't forget any of them.

A few minutes later, he crossed the room to stand in front of her, the wheeled cart next to him.

"How are your shoulders?"

"Better."

"Well enough for you to place your hands behind your neck? If not, you may simply leave them by your side."

"I'll try." After a slight twinge, she was fine.

He rolled back his sleeves, exposing his forearms, and once again she had the crazy image of him being a pirate.

"You've been playing with nipple clamps at home."

"Mostly when I'm on the phone with you, Sir."

"We'll see how you do with the clovers."

She wrinkled her nose.

"Is that a silent protest?"

"They're the nasty ones, Sir."

"I'm aware."

Of all the things they'd played with, those were the ones she liked least. They seemed to have two intensities—painful and more painful. At least tweezers could be adjusted so they were barely there. The alligators she'd used looked vicious, but their little metal teeth didn't bite terribly hard.

"Since you've expressed your displeasure, please press your breasts together and up, offering them to me."

How had she not realized he had a sadistic streak?

"Emma?"

Not that it would do her any good, but she took her time.

"Now ask me to affix the clamps."

Instead, she pressed her lips together.

"Your choice. Safe word, or immediately do as I say."

Ice edged his words.

"Please clamp my nipples, Sir."

"Ah, Emma. When you ask so nicely, how can I refuse?"

She bit back her instinctive snarky reply.

Thankfully he played with her first, caressing her breasts, then laving the pebbled tips with his tongue, only to then release them.

"Ready?"

After drawing a breath, she nodded.

Without any delay, he set the rubber-coated tips in place.

"How's that?"

She exhaled, relieved that the pain wasn't as severe as she'd anticipated.

"You may release your breasts."

"Thank you."

"It's a little late, but you remembered before I mentioned it."

His approval would get her to behave more than her punishment; she was convinced of it.

"Will you please step out of your shoes? As sexy as I find them, I'm wanting you to be very much aware of your submissive state before your first spanking."

The clamps swayed when she bent, making her wince as she kicked off her heels and swept them beneath the bench, out of the way.

She stood in front of him again, aware of their height difference. In stilettos, she almost looked him in the eye. Now she had to tip back her head. And being barefoot on the cold floor, naked and clamped, she was terribly aware of her role.

"It's working, isn't it?"

"Yes, Sir." And if it hadn't been, her use of the honorific would have sealed it.

He once again reached for something on the top shelf of the cart. "I'm going to put this in you."

"What is it?"

"It's a vibrator."

Frowning, she accepted a sleek, stylistic pink device that was shaped like an exaggerated C. "I'm not sure I understand."

"I'll show you."

"Why was I afraid you'd say that?"

"The position I had you in earlier on the bench. Do you remember it?"

How could she forget?

"Please resume it."

With a small nod, she offered him back the vibrator.

Arms folded across his chest, taking in each of her movements, Master Philip appeared to be in full Dominant mode as he watched her climb into place.

Because each movement disturbed her clamps, she took her time and stayed as still as possible.

When she was on the top of the piece of equipment, arms behind her, breasts thrust forward, pussy a couple of inches off the vinyl, she shook her head a little to adjust her hair. Then she wished she hadn't, because a piercing pain shot through her nipples.

"You're everything, Emma. Beautiful in your compliance."

Warmth suffused her, chasing away all discomfort. Until this evening, she'd had no concept of just how powerful word choice could be.

"Stay still while I insert the vibrator."

She frowned. "How does it stay in place?"

"You may have to squeeze your muscles."

He was perfunctory. Rather than taking the time to explore or play with her, he crouched for an up-close view of her private area. Then he inserted a finger to find her G-spot. She jerked in response.

"Right there."

He knew her body as well as she did.

Before tonight, something like this might have mortified her. But now, she just forced herself to settle down and submit to her Dominant's evil little plans.

"Keep your position, Emma."

A moment later, he settled the long end of the curved device against her G-spot. Whatever he did next was going to be awful.

He continued on, placing the other end of the vibrator

against her clit. Then he squeezed the silicone together, so it conformed to her body. "How's that?"

It seemed to weigh several pounds, though in reality she knew it couldn't be more than a couple of ounces at the most.

After spreading her labia and pressing the head more firmly against her clit, he took a step back.

She tightened all her muscles, but even at that, she wasn't sure she could keep it in place. "You're asking the impossible."

"Gravity won't help, either. It'd be much easier if I allowed you to lie down."

Which he clearly had no intention of doing.

He reached into his pocket, and instantly a pulse went through the device, forcing the ribbed ends to simultaneously shudder against her clit and G-spot.

She cried out, reaching behind her for something to hold on to. "What was that?"

"Remote control. It has about two dozen settings. That was the…"

Whatever he was saying was lost as a second wave went through her, making her whimper. She was on fire, overwhelmed with response, her pussy dampening in response to his action.

"How was that?"

Emma shuddered. "Surprising."

"You're slouching."

It took amazing amounts of control to regain her composure.

"Ready?"

She wasn't sure she'd ever be. "Yes, Sir."

He stood there, one hand in his pocket, studying her… infuriating her as the seconds ticked into minutes and the burn in her nipples intensified and her internal muscles became fatigued, screaming at her to relax. But if she did, the dreaded thing conforming to her pussy might slip out. No doubt that would that lead to extra punishment. "Sir?"

"This is at my pleasure."

She clenched her ass cheeks, trying to keep herself still. "And as we know, you like to see me suffer." Her words were dry, filled with her frustration.

"Precisely." He sent a quick jolt to her most sensitive place, and as she was adjusting to it, he sent another and then a third, followed by a fourth.

She bucked, trying to escape even as she wanted more—enough to give her an orgasm. This thing was annoying more than arousing.

As suddenly as it had started, it was over, and he soothed two fingertips across her forehead.

Despite her frustration, she turned to him for comfort.

"You might protest, but your body is damp. And there's no doubt you're edging toward another orgasm."

To avoid answering, she pressed her lips together. He was right. As usual.

He fisted the chain running between her breasts, easing her toward him. She moaned, wanting the hurt to end, while at the same time craving more.

"That's it. Sit up. You don't have permission to escape my wishes."

All her nerve endings were inflamed.

Suddenly he activated the vibrator, on full speed. Shockwaves echoed through her, bouncing off every part of her mind. The unceasing energy overwhelmed her.

Vaguely she was aware of Master Philip slipping a finger inside her, forcing the frustrating end piece more firmly against her G-Spot. The pressure intensified, driving her mad, making her want to crawl out of her skin. "Sir."

"Do you want to come?"

Want? No. It was so much more than that. Without it, she might lose her sanity.

"You look so goddamn hot, humping my hand like the perfect submissive you are. That's it, Emma. Rock your hips. Grind against me. Let me see you lose control."

"Sir! *Sir!*" Misery unwound through every part of her mind.

"Let yourself go. Take everything I give you and demand more. Be that honest, dirty, slutty woman that you want to be."

His nasty words freed her. For the first time in her life, she shoved aside everything except her sexual desire. She rocked and writhed, offering her breasts, fucking his hand.

"That's it." He tugged on her the chain, and anguish rocketed through her nipples.

Unable to escape him, she tipped her head back and offered her complete surrender. He accepted and relentlessly drove her forward. She was lost…gone.

With a primal scream, she shattered, drenching his hand with her powerful orgasm.

Then he spoke, proving he wasn't done with her. "Keep going."

Emma rode several frantic, successive orgasms until he showed mercy and turned off the vibrator. Spent, she collapsed onto the top of the bench.

Murmuring words of approval, he removed the clamps. With a moan, she curled a little into herself as she waited for the tenderness to subside.

"You did well." He eased his palm down the middle of her sweat-slickened back.

"Thank you." Her words came from somewhere deep in her subconscious. "For everything." *Your caring nature.* She breathed. "The orgasms."

"I'd give you the stars in exchange for your cries mixed with gratitude."

Even though she hadn't been aware of him walking away, he dried her off with a soft towel. "You're so very thoughtful."

A few minutes later, after he'd offered her more water and removed the vibrator, she roused herself. After this, she had no doubt that she could sleep for days.

"How are you doing?"

"Exhausted. That was…" She sought for the right word. Overwhelming? "Everything."

"Not quite."

She shrugged several times, attempting to ease the cramps from her body. "Meaning?"

"I haven't lost track of your infractions. And it's time to pay up."

CHAPTER 5

Blinking, Emma met Master Philip's gaze. This time he had to be teasing. How much more could she take? Then his statement returned to her. He didn't joke about things like this. No mirth teased his lips—instead they were a single, tight line, compressed with determination. His eyes were every bit as dark and unreadable as they always were.

"Unless you'd like to pick this up another time?"

But there wouldn't be another time. They'd agreed to only one scene, no matter how much that idea now made her heart hurt with regret.

No way did she want her first experience with spanking —or at least that's what she assumed he had in mind—to come from any other man.

She shook her head. "I'm fine." Even if tonight had changed her forever.

"Good. I'd hate to have this hanging over your head."

God he was a total and complete Dominant. Each word was calculated for maximum impact.

"When you're ready, lie flat on top of the bench, then back up all the way to the end, thrusting your ass out as far as you can. And yes, before you comment, you might feel as if you'll lose your balance. I'm fine with that."

Of course he was, since it wasn't his body in question.

He continued to talk as he moved away. "For the moment, I want your body completely flat."

When her breasts touched the cool vinyl, she recoiled—from the chill, but mostly from the gentle abrasion to her swollen nipples.

"Would you like to be secured? It's your choice entirely."

Earlier she'd loved the freedom of being able to struggle against the hook he'd attached her to. It had allowed her to completely surrender to the experience instead of worrying about staying in one place. "Yes."

She took a deep breath to relax while he fetched the cuffs.

Less than two minutes later, he had her securely attached to the bench, his motions crisp yet oddly tender when he checked the fit of each cuff.

"Are all Dominants this attentive?"

"I can't speak for anyone else. But I like touching your soft skin."

She smiled.

He scraped a nail down the center of her back. "It's almost as pleasurable as marking it."

Emma struggled then, wanting to get away. His chuckle didn't reassure her at all.

"I like the way you look, bound for me, naked. Helpless to escape. Beautiful in your bondage."

His words of approval warmed her. Men had given her compliments before, but they'd never been this specific or thoughtful. He wasn't simply telling her she was pretty. He was defining what he appreciated about her.

When he stepped back, she turned her head to the side, resting her cheek on the vinyl surface as she took him in. She'd never seen a more gorgeous man. It was more than just his classic good looks—with his sharp chin line, aristocratic nose, and startling eyes. It was his air of complete and total confidence spiced with a touch of arrogance.

This was a night she would always remember with a man she'd never forget.

He placed his hand on her shoulder, silently indicating she should move down as far as she could.

"Good start. But I want your ass higher."

Emma gasped, horribly aware of how lewd the position would be, exposing her completely to him.

"Do it *now*."

No doubt he'd had plenty of women in this position, but for her it was beyond embarrassing.

Eyes closed against the humiliation, she followed his instructions.

"*Fuck*. So damn gorgeous. You're helpless to escape me. If only you had some idea how much your obedience pleases me."

She dug deep inside herself. Making him happy thrilled her, and if he wanted her like this, then she'd swallow her pride.

"I may keep you like this forever."

A wild part of her wanted just that—for the magic to go on endlessly.

"Where were we?"

Surely you don't expect me to answer that.

"How many infractions did you commit, little submissive?"

Her mind whirled. With him standing so close, threatening her first real punishment, she couldn't think straight enough to form an answer. She took a guess. "Two?"

He didn't respond, and the silence hung between them, heavy with threat.

Emma's heart thundered, and she forced herself to breathe. "Three?" It couldn't be more than that.

"That's correct. I've decided we should use a different implement for each. What do you think?

"I have no idea."

"Think of it as a buffet. You'll get to sample several different types of impact play, giving you an idea of things you like as well as things you don't."

In fear, in anticipation, her tummy clenched. "That's..." *What?* "Reasonable, Sir."

He laughed, as if her opinion had not really mattered at all. "And how many spanks with each?"

As much as she wanted to be brave and ask for dozens, she was apprehensive. "Three again?"

"Now that's reasonable."

Unable to believe he'd agreed with such a tiny number, she breathed out her relief.

"I will select the first implement, and then I will let you choose the second. How does that sound?"

More awful than I can imagine.

He crossed to the corner where he selected several things from his bag and moved them to the cart, which he then wheeled toward her. His body was angled to block a clear view, but he selected something from one of the hooks on the back and showed it to her.

"Since we've discussed it before, I'll begin with the crop. Because I'm magnanimous, I'll use one with a thick keeper so the bite isn't as terrible."

She supposed he was being generous.

He held it in front of her.

His assurance didn't matter. The thing appeared rather ominous to her. "Thank you, Sir."

"I love the way those words fall from your mouth. I'd enjoy hearing them all the time."

"Yes." It was shocking how easy it had become to address him this way. "Sir."

He laid the implement crossways on her back, right above her buttocks. Though she squirmed, she was unable to retreat.

"Now it's your turn." He stepped aside, and she took in several different floggers, a strap, a couple of different paddles, one wooden, the other pink leather.

She'd been curious about the impact from a paddle. But now that they were hanging in front of her, promising to light up her skin, they terrified her. But honestly, so did everything else that was dangling dangerously from the cart.

"What will it be?"

Attempting to delay the inevitable, she stalled. "Is that writing on that leather paddle?"

"It is."

"What does it say?"

"Princess."

She couldn't hide her grin.

"The word would look beautiful emblazoned on your skin."

"Then that's my choice."

"I was hoping it would be."

In previous conversations, he'd mentioned that he got off on providing his submissive with pleasure. For the first time, she understood what he meant, maybe not fully, but it made more sense than it had. Making him happy was indeed an aphrodisiac for her.

"Which leaves me with the third and final choice."

Wondering which horrible thing it would be, she studied the cart.

"None of these."

She frowned. Did that mean he was going to settle for only punishing her for two missteps? "Sir?"

"I'm going to use my hand. It's much more personal, don't you agree?"

In ways she couldn't even explain.

"I'm going to cover every inch of your skin."

Maybe that was the worst choice of all. "That sounds ominous."

"It's a warning."

He moved behind her and began rubbing her buttocks.

She clenched and retreated as far from him as her bonds would allow, sending the crop crashing to the floor.

"Stop overthinking, Emma." Despite the command, his words were inviting, soothing, even. "Get out of your own head and stop trying to hide. Every reaction you have, I want. From the time we entered this room until the moment we leave, you ceded control to me. I hope I've proved myself worthy of your trust."

"You have."

"Good. Then recognize that I know what I'm doing in exposing your secrets. I won't harm you. In fact, I'll treasure you."

Bit by bit, he was putting pieces of her soul back together —pieces she hadn't known were broken.

"Embarrassment has no place between us." He touched her anus, pressed against it. "Breathe deep and keep going. Can you do that?"

As always, he slayed the fear within her, leaving arousal behind.

He slipped a finger between her feminine folds. No longer thinking, she ground herself backward, silently seeking more.

"You're so responsive, and I appreciate that. You could come right now, this moment. Couldn't you?"

Helplessly she nodded.

"But this isn't about giving you an orgasm you haven't

earned." He removed his hand. "It's about me reminding you to remember your manners."

Too late, too damn late, she remembered. "Yes, Sir." Why couldn't it come more naturally for her? "Thank you, Sir."

"If you knew how perilously close you'd come to adding another set of punishment. That would have made four, wouldn't it?"

She pressed her lips together.

"And to be fair, because you would have been compounding your errors, it would have been fitting to have four strokes from each implement. That would have meant going from nine to sixteen."

That, she wasn't sure she was strong enough for. "Thank you, Sir I appreciate your patience, and your kindness. It's more than I deserve."

"Ah. You *are* learning." He resumed rubbing her skin, massaging it. Then he took her ass cheeks in his hands and vigorously shook her flesh.

The reverberations rocked her whole body and made her nipples harden against the bench. "Is this what's called a warm-up?"

"It is indeed. It's not my intention to leave marks on you. Well, not ones that last a terribly long time."

So some are acceptable?

"I want you to be able to take what I plan to give you, and that means ensuring you have plenty of blood flow to your sweet behind."

Then suddenly he stopped, and she was able to inhale deeply while he took a moment to pick up the crop and clean it with a sanitizing wipe.

"Are you ready?"

I'm not sure I ever will be. And yet, she was also anxious to begin so she could put the first experience behind her.

He delivered one strike against her right buttock and then

delivered the second to her left. The unexpected sting from the leather flap left her panting.

"How many more?"

"One." She was barely able to force out the word. "This hurts worse than I imagined it would?"

"Does it?"

She scowled. Where was the concern he usually showed?

"Perhaps that's why it's called punishment."

In that moment he was such a Dominant. "You've got a mean, cold streak."

"You may learn to love it."

"I'm not sure that's possible."

"For the moment, let's concentrate on finishing this session, shall we? How many more with my favorite crop?"

What if she said none? Then she re-thought the answer, deciding it wouldn't go in her favor. He wouldn't be averse to extending her suffering. "One, Sir."

He delivered it, searing her pussy.

With a startled yelp she lunged forward, trying to escape. And then Master Philip was there, pressing his finger against her tormented flesh, soothing it.

The pain receded almost instantly, leaving her more aroused than she ever had been, leaving her whimpering again, but from need.

"Maybe we should do more like this. I can place the rest of them in the same spot with the crop."

"Oh God, no." *Please. Yes.*

"I think you protest too much."

If he continued to play with her like this, she'd agree to almost anything.

"Now we'll move onto your selection. The paddle, wasn't it?" After returning the crop to a hook, he picked up the pink implement.

"Would you like the word Princess to appear on your

skin?" With the bottom of the paddle, he traced a line up her thigh, then across the tender spot right beneath her bottom.

And then finally, he placed the shaft against the fleshiest part of her buttocks.

"I can give you a strike on each thigh, and then one on your ass. Or would you prefer I cover both of your thighs at the same time?"

"Are you really asking my opinion, Sir?"

"This time, I am."

The way he was now drawing out the moment was making her apprehensive. While she deliberated, he moved the paddle around.

"Make a decision, please."

How am I supposed to know? "Wherever it hurts least."

He laughed. "I can control that to some degree with the intensity."

"How about on the underneath of my ass cheeks?"

"All three in quick succession, or slowly, giving you time to recover?"

"Fast."

She was not prepared for his lighting reflexes nor the way the leather burned. Each smack made her cry out.

Finally, when it was over, he tossed the paddle on top of the cart, and it landed with a loud clank.

"The letters are there."

With the way her skin burned, she had no doubt.

"They're superficial, and they'll fade within seconds." But with his thumbnail he traced the P and then the R.

His touch was exquisitely painful, and she hated it as much as she loved it.

"And now, my beautiful submissive. Are you ready for the last three?"

His question meant their evening together was almost over.

With tears filling her eyes, she nodded.

"Then ask."

"Please, Sir." She blinked to clear her vision, hoping he didn't see her weakness. "Will you spank me with your hand?"

"That was perfect, Emma." He moved to the side and took his time, delivering the first one on top of the place where he'd scratched the P into her skin.

He was masterful, brutal, beautiful, and she was losing herself in him.

Then he shifted position, placing one hand firmly on her back, forcing her down against the vinyl.

His next sizzled, so much so that she would have reared up if he hadn't kept her in place.

"Last one."

Ever.

"Where would you like it?" He traced between her legs.

No! No, no. Not there. Please. Before she could force out her response, he took the choice away from her. He laid it on top of the first one; then he rubbed away the hurt before stepping back.

"Everything about you is absolutely beautiful. I can see the imprint from my fingers, and it's fucking beautiful." He dropped to one knee beside her and feathered her hair back so that she could look at him as she struggled to bring her breathing under control. "You did well. Every bit as wonderful as a more experienced submissive. It's been an honor to introduce you to my way of life."

"Thank you." Her whisper contained her whole heart, her gratitude, her goodbye.

He smiled. "Even that was well done."

"There's a lot to remember."

Just like he had at the beginning of their time together, he kissed her forehead before standing.

He released her bonds—her physical ones, anyway. The ones that attached them emotionally were still in place, at least on her end.

"You're free to move around a little, relieve any cramps, but I'd like you to stay where you are while I rub you with some arnica cream." His voice soothed her, almost as much as the dance of his fingertips across her skin did. "It will help prevent bruising, and it should help with some muscle fatigue as well. Maybe a bath before bed."

That she would definitely do. No doubt it would take some time to process their time together. Without a glass of wine or a cup of tea, she doubted she'd sleep at all.

When he was finished, she didn't push herself up. After everything they'd been through, she was well and truly spent.

"I've got you." He helped her from the bench and then carried her over to the chair in the corner of the room.

At some point, without her realizing it, he'd tossed a blanket over the back, and he plucked it off and wrapped her in it when he sat.

She needed no encouragement to settle into his arms. "I think I could get used to this."

"Good." He toyed with her hair. "It's part of the connection. For me, scening isn't complete without it."

Even though she wasn't a snuggler, she stayed there, taking comfort from the gentle rise and fall of his chest beneath her, accepting comfort.

For a few minutes she just allowed herself not to think at all.

"How are you doing?" A stray tear clung to her lashes, and he wiped it away. "Do you want to talk about your experience?"

"No." The word emerged squeaky, and she cleared her throat. "I'm not sure I can…at least not right now." Repeatedly he'd told her how important it was for them to be honest with each other. But her heart was involved, and she wasn't sure she could trust herself. Even though she barely knew him, she was starting to care for him. The realization was absurd, and something had to be off-kilter for that idea to even float around her mind. It had to be a result of endorphins or one of the other weird brain chemicals spilling through her system. It was impossible to fall in love with someone in less than two weeks, no matter what they'd shared.

Regardless, she was overwhelmed. Above all else, she needed time alone to process everything.

Afraid of confessing her ridiculous emotions to him and putting them both in an awkward position, she removed the blanket. "Thank you. It was an amazing experience." She slid from his lap.

Surprisingly she wobbled a little, and he placed his hands around her hips, holding her tight until she was steady.

"Would you like to go to the bar? I'm happy to buy you a drink or a soda, even a meal if you'd like...give you a little time to think and then talk when you're ready?"

"I've got an early morning. But I appreciate it."

He continued to hold her, seeming as reluctant as she was to end the evening. "It really has been everything I could hope for. You were..." God, what was wrong with her? How could leaving him be so difficult? "The best Dominant possible for my first experience." She offered a gentle smile.

"The honor really was mine."

"I'm good. You can let go of me now." The urge to run built in her.

With a small nod, he did as she requested.

While she dressed, pretending her fingers weren't shaking and that her heart wasn't threatening to explode, he cleaned the room and the toys they'd used before repacking his bag.

As he rolled down his sleeves and reached for his phone, she slipped into her shoes.

"You're sure you're ready to leave?" He looked up from the screen.

"I am."

"Would…?"

She tilted her head to the side. Was he distracted? Surely that was the case, because he wasn't a man to consider his words.

"Would you like me to take you home?"

No. If he did, she might beg him to stay. How mortifying it would be when he informed her that she'd misunderstood everything? "Thank you. I've taken you away from your real life for long enough."

"It's no problem."

"I'm fine." Was that force or desperation in her tone? "Really."

"Very well." His nod was curt. "In that case, I'll let Cressida know you're ready."

That sounded so final.

After he slung the bag over his shoulder, she followed him from the room and down the stairs, marveling at how an hour or two together could change her so completely. She was no longer an innocent, and what had seemed so foreign was now normal.

He led her out of the dungeon and pushed through the etched glass door back into the reception area to claim her purse.

"You're welcome to call me anytime with questions or to talk about what we shared."

"Thank you." She smiled. "And I mean that sincerely, not just because I think I have to say it. I'm so glad you talked to me on the elevator."

"I am as well. Thank you for trusting me."

She clutched her purse.

"Before you go." He opened his bag and pulled out a tube. "It's the arnica. I want you to massage more in before you go to bed tonight, and then have a look at your bottom in the morning. If there is any trace of a bruise, or if you're sore anywhere, go ahead and use it again."

"That's thoughtful of you." She accepted it and tucked it away.

"I'll see you out."

Trinity smiled as they walked past. "Thanks for coming."

Acting as if everything was normal and that she wasn't holding on to her emotions by a thread, Emma said good night.

Outside, Master Philip placed a protective arm around her shoulder as they waited for the sedan to slide to a stop at the curb. Then he opened the back door of the vehicle and offered a hand as she slid inside.

One final time, he eased a knuckle over her cheekbone, then down the side of her throat. "You're exquisite."

Then, with a small salute, he stepped back and closed the door.

Before pulling away, Cressida glanced in the rearview mirror. "Straight home, Ms. Monroe?"

Unable to resist temptation, Emma looked back to see him still standing on the sidewalk beneath one of the historic lampposts, hands in his pockets, frowning. "Yes. Please."

What was she supposed to do now? For him, this was an everyday experience, but her entire world had been upended. He'd given her a taste of BDSM, and it wasn't even close to being enough.

∼

What the actual fuck is wrong with me?

Philip pushed the Up button on the elliptical machine, until its speed was somewhere between punishing and impossible.

The day he walked out of court with his divorce papers signed after the proceedings had dragged on for years, he vowed he wouldn't spend his time consumed with thoughts of the fairer sex.

In retrospect, it had been complete stupidity to play with Emma—not because he hadn't wanted to, but because her responses had been beautiful, stunning. Since she stepped on the elevator, innocent and curious, he'd lived for her sighs and thirsted for her whimpers. Last night, everything about her had been perfect.

Until her, he'd never played with a neophyte before, and the experience had been nothing short of pure pleasure.

His ex had made him into a man relentlessly focused on his goals and on his future—never reflecting on the past. So why the hell couldn't he stop thinking about last night and Emma—the way she had shamelessly come undone for him. The way she surrendered was the stuff of Dominant dreams.

He'd sent her a text message when the chauffeur app had informed him that she was home safe.

He wanted to know she was okay. That was his duty to her. Any Dominant who gave a shit about his obligations would do the same.

But the way he'd held his phone, waiting for her response, reminded him of the way he'd behaved in high school, rather than the person he was now.

Her reply had taken forever, long enough for Cressida to drive him home and for him to pour a Scotch from his private reserve. At that point, he began to worry and think that perhaps his concern was well-placed.

No doubt scening with him had been a lot for her. He had high expectations and pushed her. Too far?

Once he cradled her in his lap, she distanced herself from him—becoming emotionally withdrawn. Other than comforting her, asking if she was okay, offering dinner, conversation, or drinks, he hadn't known what to do.

When she finally replied, her response was as short as her replies had been at the club.

I'm fine. Taking a bath and then going to bed. Good night.

What the fuck? And how was he supposed to respond? Then reality smacked him hard. She didn't want him to.

Why the hell not? He'd been a Dominant a long time. He knew for a fact she hadn't been faking her reaction to him. She'd been as invested in the scene as he had.

Thinking, he carried around his phone.

Was he stupid for letting her go home alone? Really, what choice had there been? He'd made the offer, and she refused. She was an adult, capable of making her own decisions, which clearly she had done. They'd both agreed to one evening, a few tantalizing hours together. So he should have been able to compartmentalize the experience and file it away and go on with his life. But the cold, hard fact was, he didn't want to.

Chatting with her in the evenings had filled a hole in his life, one he hadn't realized was there. He no longer worked as many hours, and he was more creative when he arrived at the office. Even though it had only been a short time that he'd known her, it was already difficult to imagine a future without her.

Unable to let her last text be their final communication, he'd reached out again.

I'm here for you anytime.

Nothing.

So he reverted to his natural role.

Remember to use the arnica.

No matter how many times he checked, his notification light was off.

After the second shot of liquor warmed his insides, he'd replayed the details of their outing, recalling the sight of her as he'd bared her body to him. Once he'd placed the vibrator inside her, she'd gotten out of her head, forgetting her inhibitions. She'd been so sexy with her back arched and hair hanging wildly everywhere. The memory of her pants and screams had whispered in his ear. Unbelievably aroused, he'd masturbated in the shower.

The relief had been temporary. When he woke up this morning, he'd jacked off again. When that didn't satiate the angst crawling through him, he grabbed a duffel bag and headed for the elite fitness center near his office.

Fortunately he had a card that allowed him access to Next Level twenty-four hours a day, and when he arrived, he'd been the only person in the place.

Now, bright light flooded the area, and music reverberated off the walls with a powerful thump. Which no doubt meant it was almost five a.m. He glanced over as Sean Finnegan, the center's owner, walked past, lifting a hand but not interrupting.

With a tight nod, Philip continued at his grueling pace.

As other people entered, headed for the spin area, his muscles began to fatigue. His T-shirt was drenched, and perspiration clung to his face. After adjusting the machine's speed for a cooldown period, he grabbed his hand towel.

Five minutes later, his heart rate in a much safer zone, he hit the Stop button, then wiped down the equipment before moving to the free weight station.

Outside, the sun was rising, bouncing and refracting off a nearby building.

He was re-racking his weights after a final set when

Mason walked over. Judging by the state of his clothing, he'd just finished up his cardio.

"How'd it go last night?"

"None of your fucking business."

"I see." Unperturbed, Mason began adding plates to his barbell. "Spot me?"

Philip joined Mason at the weight bench.

"Been thinking about the 1212 Building."

"You mean other than selling it as Thoroughgood suggests?"

"It's in a good location and has good bones. It just needs a rehab."

Or a bulldozer.

"We could make it into one of the Crescent City's crown jewels."

Was his wallet deep enough for that?

"I've got ideas, and I've started drawing up some of them. Thinking about proposing a mixed-use concept." Mason repped out a dozen impressive bench presses. No wonder he was capable of swinging a fucking hammer all day.

When he was finished, Philip placed his hands under the bar as his friend racked it.

"You've got good views from the top few floors. They could be lofts, and you could offer concierge services."

"You think that'd fly in the CBD?" he asked, referring to New Orleans's Central Business District.

"I do. You could run it by Thoroughgood. Barring that, maybe a boutique hotel of some sort."

With the proximity to the French Quarter, that was a possibility.

"And then there's the bottom few floors."

"Go on."

Before responding, Mason dove into his second set. Then,

after he'd recovered, he outlined his next ideas. "You've got a coffee cart in there now, right?"

That was boarded up at two o'clock in the afternoon, right when he needed his midday pickup.

"Make it a full coffee shop, maybe with an expanded breakfast and lunch menu—grab passersby. Have quiet corners for meetings, separated by artistic partitions for privacy. In the afternoons, add wine and fine whiskies, maybe with some jazz."

It could work—breathing some life into the dozens of floors. When he'd gotten pissed off and purchased the historic spot, he hadn't realized what a nightmare he'd be walking into. All this would take money, and a lot of it. And perhaps this was a place the consortium might be helpful. At this point, he had no qualms with relinquishing some of his ownership shares.

"Maybe some shared office space that people can pop in and rent by the day or even by the hour. Have a notary on staff—maybe the person who runs the coffee shop. Have an office concierge who can arrange meetings, handle AV needs, make copies. I've heard of real estate agents and title companies who want to close their own offices but need these kind of services. Add a bank, perhaps. A couple of places for impulse retail therapy."

The lobby was a vast, empty marble space that echoed with footsteps. Adding a bunch of potted plants hadn't deadened the noise or breathed life into the sterile environment. And that was what was needed. Life. People. Energy.

"You could have a spa on one of the upper floors, where visitors would have a premium view. Which brings me to my next idea."

Mason had given it some thought.

"Go on."

After he completed his workout, he sat up and nodded

toward Sean, who was headed in their direction. "Talk to Fin about opening a new gym in your place."

Scowling, Sean stopped next to them, legs braced shoulder width apart, massive arms folded across his chest. "Health world."

"I stand corrected."

"You said that on purpose."

"Figured it would get your attention." Mason grinned.

"Asshole."

Philip was intrigued. Sean Finnegan—known as Fin, not just because it was short for his surname, but because he'd been a Navy Seal and had the ability to swim underwater for ridiculous amounts of time, like a shark—had taken his fitness skillset and added in a degree in architecture. He'd built some of the most luxurious workout spots in the world, and he wasn't afraid to make constant improvements. His services weren't cheap, but having a world-class fitness center in the 1212 Building would earn it a marketing splash.

"And a swimming pool, potentially?" Mason wiped his face.

"Just acquired a design firm. And in addition to a hot tub, maybe we add in ice bath features."

Philip shuddered. "Worth considering." That part was a fucking lie. He didn't care how good it was for his body or mental constitution—he wasn't jumping into forty-something-degree water, let alone paying for the privilege.

Mason stood. "I've got an opening in my schedule next month."

"I'll have my assistant set up a meeting." It could work, especially if Philip could get the consortium involved to ease some of the financial woes. "Get an idea of the costs."

"It'll be a small fortune." Mason beamed.

"Never doubted that." After saying his goodbyes, Philip headed to the locker room that could have appeared in a glossy magazine. Previously he'd noted the high-end fixtures and flooring. This time his brain added in dollar signs to everything he noticed. If Mason had his way, Sean would be blowing through Philip's money as if it were confetti.

On the other hand, membership fees could be lucrative.

After he'd grabbed his bag and hit the shower, thoughts of Emma returned—not that they'd been far away to begin with.

He stepped under the lukewarm spray and scrubbed his wet body with a washcloth. Yeah. He and Emma had agreed to only one night. And he had been concerned about her after she left. But there was something more… It bothered him that she'd stopped responding to his texts. Worse was the glimpse of tears he'd caught in her eyes.

He'd had subs cry before. It was a natural enough phenomenon after her brain had been flooded with endorphins. Yet something else had haunted Emma's expression. Sadness, maybe?

As he rinsed, the soapy lather arrowed toward the drain, taking his protestations of denial with it, leaving behind a truth he couldn't deny.

Over the past few weeks, he'd developed an emotional connection with Emma, and if his guess was correct—and he'd never been more certain of anything—the feeling was reciprocal. One night wasn't enough. He wanted forever, and he never intended to let her go.

After turning off the shower and toweling dry, he dug his cell phone out of his bag to place a phone call—taking the first and very deliberate step in claiming her as his own.

CHAPTER 6

"So…" Shelby reached forward to pluck a cashew from the crystal bowl in front of her. "How was your visit to the Quarter?"

"It was…" Emma paused. "I'm not sure where to start."

She was saved from an immediate answer by the arrival of the server.

"Good afternoon, ladies. Have you made a decision?"

At least this part was easy. "Cat Five." It was the Maison Sterling's signature—and most lethal—cocktail. It was a hurricane, crafted from premium juices that were blended with Barbados rum. Since it was recommended on all the Where to Drink in New Orleans lists, a lot of people stopped in for one, but they staggered out afterward.

"I'll have what she's having." Shelby seconded the order.

"Can I bring you anything to snack on?"

Emma answered. "I think we're going to wait for our friends to arrive."

"Sounds good. I'll be back in a minute."

Then they were alone again at a table tucked near a corner of the old-world bar, away from other people. Soft jazz filled the air, making conversation easy. Even in a city filled with luxury, this hotel stood at the top.

"So, you hated it?"

"No." Emma shook her head, then settled back into the buttery-soft leather chair.

"Okay…so you loved it?"

That was more like it.

"Which is why you didn't sleep last night?"

Emma scooped her hair back from her face. "I look like hell. You're just too nice to actually say that."

"No. Not at all." Once again, Shelby protested. "You just don't seem as bubbly as usual."

"You're right about that." After arriving home, she'd spent hours pacing, then riding her exercise bicycle. Every nerve ending had been on fire, and her emotions had been upside down. Each time she'd had herself under control, Master Philip would text, or she'd recall something about their time together. Then her thoughts would tumble again. Although she'd followed a hot bath with a glass of wine, she'd still been awake at three a.m. Which meant she'd barely made it through the workday. "It was…amazing." Even that word fell short of describing her experience.

"And he treated you well?"

"I felt a little like Cinderella."

"Oh?"

"He sent a car for me."

"Oh-la-la."

She grinned and picked up an almond to plop into her mouth. "And he helped me out of the car when I arrived at the club."

"Such a gentleman. So I assume you met everyone? Trinity? Tore? Mistress Aviana?"

"Yes! Her throne is something."

HIS TO CHERISH

"Wait till you see her on one of the special nights when she has two submissives tied to the arms."

Disappointment roared through her. She doubted she'd have the opportunity to visit the club ever again.

The conversation was interrupted by the arrival of their drinks. Once they were alone again, they clinked their glasses together.

Emma took a drink, then put the lamp-shaped glass down, choking and waving a hand in front of her face. "I don't think I remember them being this strong."

"They're wicked good." Proving how smart she was, Shelby took only the tiniest sip of hers. "So then what happened?"

Emma filled her friend in on the details. "First of all, he showed me around. The bar. Kinky Avenue."

"My favorite."

"Then we went upstairs to a private room."

"Did you?" Shelby grinned. "Was that because you were shy or because there were rules that Master Philip wanted to circumvent?"

After a second sip, Emma confessed the truth, because, really, she was dying to share what had happened with someone who would understand. "He wanted me to wear fewer clothes than club rules permit."

Shelby fished a handful of nuts out of the crystal bowl, then sat back. "Do tell."

As they enjoyed their hurricanes, Emma finished her story but glossed over the things she wanted to keep private.

"It sounds as if you had the most wonderful introduction possible. Are you two going to scene together again?"

Emma shook her head.

"No. We had an agreement. It was one time only."

"Really?" Shelby frowned. "You haven't heard from him?"

"He checked up on me after I got home and reminded me to use the arnica that he gave me. Like a good Dominant."

"That's more than being a good Dominant. I presume you two talked when your scene was over."

"He held me for a while."

Shelby pressed again. "And you discussed what happened?"

"Well, he wanted to, but I wasn't ready." Emma stirred her drink. "I needed to sort things through."

"And he left it at that?"

"He told me to get in touch with him at any time. I think he was just fulfilling his obligations." The fact he hadn't contacted her today reinforced that idea.

"If he called, would you play with him again?"

"That's a moot point. He won't call." Emma attempted a brave smile. When that failed, she took another drink.

"Hypothetically…" Shelby was nothing if not persistent. "I told you there's a special event coming up at the Quarter, Putting on the Ritz. It's Mistress Aviana's five-year anniversary celebration. Let's say he invites you. Would you go?"

Emma toyed with her straw before exhaling to meet her friend's gaze. "No."

"Seriously?" Shelby scowled. "Since you had such a good time, I'm shocked. Or did you find out that BDSM really isn't your thing?"

"That's not it." In fact, the experience had been so much more than she could have dreamed of.

"I'm listening." Shelby moved her drink to the side.

"You remember yesterday, when I told you I'm ridiculous? I am." At least a dozen times in the past eighteen hours, Emma had reminded herself of that fact.

"How so?"

"I think I'm falling for him."

Saying nothing, Shelby leaned forward.

"See? I told you. I'm ridiculous."

"You're not." Shelby leaned forward to touch Emma's hand reassuringly. "There's nothing more natural than being attracted to your Dominant. You gave your entire body over to him. He respected that. In all ways he was the gentleman you deserve."

That was true. "As I said, I felt like Cinderella. He couldn't have been more of a prince if he'd tried." He'd been focused on her, and bringing her pleasure, even at the expense of his own.

"See what I mean? How could you not fall for him?"

"But I don't even know him."

"Is that really true? It sounds as if you've shared a lot with him in the last few weeks. You talked every day, right?"

"But it's only been a few weeks."

"I knew more about Trevor in that amount of time than I did about some people that I've known half of my life. There's something about a relationship that involves BDSM, isn't there? It's deeper than vanilla ones."

Emma had never experienced anything remotely similar. "Especially since I had to confess my deepest darkest secrets."

"And he made that safe for you."

"Yes." He had.

"Look, I'm going to say this again. You have to do what's right for you. But when he phones you—"

"*If.*"

"And *if* you want to see him again, tell him what's on your mind, that you're afraid to get in deeper. He's an honorable man."

"Even after all that crap in *Scandalicious* about his divorce?"

Shelby waved a dismissive hand. "Ask him about it. From what I know, she talked to the press, more than once. The judge finally issued a gag order to shut her up. I don't think he gave a single interview. If you look at it, everything there is one-sided."

When Shelby's other friends arrived, they stood for hugs and to say hello. Within seconds, Emma was swept up in excited conversational buzz.

After everyone was seated, the server came over again. Hannah, because she was expecting, ordered soda water. "But I'll buy a round for everyone. Well, before happy hour is over! Someone else has to buy when the price goes up."

The first was already chasing through her, leaving her giddy and forcing her to admit she was starting to care for Master Philip.

"Have you picked a date?" Fiona asked Shelby.

"I'm thinking next fall. Hopefully that gives me enough time to get organized. I've heard it can take a while to order a dress."

"Speaking of that…we need to plan a shopping trip." Fiona was always up for an adventure. "Have you considered going to Hautest Bridal Couture in Houston or San Antonio? We could make it a girls' weekend."

Randy Fulton owned a chain of stores in Texas, and he was now dressing brides from coast to coast.

"I'm in. We can do a spa day at the new Sterling hotel." Nicole had recently started dating a man she adored. Even though Emma hadn't known the woman long, she was amazed by how much Nicole was blossoming—gaining confidence as her mega-rich boyfriend spoiled her.

"If we're going to do that, we need to do it soon." Hannah cradled her belly. "Or we may end up bringing the baby along."

The drinks arrived. And the first sip made Emma blink. It shouldn't be possible, but this one tasted stronger than the first.

When there was a lull in the plans, Fiona spoke again. "You'll need lingerie for your honeymoon."

Emma agreed. "Totally."

"Which means we should go to Mademoiselle's." Fiona made the pronouncement as if it were obvious.

"Oh my God, yes." Shelby agreed with Fiona. "I love it there."

Lost, Emma frowned. "What's Mademoiselle's?"

"It's a shop, on Royal Street." After others nodded, Shelby went on. "From the outside, it appears ordinary, but there's a secret room in the back."

Was she the only one who didn't know what they were talking about?

"It caters to our lifestyle."

"You mean…" Emma raised her eyebrows. "BDSM?"

Shelby nodded. "Yes."

"I've heard of it, and I've been wanting to visit." Nicole finished her drink. "We should do it now."

"Agreed." Fiona sighed. "I need a new vibrator. Maybe one that plugs in." She'd broken up with her boyfriend/Dominant a while ago, and at their last gathering had complained about how many batteries she was going through.

Hannah signaled for the bill. "Who's in?"

Since everyone else was going, Emma nodded also. What else did she have to do? Go home and wait for a call that would never come?

After the check was taken care of, Emma stood and then reached for the table to steady herself.

Shelby blew out a breath as she pushed in her chair. "That rum kicked my ass."

"Same."

"One is my limit." Nicole nodded. "I learned that the hard way."

Together, the friends made their way through the marble

lobby. And Emma smiled her thanks when a uniformed doorman tipped a hat in their direction. *What would it be like to stay here?* Right now she could only afford to sashay through the entrance during happy hour.

Always seeming to be in charge, Fiona took off. Shelby and Emma looked at each other, laughed, then linked arms to support each other as they followed the rest of the party down the sidewalk. Fiona never slowed down as she weaved between throngs of tourists.

"How far is it?" Emma asked.

"Right now? Feels like ten miles. Maybe more!"

Hannah looked over her shoulder. "Are you two coming? I thought I'd be the slow one with this belly."

Without two hurricanes, keeping up would have been much easier.

In the heat and humidity and with the world ever so slightly off-center, the walk took forever. Up ahead, Fiona made a sharp turn into a building.

"Tell me we're there."

"We're here."

There was no sign with a name on it, but the door stood open. Like other businesses nearby, chilled air gushed from inside, beckoning passersby.

The small shop was filled with stand-up coolers stocked with water, energy drinks, beer, wine, piña coladas, even margaritas—none of which looked even remotely appealing to Emma.

Colorful dresses hung from racks. There were boxes of shoes, some with unbelievably high heels—ones she'd never be able to walk in given her current state. Some of the casual sandals were adorable, though.

As expected, masks decorated all the walls, hanging next to hand-sketched pictures of trumpet players and photographs of New Orleans's famous landmarks. The counter where the cash register was located looked like a million others that she'd been in. There were half a dozen brightly colored baskets filled with tempting souvenirs, enormous pralines wrapped in plastic, cards with angels and positive sayings on them, key rings, magnets, necklaces.

"Can I help you?" a young man asked.

Fiona answered for everyone. "We're hoping to see Mademoiselle."

"Who may I say is here?"

"I'm Fiona. With several—"

Before she had finished speaking, a petite woman emerged from the back, pushing through strands of silver circles that tinkled and danced in her wake. Although her long gray hair was pulled back and held with a clip, the ends brushed the backs of her knees. Her floor-length gold dress was cinched tight around her tiny waist, and she was barefoot.

"Mademoiselle Giselle." Fiona offered a slight bow. "Thank you for receiving us, and please forgive us for coming by without an invitation."

"Ah Fiona." She smiled. "My Fierce One. I'm always delighted when you grace my establishment with your presence." Her sweeping gaze took in the rest of the group. "And your friends. I know Hannah." The two embraced. "You have the glow of motherhood." She smiled. "How is the *bébé?*"

"Growing."

"Do you know the sex?"

Hannah shook her head. "We were hoping to find out. But the ultrasound wasn't completely conclusive."

"The perils of modern technology. Would you like to know?"

"You…? Seriously?"

"Well, I won't say a word if you would prefer I didn't. Mason may want to make the discovery with you."

"I…" Hannah sighed. "I want to know, but I'm afraid you're right."

"I will give you a gift to open after you discover for yourselves."

"Thank you."

The shop owner greeted Shelby warmly. Afterward, Fiona introduced Nicole, then finally Emma, whom she kissed on the cheek.

"Nicole, Emma, my pleasure to make your acquaintance." She waved a hand, and a dozen bangles rippled together. "Now, I presume you are here for more than a trinket, oui? Follow me."

They all did, with Emma bringing up the rear. The silver curtain tinkled melodically as they walked through, then passed a set of stairs and crossed through a doorway into another room—or rather, a different world entirely, one with mirrors everywhere, some on the walls, others in oval frames, tipped at various angles. There were even smaller ones on each surface. It was disorienting—and maybe it was meant to be that way.

A chandelier dripping with crystals, its light refracting everywhere—hung from the ceiling.

Surprising her, there were a couple of large glass cases artfully displaying collars and sensual high-end toys. There were tall wooden dressers and other antique furniture filled with lingerie. A discreet glance at a price tag on a pair of panties confirmed this wasn't a place she'd be shopping at very often—if ever. Maybe for a special occasion, like an outing to the Quarter.

As quickly as it formed, she shoved the thought aside. Since she wouldn't be going again, she had no need for fancy underthings, no matter how beautiful they were.

Fiona and Hannah moved toward a case filled with

elegant vibrators, while Nicole opened a drawer and lifted a gorgeous black lace bra.

Shelby leaned toward Emma. "What do you think?"

"It's nothing like I expected."

"That was my reaction as well."

Then she reminded herself they were here to select things for Shelby's honeymoon, which meant she got to help spend someone else's money. "Pick something out. I'll buy it for your shower."

"Buying me a private island might cost less."

Together they laughed, and Mademoiselle glanced in their direction with a smile.

Maybe ten minutes later, Shelby found a gorgeous silk nightie.

"I'll get you that."

"No. No. It's too much."

The hurricane had loosened her inhibitions. Besides, she had a bonus coming for a new account she'd signed. "You're only getting married once."

"Thank you. But really, there's no need."

"Let me do this for you."

A moment later, Nicole walked over to whisper that she'd found a wicker trunk filled with marked-down items.

Emma was intrigued.

"You should get yourself something." Shelby grinned devilishly. "You know, just in case."

"You're impossible."

But all three of them found gorgeous items they had to have. "And you're right. I'm only going on my honeymoon once." Shelby scooped up another two bras. "If they last that long!"

As they carried their purchases to the register, Emma noticed the floor for the first time. It was crafted from wood, like many buildings in historic New Orleans. But in the center of the room were a number of white hexagonal tiles, inset with black ones to create something that looked like an owl. She frowned. It appeared identical in shape to the one that had been on the bag that Master Philip had brought to the club.

Shelby turned back to look for her. "Are you okay?"

"The owl." Emma shook her head and glanced down again. *Am I making things up?* "It reminds me of something."

"Oh?"

"I think I've seen it before."

"Where?"

She was saved from replying when Fiona let out a tiny shriek from the corner where she and Hannah were playing with the toys.

Mademoiselle finished wrapping Nicole's purchases in layers of tissue paper and then carefully tucked them inside a gold bag. Even though it was unbranded, the color hinted of luxury.

"Thank you, Mademoiselle."

"I'd like you to return in the near future." The woman placed a hand on Nicole's. "Alone." She offered a card. "Call me anytime."

Nicole accepted, slipping it inside her bag. "Of course. Thank you."

When she turned, she shrugged, indicating she didn't understand what the conversation had been about.

Emma was next, and her phone vibrated in her purse while Mademoiselle was calculating the cost. Distracted, she pulled out the device and checked the message.

Did the arnica help?

. . .

She dropped her credit card. "Sorry." Scrambling for it, she picked it up off the floor and once again offered it to the store owner.

"Should I take a guess who the message is from?" Shelby asked.

"You'd be right."

Triumphantly, Shelby grinned.

Instead of worrying about how—if—to respond, Emma forced herself to concentrate on her transaction.

When she was done, adrenaline zooming through her, she nodded to Shelby and Nicole. "Excuse me for a minute. I'll be right back." She walked to the front part of the store.

Even though replying to him was potentially stupid, she couldn't help herself.

Yes. I'm fine.

For the next few moments, she looked at the sandals she didn't intend to purchase.

"Let me know if you need any help."

She smiled at the clerk.

Not surprisingly, her phone remained silent.

Until it rang.

Master Philip.

Her brainwaves slowed. This wasn't possible. Never in her wildest dreams had she expected him to call. His duty to her had ended.

A couple of people scowled at her as she stood there staring at her phone. She needed to send him to voicemail.

Instead, maybe emboldened by the double helping of cocktails, she stepped outside onto the sidewalk, close to the building so she didn't impede the flow of revelers. "Emma

Monroe speaking." It was impersonal, as she tried to control her breathing.

"Emma."

Her knees weakened. Damn it. Damn *him*.

"I wanted to hear your voice."

And his made her toes curl as desire crashed into need. *What am I doing?*

Just then tires screeched, and a car honked because a bicyclist dashed across the street.

"Where are you?"

"Ah... The French Quarter." When he didn't respond, she rushed to fill the awkward silence. "We are shopping. For my friend Shelby. You know, for her wedding?"

"I see."

"We met for happy hour. Or two. It was fun." *Why am I telling you all this?*

"Did you eat dinner?" His words were careful and precise.

"Cashews. Well, and some almonds. Maybe a few hazelnuts, but I don't like them very much."

"Where did you say you were? Specifically?"

"At a store on Royal. But I'm not sure how long we'll be here."

"And where is your vehicle?"

"It's at work. But I got a ride to the Maison Sterling."

"And you're planning to drive home? After not eating?"

He was right. Maybe not a good idea. A rideshare might be pricey, but worth it.

"What's the name of the store?"

"Honestly? I don't know. It's owned by Mademoiselle Giselle."

"Ah. I know the place. Stay where you are. I'll be there in about fifteen minutes."

She blinked. "What?"

"I'm on my way."

"Wait! No! There's no need. I mean…" She pulled the phone away from her ear and looked at the blank screen. He'd hung up on her?

She was standing there in stunned disbelief when Shelby joined her on the sidewalk.

"I'm being nosy. I've got to know what Master Philip said."

"He's coming here." Emma lowered her phone.

Shelby grinned. "That sounds like a little more than Dominant obligation to me."

"I'm stunned. Speechless."

"And again, I'm going to want to know all the details."

Still reeling, she allowed Shelby to draw her back inside where Mademoiselle was showing Fiona a few details about a discreet vibrator, reminding Emma of the one that Master Philip had used on her.

Why did every thought seem to lead back to him?

The young man who'd been working up front walked over to Mademoiselle and whispered something in her ear. When he was finished, she nodded, then addressed Fiona. "You are still deciding, oui?"

"I've narrowed it down, but yes."

"If you'll excuse me for a moment, then?" Mademoiselle walked toward one of the dressers and selected a number of beautiful matching bra and panty sets, which she began to wrap.

Emma and Shelby joined Nicole while Fiona opted for the most high-end vibrator in the history of mankind. "Maybe I'll be able to get some sleep now."

A few minutes later, Mademoiselle Giselle beckoned Emma to the counter, then slid across a large golden bag, much larger than the one she already had. "Enjoy."

"What?" Emma blinked. "I'm afraid I don't understand."

"A gift. From Monsieur Dettmer."

Frantically she shook her head. "I can't." Out of the corner of her eye, Emma had glimpsed some of the exquisite garments the owner had selected. "It's far too extravagant."

"Perhaps you should take it up with him." She inclined her head to the side. "Monsieur, welcome."

Trembling, Emma turned to find him standing there, gaze riveted on her. He was commanding, demanding, impossible.

Just like she had been from the moment she met him, Emma was helpless to resist him.

~

"Really…" What was she supposed to call him? This was the first time they'd been together without a backdrop of BDSM. "Mr. Dettmer—"

"Philip."

That felt far too intimate, and she was desperate to keep him at a distance, rather than letting him any deeper into her heart. "Mr. Dettmer. This isn't necessary."

"I agree."

They were tucked in an alcove of the Maison Sterling's nicest restaurant. After he picked her up from Mademoiselle Giselle's shop, he'd surprised her by driving here instead of dropping her off at her car, insisting he'd like to buy her dinner somewhere quiet. "Since we haven't ordered, we can change our minds."

"You've already said you've eaten nothing other than nuts."

True.

"And you had cocktails."

"A couple. That's not a ridiculous amount, and it was hours ago now. I'm totally sober." She touched her finger to her nose.

"What were you drinking?"

"A Cat Five. It's a hurricane."

He placed his menu off to the side. "And what do you think the five stands for?"

"I don't know. I thought it was a catchy name. A category five hurricane is the most intense."

"Excellent. Keep going."

Could you be any more annoying? They might not be in a scene, but he was still the same relentless, overwhelming Dominant male.

"Describe it to me."

"It's like heaven in a glass. Light rum, dark rum. A delicious floater of sweet coconut rum." Her eyes widened as realization dawned. *Surely not.* "Shots of liquor?"

"And how much do you usually drink?"

"Not that much. Maybe a glass of wine a couple of times a week.

"Let's have dinner. Then we'll take it from there."

Reluctantly, she agreed. Having a good meal was an excellent idea. "I can pay for my own."

"No doubt. But since I invited you—"

"Invited?" She scoffed.

"Insisted you join me?"

That was more like it.

"Which makes it doubly imperative that I pay."

"Fine. I'll order the most expensive thing."

He smiled, rich and wicked. "You can find those entrees on the right side of the menu."

Was he completely unshakeable?

"Relax, Emma. We're here. It's a beautiful evening. Enjoy yourself."

Was that a suggestion or an order? And with him, was there really any difference?

The server joined them to ask if they'd like to order something from the bar.

"A sparkling water with lime, please." Now that Master Philip had made it clear how much alcohol she'd consumed, she realized she'd better rehydrate so she didn't wake up with a headache tomorrow morning.

Philip selected a glass of cabernet.

Once they were settled with their beverages, they placed their food order.

She opted for the chicken and sausage gumbo.

"Excellent choice." He collected her menu before turning to Philip. "Sir?"

"Ribeye. Medium rare."

"And your side?"

"Grilled asparagus."

After nodding, he left them alone only to return a few minutes later with a basketful of warm, fresh-baked bread that she couldn't resist. She picked off an end piece, then slathered it with creamy butter. Of course, her companion had none. So she broke off the other end of the loaf. Then she considered him. "Why are you doing this?"

"Doing what?" He was being deliberately obtuse.

"Buying me expensive things." The bill had to equal a week's worth of her salary. And he'd never get to see the lingerie. "Picking me up at Mademoiselle's." She'd expected him to call or text when he arrived. Instead he had double-parked and strode inside, with the confidence of someone who had shopped there before. Surprising her, he'd known most of her friends, and he'd greeted them all politely before taking her bag and placing his fingers possessively in the small of her back as he guided her back outside to his car. Despite the fact that he held up traffic, he took the time to open the door for her.

She'd never been with a man who was so considerate. When they were scening, it had been nice, but not unexpected. Outside of the club, it shocked her. None of her other boyfriends would have gone out of their way to pick her up, ensuring she ate a good dinner and didn't drive right home after enjoying a couple of cocktails.

A small part of her whispered it was nice to be taken care of. Ruthlessly she shoved aside the renegade thought. He was being kind, but that didn't mean she could allow herself to grow accustomed to it.

"You didn't call me back last night."

"Is that what this is about?"

"Partially." He placed his fingers on the bottom of his glass and made small circles, causing the wine to rise and fall in a mesmerizing way.

"We had nothing to talk about. I arrived home safely and thanked you for a nice evening. You reminded me to use the arnica."

"And did you?"

Heat scalded her cheeks, and she squeezed the juice from the lime into her bubbly water so that she didn't have to look at him. "Yes."

"So you looked at your bottom in the mirror."

Frantically she glanced around to see if anyone had overheard his scandalous words. It shouldn't have surprised her that there were no occupied tables nearby. Because he left nothing to chance, he'd probably ensured that before speaking.

"Emma?"

She exhaled as she nodded.

"Any bruising?"

His voice was compelling, making her want to answer. "No. But I had a tiny red mark."

"I should have asked you to send me a picture."

Part of her was surprised he hadn't. "It was gone this morning."

"Good. And your emotions?"

"Also unscathed."

"You left the club rather abruptly."

"I was tired." *And needed some space to think.*

"You've had a day to reflect. Is scening something you'd like to do again?"

She met his gaze. Was that an invitation? As always, his intense green eyes were unreadable. God, she wished she didn't fall apart when he studied her so intently.

Last night she'd had a wild image of him as a pirate, but today—in his suitcoat and tie—he looked as if he ruled the world.

Emma stalled long enough that the food arrived, saving her from needing to answer.

She picked up her spoon to sample the gumbo. The roux was dark brown, and spice exploded on her tongue. "Oh. Wow."

"It's good?"

"Amazing." Since she'd grown up in Louisiana, she had tried gumbo all over the state. "This is some of the best I've ever had." To slow herself down a little, she took a small piece of bread and dipped it in the flavorful liquid.

"And it wasn't even on the right side of the menu."

Who was this man? She knew him to be hyperfocused and serious, but this lighter side of him was new, and it was even more dangerous to her resolve. "Wait till I order dessert."

"It's my pleasure."

"This is amazing, and..." She looked at him. "Thank you. But I don't know—maybe you have a misplaced sense of obligation? We played last night, and it was everything I could have hoped for, dreamed of. And then you provided aftercare. You owe me nothing else. It's okay for you to move on and forget about me."

"You've got things mixed up entirely if you believe this is about obligation."

"Then what?"

"Curiosity. I want to get to know you better."

"There's not much to tell."

"You've mentioned you're in finance."

Emma laughed. "Me?" She shook her head. "No. I'm an advisor. I have got a couple of decent-size clients, and our firm takes care of a significant amount of capital. But seriously? You're a gazillionaire. In a stratosphere of your own."

"A slight exaggeration. Perhaps that would be possible if I had a more interested manager."

"Mr. Dettmer—" He held up a hand to interrupt her, and so she tried again. *"Philip.* Joking aside, with the kind of money that you have, there's no doubt you're getting the best service possible."

"People with a vested interest do better. They're concerned about protecting the investment, and they're not as likely to move funds around to generate a profit that goes right to their bottom line."

"That's a little cynical."

"Is it? Personal experience says otherwise." He finished his steak, then took another drink of his wine. "It's the reason I move around. People get complacent—and sometimes greedy. In a perfect world, my manager would make money if I did. And there wouldn't be a thousand *convenience* fees assessed every quarter."

"You have a bad opinion of everyone in my profession?"

"Not at all, and I'm interested in why you chose your career path."

How much to reveal? "My dad left when I was little, and my mom worked two jobs to take care of me. I didn't lack for anything, but…" Maybe it was the result of the rum still warming her, but she decided to share more with him than she'd told even her closest friends. "Up until the time I started babysitting and could help out a little with finances, my clothes came from secondhand stores. When we shopped for food, it was always on Tuesday, and we went right after the grocer opened. At the back of the store, at the end of the refrigerated section, there was a place where the about-to-expire meats were placed. We'd get what we could, ground beef and chicken. Once in a while, we'd get a skirt steak for fajitas. We ate a lot of soups. Beans. For birthdays, we made each other cakes." She smiled at the memory. *Simpler times.*

"Go on."

Was he really interested?

"But each year, Mom took me for ice cream. It was the only time we ever splurged, and she'd tell me to get whatever I wanted. I remember my first banana split, with three different scoops of soft serve, each topped with something different. Chocolate, strawberry, and pineapple, but I'll admit that wasn't my favorite. The whipped cream and maraschino cherries?" She closed her eyes. "To die for. But since I rarely had treats, I usually ended up with a stomachache. It was worth every single bite."

He grinned. "You didn't have pizza parties at arcades or anything like that?"

"No. But I guess you can't miss something you never had." She shook her head. "Right?"

"A good attitude."

"I focused on what I did have. Love. A roof over my head. And my mom continued to work to help pay for my college, even though I told her not to."

After the server cleared away their plates, they ordered coffee, and she decided that she did want dessert. She had an entire future ahead of her where she could work off the calories at a yoga class.

"You're bored, aren't you?" Emma stirred a splash of cream into the hot, strong brew.

"On the contrary. I appreciate what you're sharing."

"Maybe because we never had money, I was fascinated by it. I started listening to podcasts, took a class in economics." She grinned. "Talk about a dry subject."

He pushed aside his now empty wineglass and poured a cup of coffee from the silver carafe.

"At the urging of a friend, I opened a savings account, and then signed up with an online company, the kind where you can buy stocks and reinvest the dividends."

He nodded, and she laughed. "Okay, this is absurd. You have no idea what I'm talking about, do you?" They were from totally different financial universes.

"You may be surprised to know that my father appreciated the value of a dollar. And he made damn sure we did too. I had to work outside the family business, and I had to pay room and board when I went to school. Because he was sensitive to nepotism, I wasn't allowed to join the family firm after I graduated from business school. I interned for several years…of course without compensation."

She winced. "I stepped in it. Didn't I?"

"Not at all. I won't pretend that I have any idea the struggles you faced."

Or what it was like to have power cut off one winter when Louisiana was hit by a terrible, rare arctic cold front. "Anyway, after I went to work at Larson Financial, my mom started dating. It was then that I really realized how much she'd sacrificed to ensure I had a good life."

Giving him the opportunity to change the subject, she didn't go on. Instead, he leaned forward a little, a silent sign that encouraged her to go on. "She met an oil rig worker who was a widower, and they got married. At her urging, he moved his retirement funds to our firm. That was my first decent account."

"And you've taken good care of it, I assume."

"Every day. I never want my mom to struggle again."

"You're good at your job?"

How was she supposed to answer that? "I like to think so. A couple of years ago, Mom and her husband were able to retire, and they bought a cottage in Galveston. Her best friend had moved there, and they missed each other. So we sat down and figured out how to make her dream a reality. It's great. Their group of friends has grown, and they go and do things together. They call themselves the Chunky Dunkin' Mermaids." She smiled. "Some people say they skinny dip, right? Well, these women prefer to say that they chunky dunk."

He laughed.

"They wear matching T-shirts when they go out, a bright teal color, with pictures of themselves as mermaids, complete with sparkly tails. For Mardi Gras, they decorate their golf carts in an under-the-sea theme. Seeing her happy brings me joy. And all her friends have transferred their portfolios to me."

"Not surprised. As I was saying, having someone with a personal interest is crucial to success."

"It definitely can't hurt." She nodded. "I give all my customers the same sort of service." Especially since she knew what it was like to go without.

"I may consider moving over one of my accounts."

She blinked. "To Larson?"

"No."

"I'm not sure I'm following you." Emma frowned.

"Brokerage firms are all the same. It's your services I'm interested in. The personal touch."

"You…" Once again, he had her off-balance. He had to be

HIS TO CHERISH

joking, and yet she knew Philip Dettmer meant every word he said.

"We'll discuss the logistics more in the coming days."

The idea made her giddy. Not just the realization that they'd have the opportunity to talk, but having him as a client would be a massive boost to her career. It didn't matter how small the account was—it was the prestige that mattered.

Before she could continue the conversation, dessert arrived, a massive slice of triple chocolate cake with a scoop of ice cream on the side. After sampling the decadence, she momentarily closed her eyes as she sighed with pure pleasure. "This is amazing. *Ah-may-zing.* You have to try some."

"I'll take your word for it."

"Are you disciplined in every area of your life?"

"I am. But there are areas where I'm very greedy."

Sensual tension crawled through her, and she put down her fork.

"When I want something, I'm relentless in its pursuit."

He wasn't talking about her. No way. He couldn't be. Could he?

"Do you see your mother often?"

"A few times a year. I enjoy visiting her, and they made me an honorary mermaid. I mean, not part of the actual group, but they bought me my own T-shirt, but of course, only their pictures are on it."

He grinned. "It sounds like something my mother might enjoy."

"Does she live here in New Orleans?"

"Still in the house where I was raised. My father passed a few years ago, and she keeps talking about wanting to downsize, which means moving. So far, she hasn't taken any action, but I wouldn't be surprised if she did at some point. She has shown an interest in painting and recently converted a room into a studio." He shrugged. "My sister wants to keep the house in the family because of all the memories tied to it."

"I didn't know you had a sister."

"And three rambunctious nephews. If she has her way, it'll be four soon. Which suits my mom fine. She loves her grandkids."

"Do you go to your mom's for Thanksgiving?" Which was the weekend after next.

"Sometimes I'd prefer to go on vacation or take a cruise, but neither my mom nor sister would stand for that. How about you? Do you have plans?"

Though she loved her place and was comfortable being alone, there were times during the holidays that she hated being single. She'd have liked to have her own traditions—other than taking an online yoga class before dashing out for pumpkin spice latte. "I think I'll go to Galveston this year. Mom and the splash get together—"

"Splash?"

"That's what a group of mermaids is called."

"I had no idea."

"Neither did I until I was properly schooled. A society of them is called a stirp."

"I don't believe I've ever heard that word used in casual conversation before."

"Stick with me. I can educate you on a number of fronts."

"I can't even begin to imagine." He sat back.

"Anyway, the splash is planning to have dinner at a restaurant overlooking the Gulf. They're hoping to have a table outside, and they included me in the number when they made reservations." She took another bite before admitting defeat at the hands of the confectionary gods.

The server brought the check, and he signed his name to the bottom of it.

"You don't need to pay?" she asked when they were alone.

HIS TO CHERISH

"My credit card is already on file since we're guests." He leaned forward. "I took the liberty of securing us a room for the night."

"You... *What?*"

"I hope that meets with your approval?"

Earlier she'd told Shelby that he made her feel like Cinderella. Where did it end? It was as if he'd stepped inside her fantasies and made them come true. "Under ordinary circumstances, it would."

"But tonight?"

Sharing a bed? Sleeping with him? She seized the first objection that popped into her mind. "I have to work in the morning."

"It's early still. I can take you to your car in the morning, and you'll have time to go home to change."

His plan was workable. Except for the fact that he was part of it. Last night she'd barely slept. And with his hard body pressing against hers, she'd never get any rest.

And then reality hit her. He might not intend for her to get any sleep.

She gulped. Was that what she wanted?

More than anything.

"Say yes."

Was that an order or an invitation? Either way, the result was the same. "Thank you. That's very generous."

"Shall we?"

After picking up her bags, he stood and indicated the way to the elevator. He pressed the button for the third floor, and the carriage took off with a whisper.

The suite he'd secured for them was the ultimate in old-world luxury, and she crossed the plush carpeting to pull open the draperies. Below them was the hotel's signature green awning. Beyond that was an amazing view of the

French Quarter with its famed wrought iron balconies, art galleries, gorgeous blooming plants.

A massive bed, looking much larger than king size, stood in the middle of the room. The covers were turned back, and large chocolate-covered strawberries were on the pillows.

The bathroom tile was unlike any she'd seen outside of a magazine or high-end spa. It contained a glorious standalone tub and walk-in shower. The space was about the same size as her first apartment had been.

She wanted to pinch herself.

"Come here, Miss Monroe."

He hadn't called her Emma, and his tone was soft—more inviting than Dominant—but it still sparked an undeniable response from her.

He opened the top button on her blouse. "I need to get you ready for bed."

The implications chased through her, and she had to say something before she lost the remaining pieces of her common sense. "Did you happen to bring a condom?"

Master Philip dropped his hand to his side. "Of course. But we won't be needing one."

"Oh?" Was he planning a scene, potentially?

"As you know, I have rules. And in the future, I want to fuck you hard, ragged...until you don't know where I end and you begin. But tonight is not that night."

"But... I thought..."

"That I was bringing you up here to take advantage of you?" His tone was sharp, as if she'd insulted him.

"No." She placed her palm on his chest. It was the first time she'd taken any initiative, and he glanced at the place they were connected. Then his eyes darkened. Hunger? Desire? "That's not what I meant. I just thought that since you took care of me last night, and I know you were... At least I thought..."

"That I wanted you?" He placed his hand over hers. "I did. Still do. But I assure you, I meant it when I said I love pleasing my submissives. This isn't a quid pro quo. You don't have to have sex with me because I got you off at the club or bought you dinner."

"I screwed up. I'm sorry."

"I take care of what's mine, Emma. I didn't want you driving home by yourself after you'd had a couple of Cat Fives. I thought you might want to take a bath. Relax before you go to sleep."

"Sleep?"

"Yeah. That's the only thing we're doing, even if we both want something else."

Emma wasn't sure whether she was happy about his extreme amount of self-discipline or whether she was terribly, horribly disappointed by it.

His phone chimed, and he slowly released her. "Excuse me."

While he responded to the summons, she fished out her cosmetic bag from her purse. Since she never knew when she'd need to meet with a client or jump on a video call, she always carried makeup, a brush, and assorted hair clips. "I think I will relax." Unwinding might be impossible, though.

In the bathroom, she filled the tub. A shelf held an astounding assortment of items, cotton balls, cosmetic wipes, shampoos, conditioner, soap, and two different body washes —his and hers. There was even a plastic apothecary-type of jar filled with lavender-scented salts.

Once again, she felt like Cinderella. Every need and desire had been catered to. She was in one of the city's most amazing hotels, with a sexy man who'd relentlessly claimed her last night, giving her orgasm after orgasm.

And he didn't want to make love to her. He hadn't rejected her, but his words stung, nonetheless.

She sank into the warm depths and tipped her head back.

If she could just stop thinking and enjoy the moment, she'd get so much more out of this experience. But instead she was tuned in to the sounds that he made beyond the closed door.

He either had the television on, or he was talking on the phone. With as much as he worked, it was probably the latter. Not that she knew anything about his routine. Or him.

The heat and steam finally helped to harness her runaway thoughts, and she closed her eyes, half drifting in and out of sleep.

Then he startled her with a knock on the door.

"Mind if I come in?" He held a luxurious fluffy white robe in his hands. "I thought you might want this."

"Most definitely." Maybe she'd sleep in it, to be sure her body didn't accidentally touch his during the night.

"There are slippers too."

"Okay, so I might never leave."

Was there anything more intimate than having a man lounging in the doorway, watching her take a bath.

"It's tempting, isn't it?"

"Are all the Sterling hotels like this? We're thinking about shopping for Shelby's wedding dress in Houston and staying at the new property they just opened."

"Aren't there any bridal boutiques in New Orleans?"

"Not that are owned by Randy Fulton."

"I see." And it was clear he didn't—at all. "I'm a Sterling Premier Club member. You can use my points for your room."

In stunned shock, Emma stared at him. That was the kind of offer a lover or spouse made, not someone who was little more than a casual acquaintance.

"I'll leave this here for you." He placed the robe on the vanity.

"Before you go, I have something to tell you."

"Oh?"

"I've actually never ordered off the right side of the menu."

"Another thing we're going to have to rectify."

For the second time in two minutes, he was talking about a future, when it was all she could do to survive the moment.

He closed the door behind him, she sank deeper into the water, blowing out a heavy sigh.

Philip Dettmer already had a piece of her heart, and she needed to be careful because she couldn't afford to give him her body and soul as well.

CHAPTER 7

Determined to protect her emotions, Emma tightened the belt around her oversize fluffy robe, then gathered the courage to leave the bathroom.

The door leading out onto their small balcony was open, and she padded outside to join Master Philip.

While she was in the bathtub, he had removed his suit coat and his tie and opened the top couple of buttons on his shirt, revealing a sexy smattering of chest hair.

He lounged comfortably with a glass of wine cradled between his palms. He was sexy, as steamy as a Southern summer night.

How was she supposed to survive the evening?

"I'd offer you a drink, but…"

"I think water is a better choice."

"Have a seat. Let me get you one."

She wasn't sure any man had ever treated her this well.

He went inside, and when he returned, he uncapped a bottle and offered it to her before resuming his seat.

"Thank you." She took a small sip. "I've never spent the night here. The energy is… Vibrant. So different from my life." Of course he would know that. He'd sent all that fancy electronic Bonds equipment to her home so that they could video chat.

"I've often thought I might like to live in the French Quarter, and I seriously considered it after my divorce."

As if they'd wandered into dangerous territory, the ground shifted beneath her. They needed to keep their personal lives separate. The less she knew about Master Philip, the man who would never be involved in another relationship ever again, the better. And yet she couldn't help but be intrigued.

"But I eventually settled for a house. Mostly because it was better for the dog."

"You have a dog?" *Probably something big and powerful. Maybe a German Shepherd or a Great Dane.*

"He belonged to my wife. It turned out that having a pet was too much of an obligation, and Tibby cramped her lifestyle."

His use of the word obligation didn't surprise her. She already knew how deeply serious he was about his duties.

"I couldn't allow him to be sent to the animal shelter as she planned. That's not how I do things."

Despite her resolve to remain detached, Emma wanted to know more.

"He's as bossy as hell, but lovable. You should come over and meet him."

Her heart raced. No doubt the invitation was polite, automatic rather than meaningful. Even if he were serious, she couldn't possibly accept.

Instead of responding, she took a quick gulp of water to cover her nervousness and then diverted the conversation. "I love dogs. I've thought about getting one, but sometimes I work late, and I go in on the weekends, so it doesn't seem fair."

"Tibby doesn't like to be alone, and he's not shy about letting me know when he's displeased. Since I'm the boss, I often take him to work. On days that I can't, I communicate with him through videos in the house. More Bonds technology. When he stands in front of the camera, a treat is dropped in his bowl." He shrugged. "Sounds ridiculous, I know. I didn't have pets growing up, and I had no idea it was possible to care about an animal this much. My sitter has an app, so I can virtually go along with them on walks. I'm not quite sure what I would do without her."

She was absolutely enchanted. "So where's Tibby tonight?"

"Having a sleepover at the sitter's house—he's spoiled enough that he gets to sleep on their bed. I'll collect him in the morning." He picked up his phone, swiped through a couple of screens, then showed her a picture. "Tibby. Before his last trip to the groomer."

"Oh my goodness." Emma shook her head. Rather than the large breed she'd imagined, Tibby was a tiny tri-colored ball of fluff. "I don't know what breed it is."

"It's a Havachon, a mix between a Havanese and a Bichon Frise."

"He's adorable. I think I'm in love."

"He'll like you.

Again, a hint of a future meeting.

"Feel free to sit out here as long as you want." He cleared the screen. "I'm going to take a shower."

When she was alone, she walked back into the room. Because it was getting late, she locked the door and closed the blackout curtains before grabbing her phone. There were five messages from Shelby, demanding to know what was going on.

With a grin, Emma replied that Master Philip had booked them a room at the Maison Sterling.

. . .

Damn him and his Dominant obligations.

Emma laughed.

Don't do anything I wouldn't do.

Shelby followed that with a smiley face and a wink emoji.

Emma turned off her phone to conserve the battery.

A few minutes later, Master Philip emerged from the bathroom with a towel loose around his hips. Unable to look away, she stood there feasting her gaze on him.

Heaven save me. He was even more spectacular than she'd imagined—and she had imagined plenty. His abs seemed to be chiseled from marble. Every muscle and sinew was perfectly defined, making her feel protected and helpless, all at the same time.

His gaze intent, he crossed the room to stand in front of her. He smelled spicy and masculine, and the towel couldn't disguise his erection.

He feathered his fingers into her damp hair.

"I'd like to kiss you."

Are you asking permission? Their relationship was complicated. They'd done incredibly sexy things at the Quarter, and yet, this was a different kind of intimacy—man to woman, rather than Dominant to submissive.

He arced his thumb down the curve of her jaw, making it clear it was a question, and whatever happened next was up to her.

She wanted his taste, his possession—yearned for it. If she

HIS TO CHERISH

was honest with herself, she'd admit this is what had kept her awake last night, thinking of him, not being able to shove thoughts of him aside. "Yes."

He slanted his mouth over hers, capturing her lips, seeking entrance.

She gave herself over to him as he explored and teased, tantalizing her senses. Then he deepened the kiss, overwhelming her.

Emma grabbed hold of his shoulders for support, but as always, he took charge, even as he took care of her. He wrapped his arms around her, drawing her closer until her stomach pressed against the hard ridge of his manhood. Anything he asked her, she would happily give.

Too soon, he drew away, leaving her mouth slightly bruised and swollen and her breath ragged.

She clutched the lapels of her robe, then dragged them together, as if the futile action could shield her vulnerable heart from his relentless onslaught.

He feathered his first two fingers across her lips.

"You're exquisite.

Before she had time to wonder what he was doing, he scooped her off the floor and strode toward the bed. *Oh my God*.

"Better move the strawberry."

He lowered her so she could move the temptation from the pillow to the nightstand.

"I'm not sure how I'm going to keep my hands off you."

Don't. She was ready for him, throbbing with need. "There isn't an ounce of alcohol left in my system."

"Sorry. I'm a man of my word." He let her go.

Unsure what came over her, Emma unknotted her belt. "I prefer to sleep naked." The lie was so big she was lucky that her nose didn't grow from it. "You don't mind, do you?"

"I wouldn't have it any other way."

She shrugged out of the robe and tossed it toward the end of the bed. The chilled air from the overhead vent made her nipples pebble. Or maybe it was a reaction from the fierce hunger that tightened his face. His hard dick proved he wanted her. And a naughty part of her decided to do everything possible to ensure he couldn't resist her.

"I'd like to look at your ass."

"Oh?"

"See for myself whether all traces of my fingerprints are gone."

No matter how well she played the game, he was better. "Of course, *Sir.*" He groaned, and she attempted to hide her triumphant smile. "Would you like me to bend over?"

"Emma." Her name emerged as more than a growl. It was a warning. One she intended to recklessly ignore.

"Should I keep my feet together, Master Philip? Or should I spread them?"

When he spoke, the words were an uncompromising growl. "As far apart as you can. Grab your ankles. Don't let go until I say so."

All of a sudden, this wasn't funny. He was in charge.

She inhaled as reality blurred, fading into the sweetness of submission.

"Turn around. *Now,* please."

Slowly she assumed the position he'd asked for.

"Perfection. Holding yourself like that is a form of bondage, isn't it? You're unable to move without my permission."

Her hair dragged on the floor, and she was totally exposed to him. If he wanted, he could take her that way. The idea turned the pattern on the carpet into ribbons that swirled beneath her.

He was so close to her, and the fabric of his towel was the

only thing separating her pussy from the demand of his cock. Hot desire made it impossible for her to breathe.

"You're beautiful."

"So are you, Sir."

His touch agonizingly light, he skimmed his fingers across the backs of her thighs and buttocks. "I don't see any marks." Then he captured each of her ass cheeks and squeezed hard.

"Oww…" She gasped, bending her knees and almost letting go of her ankles.

"Be a good girl, Emma. Stay where you are."

Response flowed through her.

"Maybe tomorrow I'll have something to look at." He repeated his action, and surely he'd created bruises. But this time he offered no relief. He didn't rub away the ache.

"The arnica is in my purse, Sir."

"It can stay there."

Which meant he wanted her to wear his mark, something she would proudly, happily do.

"You may stand."

She did, and faced him again, unable to believe he hadn't entered her, taking her the way she wanted.

"I too sleep naked."

Then…*fuck*. Confound him, he dropped the towel and echoed her words. "You don't mind, do you?"

Her mouth dried. He was like an ancient pagan god. His enormous cock angled insistently toward her. "Do you have a condom?"

"We won't need one."

"Uhm, I'm not on birth control."

"I keep my word. Always." He pulled back the sheets. "There is nothing I want more. But we are not making love tonight."

"You are annoying, Sir." She wanted him inside her, deep and hard. "*This* is annoying."

"It's no easier for me." Though he chuckled, he showed no quarter. "When you give yourself to me, and you absolutely will, you will offer me everything—your breasts, your pussy..." Then he trailed off. "Your mind. You will be completely sober."

"I understand that rule for scening together." Frustration made her a little dizzy. "But this is just sex."

"Oh no." His laugh was brutal. "There's no such thing as just sex with you, Emma. It will be lovemaking. It will be fucking. It will be conquest. You will have no doubt who you belong to." He left her to turn off the lights, plunging them into total darkness, disorienting her a little bit.

She curled up into a ball on the far side of the bed. But he reached for her and dragged her back, pulling her against the hard planes of his body.

"I'm not much of a snuggler."

"Such a little liar. It worked well for you last night after our scene."

This time, her fib had been one of self-preservation. How would she sleep with his cock pressing against her?

He brushed her hair aside and kissed her neck. "Go to sleep."

Was that even possible? Despite herself, once she was in his arms, tension eased from her body. As he cradled his still-hard dick between her ass cheeks, she marveled at his restraint. This hadn't happened with any other man. Of course, Master Philip Dettmer was unlike any man she had ever met.

Sometime during the night she woke up cold. She wriggled farther beneath the covers, then went rigid when she realized she wasn't alone in the bed. Next to her was a dashing billionaire Dominant.

Wordlessly he reached across to pull her against him. When she stiffened her body, he slid an arm around her. And then he stroked her belly before moving lower to bring her fully awake.

He knew how to make her respond, not that it was difficult because she'd been aroused for hours. Without saying anything, he slipped a finger between her feminine folds to tease her clit. The nub hardened under his deft touch. She spread her legs, granting him greater access.

Whispering encouragement against her ear, he fondled her. "Come for me, Emma. Come from me."

As intimately as a musician knew his instrument, Master Philip knew her body. And he played every note perfectly.

Her pleas became wails as she begged for more.

"That's it."

Under his expert touch, she cried out as she shattered.

"Maybe that will help you sleep."

Though she couldn't see what he was doing, the sound told her he was sucking her essence from his fingertips.

"Delicious."

Sated, soothed as much by the knowledge he desired her as by the fabulous orgasm, she drifted back to sleep and knew nothing until she blinked her eyes open hours later.

Master Philip sat at the desk across the room with a small light on, its lampshade tipped to the side so as not to disturb her.

She put her elbows beneath her, sitting up a little to watch as he tapped out a note on his cell phone. He was dressed only in his slacks. It was a sin that he always looked so sexy.

With a slow smile that made excitement crash through her, he turned toward her. "Morning."

"Is it?"

"A little after five."

"Way too early for me." She fell back onto the pillow until she recalled she had to get up and go to work.

It would take them a while to check out and for him to drop her off at her car. Then she'd still have to drive home and get ready for work.

"Are you a coffee drinker?"

The room had a maker and a couple of pods. "That little thing isn't going to suffice."

"For me either. There's a specialty roaster in the lobby. Would you like me to get you one?"

"You're a superhero."

"At some point, I'll remind you that you said that."

Emma sat up and dragged the sheet with her, clasping it against herself. Not that it mattered. No doubt his misplaced sense of duty would protect her modesty.

"Do you like anything particular?" He shrugged into his shirt.

"The biggest latte they have. Vanilla."

"You are decidedly *not* vanilla, Emma."

His wicked grin shot heat through her, flooding her with the memory of how he'd masturbated her in the middle of the night. He was correct. That had never happened in any other relationship. *Definitely not vanilla.*

"Something to eat? A croissant breakfast sandwich?"

If she was going to be decadent, she might as well go all the way. "Please."

"I'll be back in fifteen minutes, maybe less." He finished dressing. Though he didn't add a tie, he buttoned up his shirt all the way and slipped into his suitcoat. Once again he was a competent businessman instead of a fantasy lover.

So, while she might be Cinderella, this was definitely the morning after the ball.

Before walking out of the room, he paused, then returned

HIS TO CHERISH

to her to tuck wayward strands of hair behind her ears. "I love the way you come for me, Princess."

Then he was gone, and the door closed behind him with a resounding click.

To jumpstart her brain as well as her body, she tossed back the covers and dashed to the bathroom. She couldn't afford to spend the entire day in bed thinking about the enigmatic Mr. Dettmer.

Except... A couple of tiny spots on her rear end were a little tender from where he'd grabbed her ass last night. But no matter how she contorted her body, she couldn't catch a glimpse of any marks in the mirror.

Giving up, she settled for a quick, bracingly cool shower, though she would have preferred the luxury of a hot bath.

After turning off the water, she wrapped up in the robe before applying a coat of mascara. Then she fished a small brush from her purse and attempted to tame her humidity-curled hair. When that failed, she decided it was going to be a messy-bun day.

Before she expected him, Philip returned.

When he caught sight of her, he stopped. Then a moment later, he shook his head and placed the cardboard carrier with food and cups on top of the dresser next to the television. "You know, I could get used to waking up next to you."

How did he always know the most perfect, dangerous words?

"Did you look to see if I left marks on your ass?"

"I tried." She cleared her throat. "The bathroom mirrors weren't angled correctly."

"Then allow me to look."

Of course he would suggest that.

Emma gathered the thick material of her robe and drew it up to her waist.

"Your back to me, and then bend, please."

In response to his soft, uncompromising command, her pulse slowed. When he spoke, it was as if her brain short-circuited, and she went somewhere else, became someone else. All she wanted to do was please him and be his.

He took two steps toward her, then palmed her buttocks. Instantly her body was on fire for him.

When he dug his fingertips in, she gasped.

As soon as the slight pain registered throughout her entire body, it vanished, leaving sexual hunger in its damnable wake.

"The smallest of marks. You won't even notice them, perhaps until you sit."

Which meant that all day, at her desk, she'd have reminders of him and their time together.

Emma hated it when he flipped the material of her robe down, leaving her unfulfilled and restless.

As she stood and faced him, he moved away to pick up his coffee, before taking a seat at the desk. "You have plenty of lingerie to choose from this morning."

She struggled to find her equilibrium, something increasingly difficult the more time she spent with him. "You spoil me."

"You deserve it, and more. It's my pleasure." While still regarding her, he took a drink. "I'd like to select what you wear today."

Another new experience for her.

"Show me your purchases."

With a nod, still in a partial submissive state, she forced herself to cross to her golden bags. She started with the sale items that she'd bought—a gorgeous bra and panty set, ivory in color, and covered with tantalizing black lace.

"Excellent choice. I like how low cut the panties are. They'll barely cover you. Which is perfect."

That hadn't been her intention, but he was right. "The

things you bought me are in the other bag." Of course, everything had been packaged perfectly, wrapped inside tissue paper.

His first gift was exquisite, a rich royal blue. The cups were shallow and uplifting, which meant her breasts might spill from them.

"Mademoiselle chose well."

"She did." Emma might have selected the items herself if she'd had discretionary funds available.

It shouldn't have surprised her that he'd been ridiculously generous. There were three more presents, black, purple, and red.

"Show me the purple panties."

She picked up the scrap of fabric, scandalized when she realized it was a G-string.

He grinned. "I think we'll save that for another time because I want to be able to enjoy the sight of you in it."

"It's…"

"Yes?"

"More daring than anything I've ever worn."

"Perfect. So, as for today, why don't you wear the blue?"

The cobalt color would limit her choices of what to wear to work. Her customary white shirt was not an option. But it didn't matter. She was secretly thrilled that he was behaving in a Dominant way and influencing her life in subtle, sexy ways.

He sat down in the office chair again and steepled his hands…waiting. Watching.

Since it would be ridiculous to dash back into the bathroom to get dressed, she dropped her robe. And then pulled on the panties that were a perfect fit, hugging her curves.

"Made for you."

Her fingers were a little nerveless because of his interested stare, making her struggle to fasten the bra strap behind her.

"Allow me."

Within seconds he was behind her. His actions were unhurried, leisurely as he secured the hooks. Then he skimmed his fingers down her spine, ending where the fabric of her panties met her skin.

"You're every bit as gorgeous as I imagined. I have to admit, I have good taste."

With a grin, she turned to him. "I'm not sure how to respond to that."

"Just agree with me. I'm always right."

"Of course you are."

He crossed the room to pick up her latte.

"Thank you." She accepted the cup from him.

What a surreal experience to be standing in the middle of one of the city's best hotels, sipping a hot rich beverage while wearing extravagant lingerie.

Just as he had said he could get used to waking up next to her, she could get used to this. Maybe too easily.

Across the room, his phone rang. He excused himself to take it, and he stepped out onto the balcony.

While he was gone, she finished dressing, hating that each moment took her closer to the time that she had to leave him.

When he reentered the room, she was ready to go.

"Sorry. Work calls. Are you ready?"

Within minutes, they were in his luxury SUV, zipping through New Orleans's quiet streets to her office building.

Not surprising her, he didn't just drop her off. Instead, he walked her to her car and placed the bags from Madame's shop in the trunk while she placed her cup in a holder and tucked the uneaten sandwich in the console.

When she was inside with her hands curled around the

steering wheel, he leaned in toward her. "I meant it when I invited you to meet my dog."

"Tibby?"

"And you never answered me when I asked if you'd like to scene again."

Was her unspoken answer not clear enough? She shouldn't, but she wanted to.

"Saturday night. Have dinner with me. I can cook, or I can make reservations, and you can get outside your comfort zone by ordering off the right side of the menu."

Extravagant gifts and the way he treated her were much more than a simple scene. "Look, Mr.—" She stopped herself and tried again. "Philip. What I mean is…thank you." This wasn't her life, and the sooner she woke up to that reality, the better. If she wasn't careful, this Prince Charming would break her heart.

"Consider it? No strings, just mutual enjoyment."

She gave a half smile.

"What could it hurt?"

What, indeed?

With tenderness, he tucked a wisp of her escaped hair back into her bun. "Hope to see you this weekend."

Emma prayed that her long-neglected sense of self-preservation would keep her from accepting his oh so tempting invitation.

CHAPTER 8

At exactly nine a.m. on Friday, Emma's desk phone rang, and the identification screen showed Philip's name. Heart racing, she scowled. How was that possible?

As far as she knew, he didn't have this number. Which meant he'd gone to some work to secure it. But that didn't explain why he was calling her office rather than her cellular device.

Instead of lunging to get to the call before he hung up, she took a breath and answered professionally. "Emma Monroe."

"Philip Dettmer here."

Professionalism be damned. It was the first time they'd talked since he'd dropped her off at her car two days prior, and her heart raced as if she were jumping rope. But what the hell was she supposed to say next? *"I know?" "How can I help you?" "What can I do for you?"* Damn, she would have preferred a text.

"I'm following up—"

On dinner since I never gave you an answer.

"On the possibility of moving one of my accounts to your brokerage."

Holy hell. She kicked herself for not contacting him. After all, she generally wasn't afraid to reach out to people or even make cold calls. But then again, she'd never expected a billionaire to actually want to do business with her. "I apologize. I should have reached out."

"Yes. You should have."

She winced. Deservedly. "I didn't—"

"After everything, if you thought I was merely being polite or even joking, perhaps I should reconsider?"

"*No!* Absolutely not." She shook her head at her own idiocy. "I'm honored. Flattered. And I promise you'll receive the very best care possible."

"I expect nothing less." His voice held a chilly spike that she was unaccustomed to. For the first time, she was seeing his ruthless business side, and it was a little disconcerting.

"Yes. Right." *Don't stammer. Do not stammer.* "Is now a good time to talk about your objectives and risk tolerance? And your expectations? Or would you like to make an appointment for us to sit down and discuss these things in depth?"

"I'll want to hear what you're going to do to take care of my account and present me with your ideas and strategies. Call my office and have my assistant add you to my calendar sometime in the next two weeks. If I'm going to make a change, I'd like to have it in place for the new year."

"Of course." She wanted to pinch herself. Landing this kind of account was every associate's dream. "Thank you for the opportunity. I won't let you down."

"You never have." After providing her with his work number, he offered the usual requisite words of farewell, then ended the call.

Shell-shocked, she sat back in her chair. He'd hung up without ever mentioning the fact that he'd invited her to his house the next day.

So that she wasn't an idiot a second time, she called his administrative assistant to get on his calendar. The woman informed Emma that his first available appointment was the Tuesday after Thanksgiving at ten. Immediately she agreed and sent him a calendar notification with a request for confirmation.

He responded within minutes but changed the location from her office to a coffee shop across town.

She'd meet him on the moon if that was his preference.

At least that was handled, and she had some time to prepare for the meeting.

For the rest of the day, concentration was impossible. She spent half her time thinking about strategies to ensure she won his business and the rest of it trying to decide what to do about tomorrow.

Since the moment she first met him, her life had become a series of *am I really going to do this?* moments.

So far she had no regrets, but she was skating ever closer to the edge. Going to his house, getting to know him—and his dog—was tempting fate.

Why hadn't she fallen for a man less complicated?

And the truth was, she didn't want that. She yearned for the wild exhilaration that Master Philip provided. Even if this relationship lasted only for a short time, the memories would outlast the pain. *Won't they?*

Right at quitting time, she yielded to temptation and picked up her cell phone to send him a text message.

If the invitation still stands, I'd like to meet your dog. What time?

His reply was instantaneous.

. . .

Six? Am I cooking, or are we going out?

Let's go out. Safer that way.

Pack an overnight bag.

She placed the phone on her desk, screen side down. Those were the words she was alternately dreading and expecting.

Emma busied herself by cleaning her desk and grabbing her purse; then her phone chimed again.

I'll send a car.

Her instinct was immediate. *No.* She wanted the freedom to come and go as she wanted.

No need. I'm fine with driving.

She took a moment to think before sending something more cheery.

Thanks!

He sent his address and a final message.

. . .

Wear something nice. Preferably a dress.

~

Emma swallowed her nerves and smoothed the front of the dress as she tried to gather the courage necessary to push open Master Philip's gate and walk up the path that led to his front door.

Since she had looked up his street address, his house didn't shock her as much as it otherwise might have. She didn't know exactly what kind of home a billionaire typically lived in, but she had expected something much bigger, maybe ostentatious, perhaps on acreage. At any rate, she expected it to be more private, like an estate with big wrought iron gates. His choice of neighborhoods was interesting too. She'd been prepared for him to rattle off a street number in the Garden District.

Instead, his corner-lot Victorian was north of Saint Charles, and not too far from Audubon Park in the middle of a busy neighborhood where kids played on lawns, moms and dads pushed babies in strollers, and plenty of tourists zipped by on motor scooters.

But then, she should have known better than to expect that Philip would ever be what she expected.

Ordering herself to quit stalling, she entered the property, passing the lush tropical landscaping before walking up the steps. The covered porch was large and inviting, with chairs and tables, as well as plenty of potted plants. It was a perfect place to enjoy the sights while sipping something cool.

But that's not why you're here.

With a slow thud of her heart, she stood in front of the camera located next to the bright-aqua-colored door and pressed the lighted doorbell. An explosion of sound erupted from inside, peals of churchlike dings, yips and barks, and if she wasn't mistaken, several different voices. Taken aback, she frowned. Perhaps he just had a television blasting?

Philip answered the door and stole her breath. She'd never seen him so casual in jeans and deck shoes, wearing a summer-weight linen shirt while holding the most adorable dog she'd ever seen.

"Emma." His smile was welcoming and inviting but was followed by an immediate wince. "In advance, I owe you an apology. Forgive me for what's about to happen."

A woman popped her head around the corner.

"Oh my God. I…uh…" She tightened her grip on her purse and now unnecessary overnight bag. "I didn't know you had company. I'll be going."

"No. Wait. It's not what you think."

Pretending as if her heart were still in one piece, she nodded.

"The annoying woman—"

She waved wildly.

"Is my sister, and she is here with her three kids."

"Invite her in, dum-dum!" the woman called out.

"I swear to you, I didn't invite her over, and I've been trying to get rid of her for over an hour."

His frown of exasperation melted her.

"Oh, shit! Rex! Philip, don't let Rex get out!"

"Please, come in. Quick."

Another dog, a small flash of fur, darted toward them, and a young boy scrambled after it, making it race faster. Automatically Philip stuck out his foot to block the threshold.

Emma hurried inside as he brushed the animal back with his foot and then slammed the door shut, avoiding a disaster, but sealing her within the pandemonium.

"Titus, bring Rex to Mommy!"

"Yes, ma'am!" The youngster gave Emma a quick smile,

then scooped up the pup and headed farther into the house, leaving her and Philip momentarily alone.

"I'll get rid of them as soon as I can. This is not how I intended for our evening to go."

Tibby had his nose in the air and was paddling his front feet, apparently trying to get closer to Emma. "Is it okay for me to pet him?"

"He'd like that. You can put your belongings on the hall table."

After she did, she placed a hand in front of the dog's nose so that it could smell her. After a few requisite sniffs, Tibby licked Emma's hand.

"Hey, look at that. He likes Emma." Philip's sister shouted. "Even though he hated Simone."

"Jesus."

Philip's sister walked down the hallway. "Are you going to introduce us?"

"If you were to do a google search on annoying younger sisters, this is the result you'd get. Emma, please meet Diane, who was just packing up to leave."

"No I wasn't."

Rather than offering a hand to shake, Diane swept Emma into a big hug.

"I'm so happy to meet you. It's been too long since my brother has had a woman in his life. I was afraid that bitch had hexed him forever."

"Diane—"

"Shut up. You know it's true."

Just then, a toddler wearing nothing other than a diaper tore down the hallway toward them.

"Do you mind?" Philip handed the dog to her.

Unconcernedly Tibby snuggled into Emma's waiting arms while Philip swept up the rambunctious boy.

"Unka Flip!"

"What's up, buddy?"

He proudly displayed a red lump of modeling compound with a second blue piece mashed on top of it.

"Fabulous! You're an architect." Philip grinned.

First the dog, and now he was holding a youngster, not even seeming to notice the little bits of clay that were falling on his shirt.

"Emma, this is my nephew, Tyson."

"You need to learn the difference." Diane rolled her eyes. "That's Tyler."

"Identical twins." Philip sighed. "You should dress them differently."

"Where's the fun in that?"

"Unka!"

Another toddler joined them. Tyson, Emma presumed.

"Hunger!"

"Your mom can get you a snack. Right, Mom?"

Rather than answering, Diane looked at Emma. "I understand you guys were planning to go out to dinner. And since we haven't eaten yet, I was thinking that maybe—"

"No." Philip's interruption was swift and firm. "Absolutely not. You're not going with us. It's nonnegotiable."

Tyson's eyes filled with tears, and he tugged on Philip's pantleg. "Hunger!"

"We know, baby." Diane's tone was both soothing and firm. "And at this time on a Saturday night, lines are long everywhere. Since we all need to eat, I think we should order pizza."

"Pizza!" The older boy joined them again.

"Do it from your own home, Di. In fact, call now. By the time you arrive, it will be on your doorstep. We can load your car, and you can be on the road in five minutes."

Since Diane refused to be dissuaded, Emma instantly liked her.

"There's a place right around the corner. Mama Maria's Winged Pies. They're the best in town."

It'd been over a year since Emma had indulged. "What kind of pizza were you thinking about?"

"Jesus." Philip placed Tyler on the floor. "For God's sake, Emma, don't encourage her. We have reservations."

Diane carried on as if he'd never spoken. "The boys like pepperoni and cheese. But I love one of their specialties, the Primal Pie. Seven meats and drizzled with their famous sriracha sauce."

On cue, Emma's tummy rumbled. Because she'd been planning to eat a nice dinner, she'd skipped lunch. "Sounds amazing."

"Emma—" A warning was laced in Philip's voice.

"Ignore him. He's all bark." Diane was more confident of that fact than Emma was.

"You're being nosy. I didn't bring Emma here so you could interrogate her."

Diane shrugged. "It's not my fault the kids need to eat."

"Actually, yes. It is your own damn fault you didn't take them home before dinner time."

"Uncle Philip, you swore." Titus's eyes were wide.

"Christ." Philip sighed.

"That's two dollars! Mom, Uncle Philip has to put two dollars in the swear jar."

"Keep it up, big brother. If you don't shut up soon, we can pay the bill with your fines." She grinned. "Where's your credit card?"

"Your husband works for a living." Even as he spoke, he pulled his wallet from his back pocket. "Use his."

"How inhospitable of you, with you having a guest and all."

Philip touched Emma's wrist. "We can still go out." He

shot his sister a hard glare. "Leave this motley crew here to eat and clean up their damn mess."

"Three dollars, Uncle Philip."

"And miss this?" Emma shook her head. "Not for anything."

"High five." With a grin, Diane lifted her hand, and Emma responded in kind. "Are you in for the Primal Pie, or do you want something else?" Pretending her brother wasn't standing there, Diane addressed Emma.

"Sounds interesting." Good thing she liked spicy food. "Maybe one slice and another of the pepperoni?"

"Perfect. And you"—Diane snatched the credit card from Philip's hand—"can eat whatever I get you." She headed toward the back of the house. "Come on, boys. Let's clean up the toys and set the table so we can eat."

When they were alone, Philip sighed. "You've been here five minutes, and we haven't even let you leave the foyer."

"I'm totally fine. Your sister is great—I love her already."

"Forgive me if I don't agree with you."

"I've always wanted a sibling. At times growing up, I was really lonely. Mom did the best she could, but still..." She looked toward the back of the house where all the noise was coming from. "This is the stuff of dreams for me. Really."

"There's no need to let her steamroll you. I wanted to treat you to a nice meal tonight."

"And miss this excitement?" She grinned. "No way."

"I'm warning you, the boys can be a little much."

"Maybe for some people. But I like kids. We can go out anytime, but this is an opportunity for you to be with your family, and for me to get to know you all better."

"You're kinder than her behavior merits. Thank you. At least let me give you a tour. And you don't have to carry His Highness around."

"Is it okay if I don't put him down?"

"He'll object if you do. I'm afraid he's going to be even more spoiled."

"One night can't hurt. Right?"

"With this one? You have no idea. Let's start with the upstairs so that I can get you alone for a minute."

"Show her your secret room!"

"Fuck."

"Four dollars, Uncle Philip!"

"Secret room?"

"We'd better get upstairs before I have no money left to invest with your firm."

"On the other hand, if you have me manage your portfolio, you'll have enough funds to stuff the swear jar all you want."

"Well played, Emma." He nodded. "Well played."

While keeping her fingers lightly curled around the polished banister, she followed him up the glossy wooden stairs and into a guest bedroom with a four-poster bed and en suite that reminded her of a spa.

His office was next, everything clean and organized, suiting him perfectly.

Finally, he showed her to the primary bedroom, with a large bed set in a small alcove with windows on all three sides.

The attached bathroom was spectacular, with beautiful black-and white tiles on the floor, a glassless shower, and separate soaker tub. "I feel like I'm back at the Maison." Only this space was much larger. "Everything is perfect. It's like classic New Orleans style, but everything is so modern and bright." And the ceilings were at least twelve feet tall.

"When I bought this place after my divorce, it hadn't been renovated. The work took a little over six months. Tibby and I stayed at an apartment, but I think he's much happier here."

No wonder. There appeared to be a box of dog toys and a Tibby-size bed in every room.

Philip bent to grab a ball that he tossed down the stairs. Tibby wiggled, and she placed him down to chase it. "Clever."

From the kitchen area, Rex barked excitedly.

"Do you really have a secret room?"

"I do. Diane calls it that because she's never seen it, so her mind spins as she tries to figure out why I won't let her in." He shrugged. "At this point, I mostly do it to annoy her. Come with me, and I'll show you. It's where I plan to corrupt you later this evening."

She shivered. "Is that a promise?"

"Most decidedly so."

At the far end of the hallway was a narrow carpeted staircase, and he led the way up. The only thing on the third story was a closed door with a black pad on the wall next to it. When he placed his thumb on the device, it lit up; then there was a quiet *snick* as the lock released. "No one but me has access, which means it's totally private." He pushed the door open. "After you."

Her heart sped up as she imagined what she might see.

The brightly lit space had warm polished wood floors. Up here, the ceiling was not as high as in other parts of the house, and the far ends of the room were angled in dormer style.

An oversize television was mounted to one wall, as were numerous speakers. There were several pieces of exercise equipment, including a rowing machine and a popular exercise bike.

It appeared to be an enormous, well-thought-out workout space, even more wonderful than a high-end gym. There were mirrors everywhere, lots of overhead lighting, a weight bench, barbells with plates in every possible size. In addition to the area being big enough for her to comfortably practice yoga, he'd decorated with several large, tasteful pieces of art.

"What do you think?" He entered behind her and closed the door.

She turned around and blinked. "I'm a little confused as to why it's so secret."

"My real estate agent called it a bonus room. So that inspired me." He pushed a button that lowered the blinds, filtering out the remnants of the early evening sun while ensuring they enjoyed complete privacy. "Have a look around."

Curious, she walked toward an open door across from her to discover a small bathroom with a luxurious shower. "Okay, this space is officially fantastic."

When she turned back toward him, his arms were folded across his chest. His head was cocked to the side, and he wore a devilish grin.

She scowled. "What am I missing?"

"Open that antique wardrobe over there." He nodded.

Emma pulled open the doors to discover the bag he had brought to the Quarter. Once again she recognized the owl on its side, and it matched the one on the inlaid floor at Mademoiselle's shop. She was going to ask him about it, but her attention was seized by the numerous BDSM implements that hung from hooks.

Inhaling sharply, she took in the rest of the items. Three shelves were stocked with nipple clamps, butt plugs, bottles of lubricant, cuffs, rope, and a couple of things she didn't recognize.

"I like to be creative. The weight bench, for example—it can be customized to be as useful as a piece of equipment at a club. Everything is hidden in plain sight." He took down a piece of art to reveal metal slats that were screwed into the wall. "It would take me less than ten seconds to have both of your wrists secured and have you completely at my mercy."

"Oh."

"I could have you facing away as I spanked you." He took a purposeful step toward her. "Or facing me as I cropped your breasts or ate your beautiful pussy until you couldn't stand any longer. I can almost imagine your whimpers as you beg for mercy."

She was dizzy, and she reached for the handle of the exercise bike to steady herself.

"Even that piece of innocuous equipment. I could sit on the seat and ask you to straddle me. Make no mistake, this may not be an ordinary dungeon. But here, with the door closed, us locked inside, you're my helpless submissive."

"Philip…"

"Master Philip when we're in this space."

God. His eyes had darkened, and his tone had roughened. She craved his Dominance, his touch.

"We may have company for the next hour or so, but I wanted to be certain you knew what is ahead of you for the rest of the evening."

Anticipation made her shudder.

"Lift your dress and show me your panties."

She'd selected a thong for tonight's date.

"Very nice choice. Beautiful." He inhaled deeply. "Now take them off."

Her hand shook as she lowered the fabric. And then her heel caught. It was a good thing she was able to hold on to something; otherwise she might have lost her balance completely.

He offered no help, seeming to enjoy how flustered he made her. "Good. Now tuck your dress up somehow. I want your ass exposed."

Could they really be doing this with other people in the

house? Because of his security system, they were completely safe, but it was still scandalously unnerving.

"Go select a butt plug and a bottle of lube and take them into the bathroom."

This couldn't be happening. It was totally, deliriously exciting…until she had to choose from the terrible array of plugs in front of her—fat glass ones, some crafted from silicone, even several stainless options. All of them looked way too big for her, and like the coward she was, she picked up the absolute smallest one before grabbing some lube.

He followed her into the bathroom and nodded when she placed the items he'd requested on the counter. "Please put your palms flat on the wall above the towel rack and stick your ass out as far as you can."

"Yes, Sir." Unnerved, she did as he asked.

She kept glancing over her shoulder trying to see what he was doing. Deliberately, he blocked her view. And then he crossed to her, cradled her head in his hands, and positioned her where he wanted.

"Don't worry about what's going to happen. Just ignore me and let yourself go. Enjoy the experience."

Easy for him to say when it wasn't his ass in question.

Then there was a wetness against her anal whorl, and she reflexively struggled to get away.

"It will be easier if you don't fight."

And yet it was difficult not to.

He worked a finger inside her, stretching her, preparing her. It was exquisite and too much, all at the same time.

Then he eased out, and water splashed into the basin. She tried to make out the next sound…something thick being pumped? The lube?

Moments later, something more rigid and bigger forced her anus wider than it had been earlier. She gasped and tried to stand, but he placed a hand between her shoulder blades, keeping her in place.

"Don't make me secure you. But I can if you prefer it?"

Frantically she shook her head. "I'll stay still." At least this way, she had some hope of escape if it became too much.

"I'm proud of you."

His words sustained her.

When he bore forward, she whimpered, then pressed her lips together, in a vain attempt to remain silent.

"It's okay if you cry, or even scream. No one will hear you. The room is completely soundproof, handy for working out with music blasting."

He slid the horrible little toy in, then eased it back out, and then began fucking her in earnest.

"Oh. *God.* Damn it. Damn. Damn. I can't." She bit her lower lip, fighting to stay in position instead of bolting. "It won't fit. I can't do it."

"Of course you can. It's barely bigger than my finger."

She yelped as the plug got thicker. "Master Philip!" Then despite her intentions, she tried to pull away.

He grabbed hold of one of her shoulders, pulling her backward, even as he continued to insert the thing in a slow, decisive movement.

Then all of a sudden, it was over. The discomfort vanished as the thing settled inside her.

"Perfect." He wiped her with a wet towel, then landed both of his hands on her ass cheeks, harshly enough to bring her to her tiptoes with a gasp. Then he jiggled around the base of the plug until he was satisfied. "How does it feel?"

Miserable. "Abominable."

"Even better, then. For the rest of the evening, you will be filled for me, and I will enjoy every minute that you are tortured."

Right at this moment, she wasn't her Dominant's biggest fan.

"You may stand."

She turned to him and squeezed her buttocks several times in quick succession as she tried to get accustomed to the thing.

"You may thank me, or we can do that again with the bigger plug."

Anything but that. "Thank you, Sir. I appreciate this very much."

"What do you appreciate?"

Resisting the impulse to snarl, she tried to answer appropriately. No way did she want anything bigger up there. Not that it would fit, anyway. "The kindness you showed by letting me use a small plug. By taking your time entering me."

"And?"

The cruel man wanted more? "By filling me in a way that guarantees every thought is centered on you."

"You're welcome." He kissed her forehead.

After washing his hands again, he untucked her dress and let it fall back into place. "I'm sure the pizza will be here soon."

Not that she'd be able to eat, anyway.

"We should get back to our company."

"Yes, Sir."

Her thong was still puddled on the floor. "Am I allowed to put it back on?

"Afraid not."

Which would make her doubly uncomfortable. With an obedient but reluctant nod, she followed him from the room.

The plug shifted each time she moved, which made the two flights of stairs an uncomfortable challenge. "You're positive this thing will stay in place?" Maybe she should ask him to reconsider his underwear decision.

"If you're concerned, we could switch it out for a larger one."

"No!" Even the threat made her tighten her butt cheeks. "This one is fine."

"I thought it might be." He reached the foyer and watched as she descended from the final step. "I'm confident you'll figure out a way for it to stay where it should."

She wrinkled her nose. "If we had gone out to dinner, would you still have made me wear this thing?"

"Absolutely. Let me show you the main level."

In the large formal living room, the dogs were wrestling with a pull toy, their tiny paws scrabbling on the hardwood. Happy noise from the back of the house reached them. "Your house is so comfortable." Lived-in, when it could have easily been formal or stuffy. Near the window was a nook that would be perfect for reading.

"I'm glad you like it."

The back area was open concept with clear views of the dining area and den. He showed her into the kitchen with chef-inspired appliances and an oversize island. The counters were crafted from gorgeous marble, and the cabinets were a soothing gray-blue color. Diane stood in front of the pantry, and she handed the oldest boy a package of paper plates.

One of the twins—Tyson, Emma assumed, because he had a shirt on—toddled over. "I halp?"

"Thank you." Diane bent to give him a handful of napkins. He dropped several, then made his way to the den rather than the dining room.

"Tyson! Stop. Give them to Titus." She shook her head. "It's never ending."

"Looks like a challenge." Being in the midst of the chaos and love sent a pang of emptiness rippling through Emma, and she forced it away. "Anything I can do?"

"We're almost ready. We go through some version of this every day. I really want the boys to participate in chores." With a sigh, Diane glanced at the line of paper littering the floor. "Though it would be much easier to do it all myself. How about you? Do you want kids?"

Stunned by the question, Emma blinked.

"As you've already seen, my sister's life passion is minding other people's business. It's perfectly all right to tell her to quit being nosy. I do it all the time."

Even though she didn't think about it often, Emma did want her own family. So what was she doing here with Master Philip? What they shared was incredible, but he had no interest in a long-term relationship. She should get serious about dating a man whose dreams and goals matched hers. *Right?*

When she realized Diane was still watching intently, Emma nodded. "When the time is right, yes. Several."

"I've been wanting another myself."

"Really?"

"I want them to grow up close together. And I have a friend with a newborn, and that makes me miss having an infant. They're so sweet and innocent. Bernard—that's my husband—thinks the three we have is enough, but four's a much better number."

"Would you like a glass of wine?" Philip inserted himself into the conversation. "I think you may need it."

She frowned since he'd made it clear that alcohol and BDSM didn't mix.

As if he'd read her mind, he responded. "It's early. A small glass won't hurt. And no doubt the alcohol will be absorbed by about ten pounds of dough and cheese."

That part was true. "Red, if you've got it. Thanks."

"None for me," Diane interjected. "Thanks for asking. I still have to drive home."

"Good God. I didn't ask because I refuse to make you feel anymore welcome than you've already made yourself."

Emma accepted the glass of wine he offered and took a sip to cover her smile. She hoped they knew how lucky they were to have each other.

"Philip, do you mind finding something on the TV for the boys to watch?"

"You're capable of figuring out how to operate the remote control."

"I want you to go away so I can talk to Emma alone."

"That's a spectacularly bad idea."

"If she's seeing you, she's more than capable of holding her own with me. Stop fussing."

As if Philip Dettmer ever fussed.

"Your sister is right. It's safe to leave me alone with her for a minute."

"I mean it. Tell her to mind her own business." With a shake of his head, he pointed at his oldest nephew. "Hey, Titus. Help me find something age-appropriate for you to watch."

When the older boy scrambled after his uncle, the twins followed.

"I'm a little jealous of the wine. If I didn't have to drive across the causeway, I'd have a great big glass."

"You live on the North Shore?"

She nodded. "Covington. More house for the money, and a much bigger yard. But there are times it feels as if I'm a million miles away from Philip and Mom."

"I considered living over there too. But the drive in every day deterred me. Not that it's that far, and people all over the country have much longer commutes, but—"

"So you know exactly what I mean. You met Philip at work?"

Just how much information had she gotten from her

brother? "Yes." Beyond that, Emma didn't elaborate. Technically the elevator *was* at her workplace.

"And you're in finance?"

"Philip is too generous." She rested her hips against the end of the counter, and the act made her once again aware of the plug. "I'm a financial advisor, but not one you'll ever find written up in a magazine or anything. I help regular working people with their retirement funds. It's a passion."

"Well, you must be good at it if Philip is considering moving part of his portfolio."

"Oh my God. I never asked him to." Did Diane think she was trying to make money off her brother? "I swear."

Diane rolled her eyes. "If I thought you were a fortune hunter, I'd have had your head on a platter before now."

That, Emma believed.

With a clatter of nails against hardwood, the two dogs entered the kitchen, with much less enthusiasm than they'd shown before.

"I love my brother, and I don't want him to get hurt."

"It's more likely to be the other way around." Maybe she shouldn't have admitted that, but it was the truth.

"How's that?"

Sound blasted from the television before diminishing beneath Philip's shouted apology.

Sharing anything else would skirt the line of what she considered personal. "And you don't need to worry. We're just…" *What? Lovers? Scene partners?* "Friends."

"Mmm-hmm." Diane grabbed a diet soda from the refrigerator and pulled up on the tab. "You're the first woman he's invited over since that bitch left him."

"Mom!"

"Swear jar, little sis!"

"Okay, okay!" she called back to Titus and Philip. "How the heck did they even hear me over the television?" She opened a cupboard and pulled out three tumblers with dinosaurs on them. "Can you grab the milk for me?"

Which was clearly a way of drawing Emma into the kitchen for a little more privacy. Diane was more than nosy—she was clever.

Diane began pouring the milk into the glasses, then sealed two of them with lids and stuck straws through the openings. "Anyway, what has he told you about his ex?"

"Not much. And it probably should stay that way."

"I like you even more now." She grinned. "You're honest. Simone? Not so much. She wouldn't have recognized the truth even if it knocked her upside her head."

Emma slid her glass on the counter.

"I'm sure you've looked him up. And I'll say this. My brother is a fool. He never responded to the"—she cupped her palm in front of her mouth and whispered behind it—"shitty things she said about him." Diane dropped her hand. "What's in *Scandalicious* isn't the truth, not even close to it. They ought to be shut down for the crap they publish."

The doorbell rang, and the household exploded with a fresh cacophony of noise—dogs, kids, and Diane calling out for Philip to handle it. Emma hadn't been this happy in a long time.

"Look..." Diane seized one last opportunity to have her say. "I love Philip fiercely."

"It shows."

"He deserves a good woman, one who's trustworthy. I hope you're it."

"As I said..." Emma shook her head. "We're just friends."

"Uh-huh. That's why he showed you the secret room."

Philip's arrival with six different boxes prevented any further discussion.

With a wink, Diane went to help.

"Can we eat in the living room?" Titus asked.

"It's okay with me." Philip grinned. "It's a special occasion, right?"

Diane sighed.

"You deserve it." Philip was unapologetic.

"Grab us a few towels for the floor."

While he was gone, Diane explained her frustration. "I normally insist on eating meals together with no electronics—and that includes TV."

With a revenge-filled grin, Philip returned. "You shouldn't have crashed my party."

"Your house. Your rules." She accepted the towels. "And you'll get to clean up the mess."

Laughing at their bickering exchange, Emma went to help, spreading a couple of the towels on the long coffee table and several more on the floor beneath cushions.

While Philip fed both dogs, she and Diane filled paper plates with pizza and boneless chicken wings, though Diane refused to let them bring any of the honey barbecue sauce into the living room.

"Thank you for the help."

"Of course. Your kids are great."

Philip finally took his place at the head of the dining room table, and after selecting the smallest piece of pizza, Emma joined him. Even though the seat was padded, she winced as she sat and the plug made its presence known. She adjusted herself until she found a position that was somewhat comfortable. Philip never took his gaze off her.

Diane offered each boy a glass of milk before flopping into a chair across from Emma. "Now I really am hungry."

Emma picked up her first slice and took a bite of the Primal Pie. "This is…" The taste was magnificent, savory and decadent, and then a wave of heat hit her. "Wow."

"It's a good thing they don't deliver to the North Shore. I'd eat it every day. You know, we could make this a regular type of thing—like once a week or so. The boys love visiting their uncle, and—"

"They need to see their grandmother as well. Have your date night there."

"Let's set something up. Mom was saying she hasn't seen you recently. And you can bring Emma with you."

"See why I apologized in advance?"

For the next half hour or so, Diane regaled them with childhood stories. But every time she skirted close to revealing information about Philip's marriage, he shut her down.

Then Titus wandered in. "Can we watch something else?"

Before Diane could answer, Philip stepped in. "No. Your mom said you need to be going home."

She tossed a wadded-up napkin at him. "Did not."

"I'll help you load up."

Diane rolled her eyes. "He's not this helpful any other time."

While Philip shoved toys into a bag decorated with cartoon figures, and Diane insisted Tyler actually put some clothes on, Emma busied herself with cleaning up and packaging the leftover pizza so Diane could take it home.

Loading the SUV took some time, with all the belongings, food, three kids, and a dog.

"I loved meeting you." Holding the keys, Diane gave Emma a quick hug. "Enjoy the rest of your evening. And be patient with him. He deserves it."

"Bye, Sis." He accepted her hug, then opened the driver's door for her. "Be safe. Text when you get home."

"I can take a hint."

He closed her inside the vehicle, then stepped back to drape an arm around Emma's shoulder. "At last."

It took a couple of minutes for Diane to get situated, but

then she backed out of the driveway, waving and blowing kisses before accelerating down the street.

Once Emma and Philip were alone in the foyer, he sealed them inside and turned the lock. "That was more than you bargained for."

"Don't apologize. I enjoyed it. The boys are great, and your sister has a big heart."

"I'll make it up to you. Any restaurant in the city. Hell, in the state. I'll even fly us to New York. Even Paris."

She laughed. "Really, no. That food was seriously good. I may order takeout so I don't have to cook for the next week."

"In a city filled with epicurean delights, I treated you to pizza."

"And a boneless chicken wing with dunking sauce."

"I have a lot to make up for." He shuddered. "And now that we're finally alone…" Making her breath catch, he backed her up against the wall. "We have some unfinished business."

CHAPTER 9

Passion—no longer needing to be restrained—flared in the depths of Master Philip's stunning green eyes, sending her insides spiraling.

"I want you naked."

"Here?"

"And now." He captured the hem of her dress and drew it up. Once it was off, he tossed it onto the table next to her purse and overnight bag. Then in a single, swift move, he had her out of her bra.

His gaze intent, he palmed her breasts, capturing them and squeezing them, making her knees bend. Blindly she grabbed hold of his shoulders for support. She had never been this deliriously turned on before. "I need to have you inside me."

"Yeah. I want it too."

Tibby barked, then dashed toward the rear of the house.

"That's it." Philip shook his head. "I'm having a doggie door installed next week. Tomorrow even." Then he took her hand. "Come with me."

He drew her into the living room, and this was another new experience, being led naked through his house.

"It's a kneeling bench from an old church." He pointed to an antique piece of furniture tucked into a corner beneath some built-in shelving.

Though she noticed it earlier, she hadn't paid too much attention to it since she'd had no idea what it was. "Hiding in plain sight?"

"Always the best plan. I'd like it if you waited for me here." He moved the bench to the center of the room. "Tell me you will do as I ask."

A few words and a masterfully phrased command sent her spiraling into a submissive state, turning her into somebody else.

"Emma?"

"Of course, Sir." She nodded.

"I'll be back in a few minutes, after I take His Highness out and put him to bed. I know you may grow uncomfortable."

"And that's okay with you."

"Of course." His smile was quick, and she basked in the glow of his approval.

Aware of his power, she knelt on the strip of smooth, not overly padded leather. The plug made its presence known again, and she adjusted her weight a couple of times.

"Now put your hands behind your neck."

As if being on the bench weren't difficult enough, now he wanted her to balance herself without using her hands.

"Please keep your head up with your gaze focused forward. Think about Dominance and submission, the way you're waiting for me, hiding nothing and offering everything. And think about the way I will claim you soon."

Without another word, he was gone, leaving her alone.

All her senses leaped into hyperawareness. She noticed

every sound—the way Tibby's nails scrabbled on the hardwood, the gentle squeak of the door, the soft rumble of her Dominant's voice.

The coolness of the evening air washed over her, and the thundering of her heart seemed to reverberate through the room.

No matter what came next, she intended to fully embrace it, the ever-widening risk to her heart be damned.

After going upstairs with Tibby, Master Philip returned, holding a metal choker, one like she'd seen at Mademoiselle's shop.

"Will you wear this for me?"

Silently she nodded.

"Hold your hair out of the way."

Within seconds, he had clicked the clasp into place. The metal was cold, sending a shiver through her, and the weight of the thing lay heavily against her collarbone. Maybe he had done this a dozen times before. But for Emma, it was a first, a searing moment she would never forget.

When he was done, he offered a hand up. "Now I'd like you to walk up the stairs, ahead of me. I'm going to enjoy every moment of watching your sassy ass wiggle."

With the silicone toy inside, her gait was awkward, and yet his little whistle of approval made it bearable.

"The only way this could be any more perfect is if you had spank marks on your rear. But I'll take care of that soon enough."

Making him happy pleased her, and she finally understood what he'd meant when he said something similar earlier on. Focusing on what the other person wanted was its own reward.

"All the way to the secret room."

When she stopped in front of the closed door, he reached around her to let them into his makeshift dungeon.

"There's a box of condoms in my bag. Bring me one."

Everything inside her tightened. This was what she'd been waiting for.

After opening the wardrobe, she crouched to unfasten the bag's clasps, and once again she noticed the owl on the side. Before she could ask about it, he spoke.

"While you're there, fetch me the wooden paddle."

"Yes, Sir." A wave of dizziness hit her as she returned to him, unsure what to expect.

He was raising the height of his workout bench, and he was no longer the same casual man she'd spent the evening with. Instead he was the Dominant who would live in her fantasies forever.

"Thank you." He took the requested items from her hands and ordered her to lie on the bench. "Lift your legs. I'd like to see how flexible you are."

"You're making me nervous."

"The more the better."

It took her a moment to settle into a position, and even then she wasn't comfortable. The plug was huge inside her, and her abdominal muscles were not accustomed to holding this position for very long.

"Scoot toward me a couple of inches."

She knew better than to argue. He knew what he was doing, and no doubt he realized that his request would leave part of her ass unsupported, which meant he wanted it that way.

Struggling, she grabbed hold of the bottom of the bench, trying to hold herself steady so that she didn't fall off—grateful he hadn't secured her wrists.

Master Philip reached over her and placed the paddle above her head. Then he moved to her side and braced a forearm against the backs of her knees, ensuring she couldn't move and leaving her pussy exposed to him.

"I love how much you like surrendering to me." He outlined her labia, and his fingers came away damp.

Emma squeezed her eyes shut. She had never experienced anything that was more right than this.

He tapped her pussy several times in a slow rhythmic way that was oddly relaxing, allowing tension to slip from her body.

Gradually—ever so slightly—he increased the tempo and pressure until she was writhing, needing an orgasm, hurting and no longer concerned about anything because she knew he was looking out for her. Her trust in him was complete. "Master Philip." She tried to lift her hips.

"Tell me."

"All evening… The way you looked at me all evening. The way the plug moved. I've been miserable." And that was only half the truth. It wasn't just that. She'd been a bundle of desire since the night she slept next to him in the hotel bed. "I want to have sex with you."

"Please." His prompt was rough, and not reassuring in the least.

Even though she begged, he was ruthless, continuing to spank her pussy in earnest, until she was choking on her sobs. It was too much, and not nearly enough.

"Imagine how happy you would be if I did this to you every day."

"Yes." *Yes.* But she wasn't concerned about tomorrow; she was only concerned about this moment.

Tormenting her, he slipped a finger inside her and angled it so that he touched her G-spot. As if hit by a live electrical wire, she lifted her shoulders, sitting up as much as possible so she could look at him.

"Lie down. I am not finished with you yet."

Even though her breaths came in ragged little bursts, she

forced herself to comply with his order. Then, confounding her, he removed his finger.

"Please hand me the paddle that is above your head."

She had to blink to reorient herself. Frustrated with him, she scowled. "You can reach it much easier than I can."

"No doubt that's true. Now do as you're told."

With an annoyed exhalation, she did.

"Thank you." He placed more weight on his forearm, forcing her legs back even farther and granting himself even more access. He tapped the length between her legs, making her scream and regret her grumpy response.

"Oh so perfect."

After slapping her cunt with his open hand, he used his mouth to soothe the ache.

Lost, she cried out as he continued the paddling in earnest, blazing her ass, marking her.

Finally when she knew she could take no more, he walked away. "Sir?"

"Stay where you are."

He returned with soft cuffs that he wrapped around her ankles; then he hooked them together.

"I'm not sure how long I can hold this position, Sir." Her muscles were already quivering in protest.

"I'll decide that."

"Beast."

"Shall I get a rope and tie your feet to the overhead bar?"

She clamped her lips together, wisely saying nothing further. Her feeble attempt to goad him into making love to her had failed, leaving her no choice but to surrender to what he did next.

With two fingers, he spread her apart and licked her.

Sobbing, she begged for it to be over. But he refused to be dissuaded, and he left her just short of a climax…time after time.

He used the paddle on her, its hollow thud echoing off the ceiling and walls, making her scream.

"That sound feeds my soul." He wielded the implement harder, blazing it across the fleshy part of her buttocks, lighting up all her nerve endings.

She was drenched in perspiration, crying and whimpering, craving something she couldn't even name.

"I'm going to take you, Emma."

Finally. She called out his name, aching to reach her arms toward him. "Please. *Please.*"

For a moment he was gone, and when he returned, he was gloriously naked, and he was sheathed in a condom. After unfastening her ankles, he moved between her legs, guiding his cockhead toward her entrance.

Because of the position she was in and the fact that she was already full of a plug, his penetration seemed impossible. "I don't think I can do this."

"Oh, I'll make sure of it."

He was in total control, playing with her nipples, leaning over to suck on them until she was delirious with desire. He stroked in and out, pulling away numerous times to play with her, tease her, rocking her ever closer to an orgasm.

She was ready for him, and she yielded, wanting to be his in every sense of the word. Even though she was tender, Emma welcomed him balls-deep.

"Beautiful, beautiful."

She opened her eyes and locked her gaze on his face. His eyebrows were drawn together in a fierce line, and his jaw was set tight as if holding back was a struggle. Whatever she was enduring, he was as well.

"I want more of you."

Within seconds, he'd removed the cuffs and picked her up. "Put your arms around my neck."

"Is this even possible?"

"Just do as I said." His words were a desperate command.

Holding on, she buried her face in the crook of his shoulder. His fingers were clenched in her flesh as he effortlessly held her. Using his powerful legs, he drove in again and again until she whimpered, climaxing around him.

Emma inhaled his woody masculine scent, memorizing it for an eternity. In that moment, she knew she was falling in love with him. She wanted this moment to last forever, but a more rational part of her psyche urged her to end it as soon as possible, while she still had some control over her emotions.

With a guttural groan, he drove in again and again, banishing all her thoughts. She was lost in him—in their experience. Then, with a helpless sigh, she came again, her pussy muscles clenching his cock.

Uttering soothing words, he held her tight. When she finally gathered enough energy to lift her head so that she could look at him, his eyes still held a purposeful gleam.

"As I said earlier, I'm not through with you yet."

He slid out of her, then carried her to a mat that he unfurled. "I want you on all fours."

Always the perfect lover, he brought her to full arousal again before taking hold of her hip bones, holding her in place as he eased inside her. The effects of the plug intensified each stroke, yet she yearned for his possession.

"You are mine."

No matter how sweet those words were and how much she wanted them to be true, they weren't. His thrusts became harder, making her breasts sway back and forth. Minutes later, when she was sure she couldn't endure any more, he gritted out her name followed by a long, slow *"Fuuuck."*

She shattered at the same time he did, but it was long moments before he loosened his grip even a little bit.

When he finally withdrew himself, she lay down on the

mat, spent. She curled onto her side while he crossed into the restroom, returning with a hand towel that he used to pat her body dry. Then he pressed a warm, damp cloth to her pussy.

"That was…"

He waited.

Incredible. "Incomparable."

His smile was as slow as it was triumphant. "I assume you're pleased?"

"Very much so." She blew out a short breath. "Thank you."

"Are you ready for that plug to come out?"

"Uhm, that's a little embarrassing. Do you mind if I do it myself?"

"There is no room for embarrassment between us."

While she squeezed her eyes shut, he grasped the base and eased it from inside her. The relief was immediate, and she exhaled a great big sigh. "Thank you."

With a grin, he returned to the bathroom. While he walked back, she took advantage of the opportunity to shamelessly study him. Master Philip was magnificent. And even though he had just orgasmed, his cock was still hard.

"What would you like to do? We can go to the living room and watch a movie, or we can talk, or we can snuggle up in my bed." He held up a hand. "Yeah, yeah. I know, you're not a snuggler."

How well he knew her objections.

He brought his discarded shirt to her and crouched to help her into it. "You never finished your glass of wine. Would you like me to get it for you? You're also more than welcome to relax and unwind in the soaker tub."

At a risk to her fragile emotions, she admitted the truth. "I want to spend time with you."

"Yeah. I'd like that too. Give me a minute to clean things up here."

Emma pulled her knees to her chest and wrapped her arms around herself. It would be polite to help him, but she was too lethargic to move. Her muscles ached from his lovemaking as well as from the various ways he'd had her contort her body.

Once the room was wiped down and everything was back where it belonged, he helped her up.

"Shall we?"

Rather than just letting her go once she was standing, he wrapped his arms around her and held her tenderly. "You're everything I could imagine. Now, let's get you taken care of."

She followed him down the stairs to his bedroom.

"Make yourself comfortable, and I will be back with some wine. Do you want a snack?"

"After all that pizza? I don't think so."

"If you change your mind, I have ice cream and key lime pie. Diane made it."

"Really?" She raised an eyebrow.

"We can have that for a midnight snack. And I have whipped cream. I have a couple of ideas what we can do with it."

"I'm sure you do." She selected the same side of the bed that she had slept on at the hotel, then crawled beneath the covers.

When he returned, he was still naked, and his cock was still impossibly hard.

He offered her a glass, then turned on the television. Rather than selecting something to watch, he chose a music channel. Soft jazz filled the room, creating an intimate air. Then he put on a robe and joined her beneath the covers.

"Is this where we have the requisite talk about how I'm doing?"

"No. This is where we do the requisite part of putting

arnica on any marks. It's also when I rub the rest of your muscles with a cream to relax them."

"Really?"

"Most definitely. I want to be sure I can make love to you again later."

"I should have guessed."

He tossed back the blankets, then parted the lapels of the shirt she was wearing. "Put your wineglass on the nightstand; then lie on your stomach."

As he moved down her legs, his touch was firm and competent.

"Pure luxury. I may have to increase the number of days a week that I practice yoga—" Her breath caught, and she fisted the sheet. For the first time she'd slipped, allowing herself to think about a possible future with him.

If he'd noticed, he didn't comment on it.

"You have a couple of good marks from the paddle. How do they feel now?" He scraped them with his thumbnail, making her gasp.

"Other than that, fine, Sir." She wasn't sure he was ever going to be able to convince her to leave his bed. "I could drift off to sleep."

"Feel free."

But then she might miss a moment of the limited time they had together.

When he was finished and went to wash his hands, she rolled back over and situated his shirt again.

From his tiny bed in the corner, Tibby made a couple of funny, adorable noises, and scrambled his front paws like he had earlier.

Master Philip joined her and tucked her beneath his arm.

"I'm in love with your dog. And Rex. They're quite a pair."

"Like father, like son."

"Really? Rex is Tibby's dad?"

"My sister collects stud fees and occasional picks of the litter."

"I had no idea."

"Simone—my ex-wife—thought Tibby was adorable. And in her customary way, she had to have him. It didn't matter that he was promised to someone else."

"Really?" Emma was stunned.

"Diane didn't think she had any other choice. Had I been there, I'd have put a stop to that nonsense. Not that I don't adore Tibby, but that kind of behavior is unacceptable. We could have waited for the next litter."

She adjusted the pillow behind her, then wiggled around to pick up her drink. "So the name Rex? Like after the Mardi Gras krewe?"

"Of course. It means King."

"Makes total sense. He totally behaves as if he's royalty." She grinned. "And both dogs are great with the kids."

He nodded. Then, maybe because of the intimacy, she tiptoed into emotionally dangerous territory. "I couldn't help but notice how great you are with your nephews."

"They're something. Keep you on your toes. And only having names that start with a T?"

"Including Tibby?"

"How'd you guess?" He grinned.

"You're a natural. Do you want kids of your own?"

Tension radiated through his body, and a pulse ticked in his temple. Her instincts had been right. This was, indeed, dangerous territory. "I'm sorry. It's none of my business."

"It's a legitimate question. And yes. I did want children. At one time."

She scooted a little farther away from him and sat cross-legged so that she could see him better and study his features.

"Before we got married, Simone knew I wanted kids.

Four of them. She said she wanted one. Maybe two. It didn't seem like an irreconcilable difference. And at her request, I agreed to wait for a while. She wanted to make some memories together, just the two of us—take some trips, get our lives established. It made sense."

That vein continued to throb in his temple, an outward sign of his pain.

"About two years later, we started trying. Every month when she got her period, she would cry, and I would comfort her. After a year of the constant disappointment, we took a break."

Emma ached for him.

"About nine months after that, I asked her if she was ready to try again. Of course, she wasn't, but to please me, she agreed to see a fertility doctor."

"Philip… You don't have to relive this." She never should have asked.

"I planned to take her to Cancun for our fifth anniversary. I arrived home earlier than planned to pick her up, and she was still getting ready. I found her pack of birth control pills on the bathroom counter."

The betrayal made his words short, clipped, and Emma winced.

"Every single day that we were married, she lied to me. She wasn't infertile, and the doctor visits never happened. Instead of talking to me about the idea of adopting or remaining childless, she opted to deceive me. It cost a pretty penny to get rid of her, but it was worth every cent." He reached for a glass of something—whiskey, maybe—and took a sip. "My nephews are enough. I'm happy to have them inherit."

She nodded, now fully understanding why he kept his entanglements uncomplicated.

"That's enough of that. Come here." He plucked the wineglass from her hand, then pulled her onto his lap and held her tight before giving her a kiss.

His touch reignited her.

"I want to make love to you again."

"I'd like that also."

"There's a condom in the drawer. Can you reach it? "

Once she had, he gave her a purposeful glance.

"Now unwrap it and put it on me."

Nervous, fumbling more than once, she followed his command as asked.

"For once, I'll let you set the pace." He took hold of her waist and helped her up, guiding her on top of him.

Because she was more than a little sore, her movements were slow and deliberate as she took his thick, hard length inside her body.

"That's right."

He didn't let her stay in control very long. With a groan, he rolled them over. Even though the style was technically missionary, there was nothing ordinary about the way he moved his hips, stroking and gyrating, driving her mad.

He demanded two climaxes before he came. "That'll hold us. At least for a little while." Then he pulled her against him, rolled onto his side, and cradled her tight. "I'm not sure I'll ever let you go."

Part of her wanted to stay forever, but for her own peace of mind she had to find the courage to walk away as soon as possible. Each moment they were together was making her fall for him deeper and deeper.

Outside, thunder rumbled, echoing the discontent inside her. She just prayed she was strong enough to withstand the storm brewing all around her.

The wind was driving rain against the window when Emma awakened alone in Master Philip's bed. Outside, dawn was breaking, and the bedroom door was cracked open a little, allowing her to see that a light blazed from the end of the hall.

Curious, she climbed from the bed and smoothed out the hem of the shirt she was still wearing.

Though he wasn't on this story, noise spilled from upstairs, and she found him in the secret room, riding his exercise bike while wearing only athletic shoes and tight shorts. From her place in the doorway, she looked at him, and memories of the previous hours flooded her. He'd uncovered parts of her that she didn't even know existed, changing her forever.

Suddenly he looked over his shoulder. When he saw her, he smiled.

"Sorry to interrupt."

"You are never an interruption."

"I heard rain, and the bed was cold without you."

"Should I come back?" He touched one of his wireless earbuds, obviously to turn off the music he'd been listening to.

The wickedness in his eyes made every memory return, and she shook her head. "Thanks. I'm good."

He laughed. "Tibby's asleep in my office right now, but he'll need his walk soon. I take him on Sundays since the sitter is off. Would you like to come with us? There's a somewhat famous coffee shop near Audubon Park. I figured we could have a café au lait and maybe a basket of beignets."

"I certainly don't need those."

"I think you worked off any potential calories."

But her protest was about so much more. Every moment they were together, and she began to feel like a family with him and Tibby, would bring her closer to heartbreak. Yet she lacked the courage to force herself to walk away.

"I need to finish up here and take a quick shower. Half an hour? Does that work for you?"

"Sounds perfect."

"Or we can make it longer if you'd like to take a bath?"

"Yeah. Actually I'd like to do that."

"I imagine you may have a few aftereffects from last night?"

More than a few.

"In the meantime, there's a pod-type of coffeemaker downstairs."

"Would you like a cup?"

"I'll wait."

Emma walked down the two flights of stairs leading to the kitchen. Several different types of coffee pods were in a glass jar, and she selected a French roast. Then she opened a cupboard to find a cup. The mug closest to the front had an owl on it—identical to the ones on his bag and on the floor of Mademoiselle's shop. This wasn't a coincidence. The owl had some sort of meaning.

While the gift from the gods splashed much-needed caffeine into the white mug she'd selected, she wandered to the back door. Sometime in the past couple of minutes, the rain had stopped, leaving all the foliage dewy and bright green. A mockingbird landed on the nearby birdbath and splashed a couple of times before jumping onto the rim.

Philip's courtyard wasn't very big, but it had large patches of grass, obviously for Tibby. There were a couple of tables with plenty of seating, all shaded by palm fronds or colorful umbrellas. It was a peaceful, perfect place to spend a Sunday morning.

After swallowing a few sips and shaking off the results of

too-little sleep and a lot of sex, she carried her remaining coffee upstairs.

In the primary bathroom, she placed the mug on a small teak table, pulled her hair into a bun, then dropped a tangerine and eucalyptus scented bath bomb under the running tap. She slid down deep into the hot, fizzy water and was soaking away her minor muscle aches from their scenes when he walked into the room, smelling of fresh clean sweat.

Of course she should have expected him to use his own en suite. But watching him strip implied an easy intimacy that made her a little uncomfortable because it wasn't real.

"You found the coffee."

"It will hold me for a little while. I hope it's okay that I used this cup. I thought it might be a special one reserved just for you."

"Even if it were, I wouldn't mind you using it."

"I'm intrigued by the owl on the front."

"Are you?" He tapped his watch face. After a soft beep, he issued an order to turn on the shower water and set the temperature to one hundred twelve degrees.

"I noticed the same symbol on the bag you took to the Quarter. If I'm not mistaken, Mademoiselle Giselle also has one on the floor of her private shop."

"Very observant."

"Are you not going to tell me about it?"

He dropped a quick kiss on her forehead, bringing his half-hard dick perilously close to her mouth. "If that's supposed to be a distraction technique, Sir, it won't work."

"No?" He slid a hand into the water to capture one of her breasts. "How about now?"

Her treacherous nipple responded to his touch, and then suddenly her whole body was on fire. Determinedly she captured his wrist. "Mr. Dettmer!"

He grinned.

"We were talking about the owl."

"Ah. Yes. That we were."

"Well?"

"It's the symbol for an organization I belong to." He entered the shower but spoke loud enough for her to hear, even over the running water. "The Zetas."

"What kind of group is it?" It couldn't be a fraternity, because apparently Mademoiselle also belonged to it. "A charitable foundation?"

"Of a type."

"What does that mean?"

"We do a lot of good work, but it's so much more than that."

"Now you've got me intrigued."

He soaped his body, and she shamelessly watched each movement, paying particular attention to the way he washed his balls and then his dick, sliding his hand back and forth as if he were jacking off. As far as a sexy show went, it was fabulously engaging. "It's a secret society."

"No way." She laughed.

Turning his back to her, he rinsed.

Water sluiced off his head and shoulders and dribbled down his back, then lower, onto his hot, tight ass cheeks.

A moment later, he turned off the faucet, then stepped out of the shower onto a mat. "You can do all the research you want, but you won't find out much information."

She sat up a little straighter as he wiped a towel across his face. "I didn't think groups like that really existed."

"This one does."

"And billionaires belong to it?"

"Among others." All his answers were guarded and vague.

"Like who?"

"Always so persistent?"

"Wouldn't you be, in my place?"

Without bothering to wipe off the rest of the droplets, he wrapped the towel around his waist before heading to the sink to shave.

Enjoying every moment, she warmed up the tub before continuing with her guesses. "Politicians?"

In the mirror, he looked up from the sink to meet her gaze. He grinned.

"I'll take that as a yes. Hollywood types?"

"A few."

She blinked. This was surreal. "Rock stars?"

"Perhaps."

"Scientists?"

His lack of response didn't dissuade her. "So you're in a secret organization that does good work, has a lot of money behind it…?"

"I can neither confirm nor deny what you've guessed."

"So what exactly do you do?"

"If I told you, it wouldn't be secret." He shrugged, then swiped a blade down his face.

"There has to be some information somewhere."

He rinsed off. "As I said, you won't find much."

No doubt he was right. "There's obviously some meaning to the owl? The eyes in the one at Mademoiselle's are pretty intense."

"Let me know what you find."

She closed her eyes and tipped back her head to rest it on the tub's rim. "This is annoying."

"I've told you more than I've shared with anyone else."

"Which is next to nothing."

"Exactly." Evidently unconcerned with his complete state of undress, he grabbed a towel from the linen closet and placed it on the bench near the mug in question. "The coffee shop starts to get busy around nine."

"You're telling me to hurry up?"

"Just providing information." He stopped on his way into the bedroom and looked back toward her. "If you want to make it on time, make sure I don't see you naked before we leave."

Was that an invitation or warning?

He whistled as he left her.

She cupped her hand to smack the water. He was as sexy as he was devilishly confounding. Until a minute ago, she hadn't been thinking about sex. Now it was the only thing on her mind.

In the end, she couldn't resist him.

When she joined him in the bedroom, she unfastened the towel she was wrapped in and slowly shrugged until it pooled to the floor around her.

"Come here." Obviously he'd expected her to make this decision. He hadn't bothered to get dressed, and there was a condom on his nightstand.

Shoulders back, she crossed the room, and he picked her up and placed her on the side of the mattress before kneeling.

"Put your legs on my shoulders."

Even the warm bath and arnica weren't enough to keep up with his demands.

"Your pussy is red and swollen." It was an observation more than an apology.

"Yes, Sir."

"My favorite combination." He finger-fucked her, then licked her, using his tongue to lick up all her hot juices.

Emma was lost, crying out his name when he stood. He used his shoulders to press back on her thighs, keeping her spread while he rolled the protection down his shaft, then claimed her in a long, single stroke that completed her.

By the time he sought his own release, she was exhausted and sated.

"Woman, you undo me."

"It's mutual, Master Philip." She smiled as she swiped a dot of perspiration from his forehead. How was it possible that the more he took, the more she wanted?

By the time she had dressed, packed up her bag, and left it next to the front door, and they actually managed to leave the house, it was much later than they planned. Despite that, Tibby refused to be hurried. He wanted to stop and sniff almost every house and greet all the other dogs that they met along the way.

The coffee shop had a line almost to the door when they arrived.

"Why don't you and Tibby find a table outside, and I'll wait in line."

Sounds more than fair to me.

He turned over the leash, then gave her a quick kiss. She found a table with an umbrella located near a bowl of water for Tibby. The exhausted pup took a few thirsty gulps before rising onto his hind legs and lifting one paw toward her.

"Aww." Cooing at his sweetness, she picked up the tiny pup and settled him on her lap. After making himself comfortable, he promptly fell asleep.

A couple arrived with young children, and since each kid was trying to claim the same favorite chair, they took a while settling in.

It was a cozy neighborhood gathering place, filled with conversation about school and sports, sending another wave through her. For the past few years, she'd been caught up in her everyday life, buying a house, working hard to build her client list.

What she had shared this weekend with Philip showed her what she wanted for her future. It just killed her that it wouldn't be with him.

To distract herself from the unwelcome thoughts that

she'd have to deal with soon enough, she grabbed her phone and entered the words Zeta Society in the web browser.

It didn't surprise her that there were few results. But *Scandalicious* had an intriguing article by a reporter who'd asked for an invitation to the organization's yearly meeting, held at a large estate located on the banks of the Mississippi River. The place was only an hour from where they were currently located. Though his request had been turned down, obviously something was going on out there, because he was arrested after he sneaked in. He had no pictures to validate his story, but he said he witnessed a massive bonfire—which was the supposed opening event of the two-week gathering.

His article stated that the organization had been formed sometime in the nineteenth century by a group of friends. If his calculations were accurate, there were a couple of thousand members, located all over the world. As she guessed, politicians belonged to the group, along with prominent people from every possible background. There were screenwriters, directors, authors, ambassadors, scientists, doctors, entrepreneurs, old-money families, royalty, and even the world's richest, quirkiest man. No doubt any meeting between them would be mind-blowing. What did they talk about? Saving the world? Traveling to Mars? How to make even more money? *Surely that.*

The initiation fee was said to be five figures, and the annual dues were at least that much. That didn't seem to matter, as the waiting list to apply for membership was several years long.

She glanced over her shoulder and looked inside the shop. Philip was next in line, which gave her a couple more minutes to read.

Evidently a reporter almost a hundred years ago had also been fascinated by rumors about the secret society. He was in New Orleans at the time and saw a group of prominent society members gathered in a restaurant. He'd secured a table close enough to overhear a little of the conversation, and in his coverage, he called the gentlemen Titans.

Back then, only males had been admitted, but in the past decades, they'd come to their senses and started admitting women. Though no name was mentioned, they now reportedly even had a female sitting on the board of directors. Surely it couldn't be Mademoiselle?

A few minutes later, Philip made his way out of the building, and she dropped her phone in her bag, so he didn't find her spying on him.

He threaded his way toward her and slid a tray onto the tabletop. He had everything they could need—beverages, plates, napkins, and a basket of beignets stacked a mile high.

"This looks amazing." The French-style doughnuts were enormous and drowning in pounds of powdered sugar.

Philip pulled back his chair and took a seat. "I see His Highness has made himself comfortable."

"It's a long walk if your legs are that short."

"More like he has you wrapped around his paw."

"Oh?" She moved one of the beignets onto a plate and offered it to Philip.

"The sitter goes much farther than this with him twice a day."

"Well…" Emma chose a treat for herself. "I'll be honest. He's sweet, so it works for both of us."

"He'll be a terror and even more demanding after you leave."

To cover her own reluctance to return to her regular life, she took a bite of the doughy deliciousness. Steam released, and a breeze whipped up, sending powdered sugar everywhere, including onto Tibby's fur.

Philip grabbed a napkin to wipe her face and chest. It was

an easy casual move that would be normal between lovers... once again reminding her of what she didn't have.

"I got us each a café au lait. Hope that works for you."

"It's perfect."

The milky chicory-laced coffee was strong and a little tart, cutting through the sweetness of their heavenly breakfast.

"I understand from my admin that you did get on my schedule to make your pitch financially."

"Yes. After Thanksgiving."

He nodded. "You'll be prepared."

It was phrased more as a statement than a question. "I will." She was less confident since she'd learned he was a Titan. The man had access to the smartest people in the world. So the fact that he was willing to talk to her was an act of kindness and nothing more. But still, she'd do her absolute best to fucking wow him.

Half an hour later, the sun was almost too hot, and it had risen higher in the sky, making the umbrella all but ineffective.

A harried server came by to collect their dishes.

"If you want to wake up His Highness, we can head home."

She scratched behind the dog's ears. He opened his eyes, yawned, then put his head back down. "I can just carry him."

"I can promise you, Tibby's more than capable of walking."

"He's precious when he sleeps, and I don't want to disturb him."

In obvious disbelief, Philip shook his head. "He can sleep twenty hours a day."

"But I don't get to do this very often." Now she understood her friends who had purses to carry their canine friends in.

"Part of the reason for a Sunday morning outing is so that he gets his exercise."

"He has a backyard."

"Between you and Diane, I know when I'm beat." He stood and offered a hand up.

The return trip happened too quickly, and once they were inside the air-conditioned coolness of his house, he asked if she wanted another beverage.

"Actually I have plenty to do at home."

"I see." His eyes narrowed slightly.

She placed Tibby on the floor, then grabbed her bag. It was better to leave now, before she got in any deeper.

"I'll walk you out."

She could have protested, but it wouldn't do any good. His sense of obligation wouldn't let him do anything else.

Saying goodbye after submitting was becoming a painful habit.

"It's been a pleasure to have you over."

"Thank you." Her attempted smile fell flat. "It's been..." So many things. *Amazing.* "Memorable."

"Meet me Tuesday night. At the Quarter?"

His casual invitation reinforced all the warnings she'd been giving herself. He wanted to scene with her. Nothing more.

"Emma?"

She should say no, but she lacked the willpower to refuse him outright. "I'll think about it." It was a bald-faced lie, and she wondered if he saw through her.

He opened the car door, and she slipped past him, barely brushing his body with hers.

"I'll confirm the time and details with you tomorrow."

A knot in her throat prevented her from responding.

When he stepped back, she closed herself in the vehicle.

He was still standing in the driveway when she pulled into traffic.

Even after such a short time together, he'd changed her life. And now her future was bleak and empty, and her heart was shattered into a dozen pieces. She'd thought she was strong enough to give Master Philip everything he wanted. She was wrong. The emotion she'd been forcefully holding back broke loose in a flood of tears and a ragged gasp of pain. She'd never experienced this kind of anguish, and she wasn't sure if she could survive it.

CHAPTER 10

Would you like me to send a car for you tomorrow?
A wave crashed against the front of the ferry that Emma was riding on, spraying water over the front of the boat. The family next to her laughed and stayed where they were, but she retreated back to where it was safer—and drier.

Her mind raced as she tried to figure out how to respond to Master Philip's text.

As she had expected, he'd checked up on her after she left his house yesterday morning. And now he wanted to confirm their plans to meet at the Quarter.

The truth was, she was scared of her fragile emotions. It would have been all too easy to shove resolve aside and agree to scene with him. Every part of her wanted exactly that.

To avoid temptation, as well as to protect herself, she'd left work after a couple of hours and set out for Galveston. Her mom and stepfather were delighted she was coming early, and they'd made lots of plans to keep her busy. Work was traditionally slow during Thanksgiving week, and she'd promised to answer her phone while she was traveling. Since she had almost a month of vacation time accrued, her boss hadn't been able to object.

But still, she'd been a coward. She'd left Louisiana without notifying Philip. Even though she'd planned to let him know, she hadn't found the right words.

And they were no easier now. In fact, they seemed more difficult, which surprised her. Being on the water generally infused her with a sense of peace. Then again, she'd never met a man like Philip Dettmer.

As the ferry rose and fell on the choppier-than-usual ship channel, she attempted a reply.

I've enjoyed our time together. Thank you. I am out of town for the holiday, so I'm unable to see you this week.

Would he think that meant she would be available the following Tuesday? Maybe she should stop letting her heart rule, and, instead, do what her brain insisted was right. End it. Permanently and unequivocally.

She spent the next few minutes composing, deleting, then trying again.

Thank you for the introduction to BDSM. It's been...

Tears blurred her eyes, making it difficult to see the words on her screen. She wanted to blame the spray from the salt water, but she knew better.

Thank you for everything. I can't see you again.

. . .

But what about the fact that she was supposed to meet up with him next week in an attempt to earn his business. How many attempts would it take for her to get this right?

Thank you for teaching me about BDSM. I will not be seeing you again. Though I would love to earn your business, I will certainly understand if you want to go a different direction.

That response brought her brain and heart into even bigger conflict. Having Philip Dettmer as a client would improve her life tremendously. And yet, being in constant communication would reopen wounds that she desperately needed to heal.

The boat approached the landing, meaning she needed to return to her vehicle. Since she'd soon be with other people, she needed to put the situation with Philip behind her.

Without further deliberation, she sent the message.

Emma slid into the driver's seat, then pressed the ignition button. Trying to still her racing heart, she curled her fingers around the steering wheel in a death grip.

As the first lane of vehicles exited, her phone rang, and his name showed up on her screen.

Fighting her own softer nature, she forced herself to decline the call. Then she turned off her phone and dropped it into the bottom of her purse.

Right now, and for the next few days, she refused to think about Master Philip. Instead, she intended to concentrate on enjoying her family time.

The drive to her mom and stepfather's historic cottage in the San Jacinto neighborhood took less than ten minutes.

Emma had barely stepped out of the car before she was swept into a great big hug, and her mother fussed at her husband to carry Emma's bag into the guestroom. She didn't have time to catch her breath before her mom said they needed to jump on the golf cart; after all, friends were waiting at a favorite restaurant on Pier 21, and happy hour would be ending soon.

"They have this amazing lobster special." Her mom, Camile, grabbed the keys to the golf cart. "And they just added a mermaid cocktail. Can you imagine? It's blue. And it has glitter on top."

Helplessly her stepfather, Justin, shook his head. "They have beer."

Emma grinned. She needed to make this trip more often. When she was here, she didn't have time to worry.

Camile insisted that Emma ride up front with her while Justin sat behind them in a seat that faced backward. As Camile gunned away from the curb and made a tight U-turn, he desperately grabbed hold of a metal bar for safety.

She navigated down Seventeenth Street, rolling slightly past each stop sign because all the foliage was still in bloom, making it impossible to see cross-traffic. Even though Camile had hurried Emma along, she slowed to say hello to neighbors and to wave at people on bicycles. Ever since Camile had met and married Justin and financial worries disappeared, she'd become a different person.

"I've told you to go down Nineteenth, Camile."

"I know."

"It's a straight-through. No stopping."

"This is more fun." At the next intersection, she braked hard again.

"It's safer the other way."

Emma laughed. They did some version of this same argument every time she visited.

When they neared the restaurant, Camile parked illegally, leading to another argument, which Justin lost.

They were still bickering, and Emma was still shaking her head, when they found the rest of the Chunky Dunkin' Mermaids.

Everyone stood to greet them, and when they were once again seated, Emma was smashed into the middle of an over-size horseshoe-shaped booth. There were already empty glasses all around, which obviously meant that they'd been partying for some time.

One of the ladies, Gina, ordered a mermaid drink for Emma but put it on her own tab—a welcome to Galveston treat.

Happy hour stretched into dinner, and for the time being, she was able to forget about her own problems. Justin switched to diet soda after a single beer so that he'd be safe to drive them home.

Three hours later, she and her mom were both a little tipsy, and they giggled when they climbed onto the back of the cart. Justin might have been brave enough to ride without a seat belt, but Emma certainly wasn't.

All the way home, this time down Nineteenth, her mother happily continued waving to vacationers who were in town for the long weekend and to celebrate the upcoming holiday art festival.

"The splash is having breakfast in the morning at the Oleander Café," Camile said when they arrived back at the house.

Because the golf cart needed to recharge overnight, Justin was patiently waiting for them to step onto the sidewalk so he could move the electric vehicle to its designated spot in the yard.

"We're going to be there at 7:45 so that we're waiting when they open. We always start with mimosas. They bring you a full bottle of sparkling wine and fresh-squeezed orange juice so you can mix them as strong as you want."

The nonstop parties, fun, and frivolity stood as a stark contrast to her normal life. In a lot of ways, the craziness reminded her of the time she'd spent over the weekend at Master Philip's house with his sister and her boys. Unbidden and unexpected, pain blossomed in her heart, and her smile faltered.

"Then the girls are going to go shopping and do an attic to basement tour at the castle." She was referencing one of the historic homes on Broadway. "You're more than welcome to join us."

"Mom, I'm going to need a vacation to rest up after spending several days with you."

"That's how you know you're having fun."

Once inside, they said good night; then Emma went into her bedroom and closed the door. From the kitchen, the sound of Justin's voice reached her, followed by her mother's contagious laughter. All of it reinforced the realization that she was all alone.

After changing into an oversized sleep shirt, Emma powered up her telephone. Unsurprisingly Philip had sent her a couple of text messages, and he'd left two voicemails. Those she deleted right away.

The text messages, though, she read, torturing herself. He wanted an explanation. Perhaps when she was stronger, she'd offer it, but for now, this was like ripping off a bandage. Eventually the relationship would end. No matter when it did, it would hurt. But the healing couldn't happen until she let go of the past.

Emma had to reassure herself of that all through a long, restless night.

She was grateful for the time with her mom and stepfather, not to mention the assorted friends. And more arrived in town each day. Wednesday night they all went to a favorite Mexican restaurant on the seawall as a group—or splash, as she was corrected—of twenty people.

Thanksgiving was spent at one the most magnificent hotels in the city, at a round table overlooking the swimming pool, and beyond it the Gulf of Mexico. Dozens of ships lying at anchor dotted the horizon.

The server kept everyone's glasses filled with champagne.

But rather than chasing away thoughts of Master Philip, the festivities brought him to mind more and more.

She wondered how he was spending the day. At his mom's? With his sister and the boys? Had he taken Tibby? And was Rex there too, stealing the show? No doubt there'd be utter pandemonium. And she would have loved to have been part of it.

"Are you all right?" Her mother leaned in with a concerned smile.

"I'm just a mile away. Soaking up the view." Emma gave a halfhearted smile and shoved aside the unwelcome thoughts. She was here, surrounded by love and laughter. And she intended to savor every moment. Besides, what was the alternative? If she had remained in New Orleans, she would have spent the day alone. Yes, she and her Dominant would have enjoyed another memorable night at the Quarter, but it would have never occurred to him to invite her to his family's celebration. She was a scene partner, nothing more. "Sorry."

"Is there something on your mind? You haven't been yourself."

"I promise—I'm fine. Work's been busy, and I have a big presentation next week." At least that was the truth.

Though her mom nodded, she wasn't satisfied for long, and the next morning when Emma got up to make herself a cup of coffee, her mother padded into the kitchen, wrapped in a gigantic robe-like hoodie. "Grab a blanket, Em, and come out back with me. Sit a spell."

Once they were outside with coffee, bundled up to ward off the north wind, her mom spoke. "Okay, we're alone. Tell me what's going on."

Even during her childhood, Emma had never been able to hide the truth for very long. But how much should she reveal? "I met a man that I like. A lot." She omitted giant swaths of the story, things that no one else could understand —not that she was sure she even understood them herself.

"Relationships aren't easy." Camile held her cup between her palms. "And it sounds like his ex-wife was an absolute lying piece of crap."

At her mother's loyal outburst, Emma couldn't help but grin. "Mom!"

"Well, it's true." She waved away the concern. "But he might need a little time or some patience. You should tell him how you feel."

That was never going to happen. In a relationship, Emma had never been rewarded for her vulnerability. In fact, it had only led to greater hurt.

She had good memories of her time with Master Philip, and that was going to have to be enough.

"Aaron was selfish and immature. But this Philip fellow doesn't sound like he's cut from the same cloth."

That was true. No doubt he would let her down in a much more gentlemanly way, even if the result would be the same.

"Talk to him."

Noncommittally, Emma nodded.

Camile stood. "Why don't you get dressed? We're going to take the ferry over to Bolivar peninsula and go beachcombing and have lunch at Steven's Stingray. They've got great margaritas."

Once again, Emma was glad to be here and grateful she wasn't alone for the holiday, but she couldn't help the apprehension that now loomed as she planned her return trip to meet with Philip about his financial accounts.

∽

"I thought you might invite Emma."

Across the counter in his mother's kitchen, Philip leveled his gaze on his sister, who was standing next to her husband, Bernard. "And I thought you might mind your own business for once."

Diane grinned. "No chance."

Just then, their mother walked in and smartly clapped her hands. "Now that Philip has arrived, we can get busy."

The meal they'd all shared on Thanksgiving the day before had been wonderful, and they'd reconvened this evening to start decorating for the holidays, something that had become a tradition. Philip and Bernard were in charge of fetching boxes and putting up a couple of the trees. Fortunately a company would arrive tomorrow to do the majority of the work—including lighting the exterior. After all, everything had to be festive for Adele's annual open house, which was held the weekend before Christmas. "There are boxes in the attic. Some in the guesthouse."

As if he and Bernard didn't know that? After all, every January seventh, they were the ones who put the hundreds of boxes away again.

"My new acquisitions are in the garage."

New?

"Diane, you and Titus can wrap the harvest decorations and bring them to me."

"Yes, ma'am."

"I'll prepare a space for the taco bar."

If Thanksgiving had been crazy, this was ten times worse.

The dogs dashed around, constantly escaping from the room that Titus kept putting them in. Philip suspected the twins had something to do with that, though they denied it when asked. Christmas music blasted throughout the entire six thousand square feet, at a ridiculously loud volume.

"So much for taking the boat out this weekend." Bernard rubbed his head after hitting it on an attic beam.

"I bet you can talk Diane into spending time at the marina if you tell her you want to participate in the Lake Pontchartrain Christmas Boat parade."

"Now you're talking." He glanced around to be sure his wife wasn't close enough to overhear. "You think she'll notice if I get someone else to do it?"

Philip laughed. But if he was honest, he envied the fact that his brother-in-law had a family to spend the holidays with, even though he good-naturedly complained about all the obligations.

Yesterday, after dinner, Philip had returned home. After checking his phone, hoping for a message from Emma that never came, he'd hit the gym, then driven to the office. The city was empty and his workplace dark. Seemed everyone but him had someplace to be.

Even after Simone's betrayal, he hadn't experienced this level of loneliness.

Since Emma left, he'd repeatedly felt the sharp edge of that unwelcome emotion.

He and Bernard carried down the first of Adele's eight trees.

Thoughtfully she was waiting for them. "That one goes in my art studio."

The doorbell chimed, and noise exploded everywhere. Both men looked at each other, shrugged, then headed back upstairs. Someone else could deal with the food delivery, the kids, and feeding the dogs their dinner.

By the time they were halfway through with the chores, Diane called their names, telling them to come fill a plate before the food got cold.

The boys were settled in front of the television, engrossed in a show about a grown-up elf.

Mom had made her famous bourbon-laced eggnog. He wasn't sure how that went with the taco bar—or if it did—but one drink told him it was way more alcohol than it was anything else. If he had a second glass of that, he'd be asleep in his dad's old study, and he'd have to haul boxes for a second day.

After filling a plate, he joined the rest of the adults in the dining room.

The twins squabbled about something, and Adele went to sort it out while Bernard excused himself to make a second trip to the kitchen, saying he'd run out of queso but still had chips left.

Which, dangerously, left Philip alone with his sister.

"So, I was serious."

Philip took a bite out of his crunchy taco. "About?" He knew exactly what she was referring to.

"Did you and Emma fight?"

"God, no."

"So she hated us all?"

"Do you ever stop?" Philip sighed. If his guess was right, Emma would have enjoyed every minute of the current insanity. "No. She liked you, and you know it."

"So it's you that she doesn't care for?"

He had no fucking idea what had gone wrong.

When Diane spoke again, there was kindness in her tone, but none of the gloating he expected. "Did you tell her you love her?"

He blinked. "What?"

"Put down your food before you drop it."

Bernard plopped into a chair. "What's going on?"

"Philip's an idiot."

"Again?"

"Thanks, man." Philip shook his head. "Appreciate the support."

"If you couldn't see the way that woman looked at you, and the way she loves you…"

Bernard grinned. "She's wound up now."

"Look…" How did he explain something that he didn't understand? "It's complicated. We had an agreement."

"Whatever." Diane waved a dismissive hand. "It doesn't matter. She broke whatever ridiculous agreement the two of you had when she fell in love. And if you let her get away, you're a world-class jerk."

"Don't hold back."

His mother took her place at the head of the table, but her arrival didn't stop Diane from speaking her piece.

"Simone messed you up."

"That bitch," Adele supplied while delicately picking up a chip.

Both Diane and Philip blinked. That may have been the first curse word he'd ever heard his mother utter. And she'd never said a bad thing about his ex.

"Good riddance to her."

Diane shook her head. "What I'm saying—or trying to say—is that not all women are Simone."

"Thanks for that."

"Look, I saw you last week. No one else did. You were happy."

He couldn't argue with that.

"And now…" She paused. "You look like shit."

"Mommy! Swear jar."

Diane scowled. "How the hell did Mom not get caught?"

"That's two dollars, Mommy!"

Saying nothing, Adele sipped her eggnog.

Diane sighed. "At this rate their college education will be paid for before they start elementary school."

Bernard grinned. "That's a relief."

"So what happened with the new woman?" Adele asked.

"Emma. Her name is Emma." And how had his love life—or lack of it—become the center of discussion? "She just said she won't be seeing me again." Which perplexed him. When he asked for an explanation, she didn't respond. Nor did she reply to the embarrassing number of voicemails he'd left her.

"She was great with the dogs, and with the boys too. Did you ever talk about a future with her?"

"In vague terms." When he looked back, his references had sexual connotations, meetings at the club, things he'd like to do to her.

"If you'd think about it for a minute, you'd figure it out. You know she wants kids, right?" Diane sighed. "While you were pouring wine, we talked about it. Remember?"

And that night in his bedroom, when they'd talked, he'd shot down the idea of actually having children, saying he was happy for his nephews to inherit.

"She's a woman looking for a husband, and a future."

That wasn't the agreement.

"She was hoping you were the one."

Philip scowled. "How do you know that?"

"I was being nosy, to use your term. You should try it sometime." She reached for the wine bottle and poured a big glass. "I don't have to drive."

At this point, he wished he'd hired Cressida for the evening.

"You may lose a really good chance at happiness here. Because of what? Simone?" Diane scoffed. "Are you really going to let her, and her treacherous lies, ruin the rest of your life?"

Bernard scooped up the last of his queso. "She has a point."

"I seem to be out of eggnog." Adele lifted her empty glass.

"I'll handle it." Philip seized the excuse to leave the table.

Since Monday, when Emma had essentially stopped talking to him, he'd allowed his frustration to get to him. He'd been more of an asshole than usual to his admin and a tyrant to his employees.

He filled his mother's glass, then took it to her. She was sipping it before he even sat back down.

She tipped it in his direction. "What Diane is trying to say, Philip"—she frowned at her daughter—"is that she wants you to be happy. We all do."

Happiness. It wasn't an idea he'd given a lot of consideration to, until now. "Thank you."

Conversation went on, and Bernard suggested the boat parade. Not surprisingly, Diane liked the idea. "How big is my budget?"

Philip sat back, again realizing how nice it would be to have Emma here. No doubt they would share a private smile, and when he got her home later in the evening, he'd take her to the secret room and claim her as his.

He'd played with dozens of submissives, had lots of first dates. But no one had cracked his heart open like she had.

He loved her. *I fucking love her.*

"Philip?"

Jesus. Had he said that aloud? He shook his head.

"Bernard was asking if you're ready to get back to work?"

For the next hour, while he and Bernard emptied the attic, Philip returned to the realization that he loved Emma.

What the hell am I going to do about it?

Half an hour later, he decided on a direct course of

action. While the other adults were in a deep discussion about whether or not to light the greenery they'd attached to the banister, he excused himself.

In his father's old study, Philip closed the door, then sat behind the desk. He knew one thing. He didn't want to spend another holiday without her. It was time to have a serious discussion, letting her know how he felt. Inviting her to his mother's open house was a perfect pretext.

After dialing her number, he settled back. When her phone rang for the fourth time, he pushed the red button to end the call.

He drummed his fingers on the glossy desktop, uncaring that his fingerprints marred the surface.

Through his life, he'd faced hundreds of obstacles. He'd gone over some, around others. When he had no other choice, he went through. And this time, that was exactly what he intended to do.

∼

Monday afternoon, Emma gathered her belongings and headed to the elevator. She wanted to go over the presentation for tomorrow's meeting without interruptions.

Near the elevator, Lori—the receptionist—raised a manila file in front of her face, using it to hide behind while spilling a secret. "Marjorie from the lobby just called up. Mr. Dettmer is in the building."

Emma's heart thudded to a complete halt.

The elevator light illuminated, and she exchanged a glance with Lori.

Then the carriage dinged its arrival. Emma was rooted to the spot as the doors slid open and Master Philip himself strode off, every bit as stunningly sexy as the first time she'd met him. Once again, he was dressed in a suit. He was clean-shaven, and his lightly graying hair was immaculately trimmed. His eyes were dark, cloaked with mystery, and he smelled of power and determination.

"Ah. Emma."

Though she moved her mouth, nothing emerged.

"I was looking for you."

Lori dropped her file folder and took forever to pick it up.

"As a courtesy, I wanted you to know I'm on my way to a meeting with Barry Larson."

Her boss. "I see." But she didn't, at all. Why would he be meeting with Mr. Larson the night before her presentation? *Oh God, I should not have ignored Philip's calls.*

"We'll be expecting you to join us." He checked his watch. "In about five minutes."

Since she couldn't find her voice, she settled for nodding.

In silence, she and Lori watched him go. Then, the moment he was out of earshot, Lori grabbed Emma's wrist. "You've been hiding something!"

She blushed. "We're simply trying to land him as a client. That's all."

"Not with the way you just turned scarlet." Lori offered her hand for a fist bump.

Wondering what the hell was going on, Emma returned to her office to collect her thoughts and gather her wits. It didn't work. Her mind was a jumble of confused thoughts, and the adrenaline chasing through her tummy made it impossible to even sit down.

Her desk phone rang. From Larson's extension.

"Ms. Monroe. If you could spare a moment?"

Wondering if she was going to be fired, she smoothed her skirt. Maybe she should have used her few minutes to begin packing a box.

She took her time walking down a hallway that she'd

never traversed before, and she arrived at a suite of offices that had a man sitting behind a counter.

"Ms. Monroe?"

When she nodded, he pointed toward a polished wood door that went all the way to the ceiling. "They're waiting for you. Go on in."

With nerveless fingers, she knocked, then entered.

Both men stood.

"You wanted to see me?"

"Please…" Larson smiled. "Have a seat." Across the desk, he sank into his massive leather chair.

She perched on the edge of hers, next to Philip, and she resisted the impulse to glance over at him.

"Mr. Dettmer is here today with some news. Would you like to tell her, Philip?"

"I've made a big financial decision."

Her heart sank. Trying to school her features, she pressed her lips together.

"I'll be transferring one of my accounts to Larson Financial."

"I beg your pardon?" Confused, she blinked. Her presentation wasn't until tomorrow morning. Yet he was here now to transfer some of his wealth to her firm, without hearing a pitch, and without involving her?

"I'll also be bringing along one of my sister's trust funds, and a couple of my mother's accounts."

"What?"

Mr. Larson nodded. "They'll all be under your management."

Her hands started to shake, and she linked them together in her lap in a hopeless attempt to keep them still. "I'm afraid I don't understand."

"Congratulations, Ms. Monroe. HR will be putting a promotion through for you immediately. We're very proud to have you at Larson, and your hard work will be rewarded."

Until today, the man hadn't even known who she was.

"You'll excuse us, Barry?" Philip's question couldn't be construed as anything other than a politely phrased order. "I'd like a minute alone with Ms. Monroe."

"That's highly—" Larson cleared his throat.

"Perhaps you could find us a bottle of champagne? I'm certain you keep some around for special occasions?"

"Of course." He loosened his tie then stood.

"A *very* nice bottle. Ms. Monroe deserves it."

When they were alone, she leaped from her chair and moved to the window to put some distance between them. "Look, Mr. Dettmer..."

He waited.

"Why are you doing this?

"Because it's the right thing. I had already decided to turn over management of some of my funds to you. The presentation was nothing more than a ploy. I was being a dick because I wanted more time with you...and I didn't come out and say that."

She wrapped her arms around herself.

"We have a lot to discuss. It's shitty of me to walk into your workplace. But..." He shrugged. "You wouldn't return my messages."

Her boss's office was not the right venue for this.

"Have dinner with me?"

His actions were over the top. Thrilling, exciting, overwhelming, the very same words that had defined their relationship. "I appreciate your trust in Larson—"

"In you."

"And me." She tipped her head to the side in acknowledgment. "But—"

He held up a hand. "One question, and only one."

"Okay." Time was ticking, and she had no idea when Mr. Larson would walk back into the room."

"Do you like me?"

Nothing could have surprised her more. "Do I...?"

"Like me?"

How was she supposed to answer that?

"My nosy sister seems to think you do."

At the absurdity, Emma laughed. "You're not unlikable."

"I'd hoped for a little more than that."

Keeping distance between them, she placed her hips on the air-conditioning unit. "I'm not sure where you're going with this."

"I love you." His words were broken and raw.

"What?" Unable to believe what she'd heard, she stood up straight.

"I couldn't figure out what the hell had gone wrong. And then I realized you want a family, and a husband. That wasn't our agreement, and when you tried to bring it up—at my house, by asking about kids—I shut you down."

"Did Diane tell you all that?"

"I figured out most of it on my own. How did I do?"

"Scarily accurate."

"You fell in love with me."

She narrowed her eyes. "You figured that out?"

"Actually, that part, Diane told me. She also said I am an idiot. And if I let you get away, I was a world-class jerk."

"Well..." Emma laughed.

"The truth is, I never planned to fall in love again. I was content with being an uncle. And then I lost you, and... It destroyed me, Emma. Please tell me you love me."

"I... *Yes.* But just being your playmate isn't enough for me."

"For me either. I want you to be mine, forever. My wife. My partner." He walked to her, tucked her hair behind her ear, then lowered himself to one knee as he pulled out an engagement ring with a ridiculously large diamond. "Emma Monroe, will you marry me?"

Marry you? Shockwaves of happiness ricocheted through her. "Yes. Yes. A million times, yes."

He slid the ring on to her finger and kissed her hand, and he was still kneeling when Mr. Larson walked back into his office carrying the requested bottle and three glasses.

Philip stood.

"It seems congratulations are in order all around." Larson found his equilibrium quickly and started twisting off the cage that held the cork in place.

"You don't mind if we take that to go, do you?" Philip plucked the green bottle from Larson's hand.

"Of course." He shrugged. "Of course."

Philip dropped his arm around her shoulder and led her from the room, sweeping her past the wide-open eyes of the admin, who reached for the phone. "Hey, Lori. You're not going to believe this…"

"Cressida's waiting."

He'd hired a car so they'd have more time together? "I need to grab my things."

They made a stop at her office. "I guess I don't need my presentation for tomorrow."

"I'm happy to listen, if you want me to."

"After all the work I went to, that might just happen." She grinned.

"We need to be someplace private, and soon." He nodded toward the window. "Otherwise, you may be the subject of more office gossip."

Pretending an interest in her stack of empty envelopes, Lori sauntered past Emma's office.

Shaking her head, Emma picked up her purse before once again turning off the light. "I'm ready." She almost added *Sir*, but if she had, any resistance she had to his charms would completely crumble.

Outside, she accepted Cressida's warm congratulations. "I couldn't be happier for you, Ms. Monroe."

"Emma. Please."

Once they were in the back of the sedan, Philip popped the cork. Sipping on the bubbly, Emma faced her future husband. "You thought through every detail."

"With some optimism, and a fair amount of fear. I don't want another moment of my life to pass without you in it."

"All that time alone?" Since he was admitting painful things, she decided to as well. "I was miserable."

"Emma, without you, I was broken."

Her heart hurt for him, and for what they'd both almost missed out on.

"Let's go home."

Home.

He pulled her against him, kissed her deeply, then whispered his promise for the future. "How long do you want to wait before trying to start a family?"

She pretended to consider, but she was actually doing a careful mathematical calculation. "About twenty-five minutes."

His eyes flared. "Make it twenty."

"You're on. Sir."

He claimed her mouth and sealed their love for eternity. Which was almost long enough.

EPILOGUE

Emma took a final look around her little house. All the remaining boxes were stacked in the living room, awaiting tomorrow's movers.

Since the day Philip had proposed to her at work just over two weeks prior, things had moved fast. He'd insisted he didn't want to spend a single night without her. So every evening after work, she returned home to pack a few boxes. When he finished up his daily appointments, Philip came over to help.

Yesterday, a moving company had taken her furniture to a storage unit, and Philip's friend John Thoroughgood had listed her house for rent. Philip had encouraged her to sell it and keep the money, but after the terrible experience with Aaron, she wanted to hold on to her house for a little bit longer.

"I support whatever you want." Which was something he said often. "But this relationship is forever."

To her, that didn't matter. She intended to take her time and make the financial decisions that were in her best interest.

"You should start a blog or podcast that focuses on finances for women."

"I'm not sure I have that much to say."

"Let's have a professional decide that." He picked up his phone.

"Who are you calling?"

"Jaxon Mills."

"Wait. *The* Jaxon Mills?" The world-renowned internet marketer?

"I'm sure he can get you on as a special guest."

"You know him?" She shook her head. Well, obviously, if he was going to make a phone call, her fiancé clearly knew the man. "Wait. Let me guess. He's a Titan."

"I can neither confirm nor deny that."

Emma sighed. "Are you going to keep that whole thing secret forever?"

"I'll be able to tell you more after we're married."

"Is that supposed to be an enticement?"

"Will it work?" He grinned.

Jaxon agreed to talk to her after the first of the year, and together they would decide whether or not she wanted to appear on his show.

And as she looked around—getting ready to say goodbye to her old life—the idea of helping other women through this kind of change held great appeal for her.

Her phone chimed.

Your fantasies await. Be prepared.

She shivered. Most evenings, he took her up to his secret room. He explored her, learned about her responses, and she trusted him more and more. Last weekend, he'd vowed he would soon fulfill her kidnapping fantasy, the thing she'd been afraid to confess to anyone else.

How soon are you leaving?

On my way. It was funny how quickly she'd adapted to living with him. She looked forward to going home and having Tibby greet her, excitedly dancing around her feet when she walked through the front door.

She grabbed her purse and keys, then drove away without a backward glance.

Shocking her, her fiancé's house was dark. His car was in the driveway, which meant he was home. Maybe he'd taken Tibby for a walk?

Emma inserted her key in the lock, then opened the front door. After closing it behind her, she flipped on a light only to have a strong, forceful hand clamped over her mouth as she was drawn backward against a strong, hard body.

"You're mine, Emma. You will give me everything I demand."

Master Philip. Desire and adrenaline pummeled her as he forced a gag into her mouth.

"Your fantasies await. Be prepared."

Against his superior size and muscles, her struggles were ineffective.

He tossed her over his shoulder and effortlessly carried her up the stairs, despite the fact that she kicked wildly.

"Enough, lass." He landed a firm palm on her ass.

Instead of walking up to the third floor, he entered one of the guest bedrooms. Sometime, without her knowing it, he'd replaced the headboard and footboard with an ornate metal one. And cuffs were attached in several different places.

Overwhelmed by the lengths he was willing to go to please her, she gave herself over to the experience.

She thrashed and fought to get away, but he quickly subdued her, straddling her body and wrestling her wrists into the waiting bonds.

"You can't escape." He unfastened her jeans and stripped them off her, removing her panties at the same time. Then he secured her ankles.

He approached her again, carrying a pair of safety scissors, and she was suddenly grateful she hadn't worn any of her beautiful lingerie. It took him mere moments to have her bared to him.

"Who's your lord and master?"

She met his gaze and shook her head. The gag prevented her from actually talking, but she had no problem communicating the fact that she wouldn't yield.

"So that's how it's going to be, is it, lass?" He walked from the foot of the bed around the side to stand next to her.

Eyes wide, she tracked his movements. Just like the first night they had played together at the Quarter, he wore a snow-white shirt that was tucked into casual black slacks. He totally was a pirate of her fantasies. She had never been more turned on.

"I have ways of making you admit who you belong to."

If he took her right this moment, she would climax instantly.

"You're beautiful when you are helpless." He sat on the edge of the bed, and she inhaled the sharp scent of danger and desire.

Slowly, he traced a finger up the inside of her thigh.

Though she tried to remain still, she instinctively lifted her hips in silent invitation.

With a short laugh, he left her, keeping his back to her so she couldn't see what he was doing.

A small hum filled the room, and he walked toward her carrying the U-shaped vibrator that he'd used on her at the Quarter and several times since. Already she knew that meant he intended to push her very limits.

He inserted the toy and adjusted the fit before setting the control so that the end riding on her clit would pulse periodically.

Next he played with her breasts, cupping them, massaging them, drawing them together, sucking on her nipples until they hardened into pouty, begging peaks. Then, making her gasp, he clamped each nipple with a clover. These weren't the most awful pair he owned, but if he tugged lightly on the chain connecting them, they would tighten.

Even as the bite seared her, he used the remote control to turn up the intensity of the vibrator, making it shake a little harder, edging her on.

"I want you on your belly. You're going to behave for me, aren't you?"

In a normal scene she would do exactly as he told her, but this was no ordinary scene. Hoping to convey an obedience she didn't feel, she nodded.

"That's a perfect little captive." He unfastened her wrists, and she remained frozen in her spot.

When he released her legs, she acted, scrambling off the bed, whimpering as the clamps swayed. The vibrator dislodged and fell to the floor with an awful clatter.

"I was hoping you'd do that." With an evil laugh, her Dominant scooped her up and tossed her down onto her stomach, forcing the breath out of her.

The clamps pulled awfully on her nipples, and she loved every moment of it.

"Fight all you want." He secured one of her ankles, immediately restricting her range of motion.

In less than twenty seconds, he had the rest of her body captured in his cuffs. "Since you can't behave, my naughty little captive, I'm afraid I'm going to have to teach you a lesson."

She turned her head to the side so she could look at him.

"And without the vibrator to distract you."

Now she was regretting her actions...somewhat.

"A cat-o'-nine tails was made for a damsel such as you." He shook out a small whip that had nine strands, each with a leather rosebud at the end.

This was something they hadn't played with before, and he must have bought it especially for this evening. The thing actually did scare her a little bit.

Her tormentor didn't release the gag as she anticipated. But he offered her a bright-yellow scarf.

"Hold this. It's your safe signal. If you drop it, the scene will end."

She nodded. Of course he would see to her comfort while still allowing her to enjoy her fantasy.

"Now, make this easy on yourself. All you have to do is tell me you're mine."

Again she shook her head.

"Then you leave me no choice." He pressed one of the buds against her clit. When she didn't respond, he exerted more pressure.

Her bundle of nerves exploded, and she gasped, wanting more.

"Gyrate your hips. Show me how naughty you are."

Though the bindings restricted her motions, Emma did as

he said. And each little movement pulled on her nipples. Her entire body was now on fire.

"Say whatever you want. But your body tells the truth."

She choked on a sob, completely giving herself over to the moment. Now more than ever, she was grateful she'd found him. He allowed her to express all of who she was, and the more honest she was, the more real, the more vulnerable, the more he seemed to love her.

"You've got a greedy little pussy, don't you? He fisted his hand into her hair. "Don't you?"

Helplessly she nodded.

"Nine lashes for you, my lovely…for not admitting you're mine."

No doubt the whip could be wielded to torment, but he didn't use a full swing. Instead, each spank fell against the fleshiest part of her buttocks with a rough, thuddy sting, bringing her carnal delight.

Even at that, by the time it had landed eight times, she wished the vibrator was still inside her. No doubt she'd be in the midst of a second or third orgasm by now.

"One more. Where would you like it?"

Since she was still gagged, she couldn't answer. Not that it would have mattered. She knew him well enough to know his question was rhetorical.

"Ready?"

She shook her head.

Master Philip placed the stroke between her legs. Gasping, she arched her body in response to the quick burn. Of course he'd spanked her pussy—that was the very first request she'd ever made of him. Could he be any more perfect?

He tossed aside the beautiful whip and seated the vibrator back inside her.

"No orgasming until I give you permission. And stay where you are."

Grateful for the scene, for him, she remained in place as he released all her bonds. Then he gently turned her over, taking care with the clamps.

"Now, little captive. *Now*. Tell me you're mine."

Tears stinging her eyes, she nodded.

With a triumphant grin, he unfastened her gag and removed it from her mouth. Then he eased the toy from her needy pussy.

"I'm yours. Forever. And ever."

After turning off the vibrator, he rubbed her muscles, working out the tension that had held them immobile while she was bound, and then he stripped off his clothes. "Spread your legs for me."

Finally. He knelt between her thighs.

Her fantasy was complete, and she needed him.

Determination glinted in his eyes, and a shiver rocked her as he slid his cockhead into her heated pussy.

"Wrap your legs around my waist. Take what I give you."

"Yes, Sir." With a sigh, she followed his order, taking, welcoming him, screaming his name when he was balls-deep.

He pulled out, then stroked in with short, shallow moves, driving her crazy. "Sir!"

"Do you want more?"

"Yes! Everything." She gulped, hanging on to his shoulders. "I want everything."

He fucked her hard and long, until her world blurred. Nothing existed but them, moving, breathing together, becoming one.

"Now, Emma. Give me your orgasm. Do it *now*."

His guttural command was the final thing she needed, and a powerful orgasm ripped through her.

"And now, take me."

He plowed in hard, claiming her; then a minute later, he changed the pace until it was lovemaking, pure and beautiful.

When he cried out her name, coming deep inside her, she kissed him repeatedly, declaring her love.

Finally, when he was spent, Philip rolled to the side to pull her into his arms. "Welcome home, Emma."

"That was…something, Sir."

"I wanted this evening to be memorable." He smoothed back her hair.

"I'll never forget it."

"You make me the happiest man in the world. I love you, my beautiful little captive, my Emma."

She snuggled into him, something she was beginning to enjoy. As he brushed her hair aside, she placed her palm on his chest. "And I love you." He was definitely her Prince Charming.

"You're going to be the most beautiful bride ever. And the sooner the better."

"There's nothing I want more."

"Let's get started on our future."

"Now?" Her voice squeaked. "Again?"

"Oh yes." He moved quickly, and within seconds, he had her wrists pinned to the mattress above her head.

His eyes darkened. First he claimed her mouth, then her body. "I'm never letting you go."

"And I swear, I am yours. Always and forever." She smoothed her hand through his hair. "Sir."

◊ ◊ ◊ ◊ ◊

Thank you for reading His to Cherish. I hope you loved Emma and Philip's story. You may not believe it, but the set-up for this story was based on a real-life experience I had with a very interesting Dominant! From the beginning, I found Philip to be enigmatic and deep, and it took some excavating to uncover his secrets in order to find a way to help him love again. He is one of my favorite and most interesting heroes.

You can enjoy Victorian Night at the Quarter in **Meant For Me**, one of my Hawkeye books. For the men of Hawkeye, the line of duty between bodyguard and client isn't meant to be crossed..

As his trainee, Mira was far too young and much too innocent for Torin's carnal demands. And now she's been assigned as his partner, placing her firmly in the forbidden category.

Even though she hated him for pushing her so hard during training, Mira has always been attracted to the older, sexy-as-sin Hawkeye commander. As danger engulfs them, Mira is a temptation Torin can't resist.

DISCOVER MEANT FOR ME

If you love contemporary billionaire Titans who are smoking hot, be sure to check out the world's most **Scandalous Billionaire**.

Lizzie has tempted Braden for years, but she wasn't just off-limits--she was forbidden. Now she's standing in his closet, holding his red tie, while his mind races with indecent thoughts.

More than a billionaire, he's different than she remembers--haunted by secrets that have hardened his soul.

★★★★★ "You'll need oven mitts to hold on to it because it's so hot!" ~Knotty Girl Reviews

★★★★★ "The story was amazing—sensual and just off the charts." ~Amazon Review

DISCOVER SCANDALOUS BILLIONAIRE

Continue reading for an exciting excerpt from MEANT FOR ME

MEANT FOR ME EXCERPT

"What do you think?"

From his place on the raised platform that had once served as a fire outlook post, Torin Carter glanced at Hawkeye, his boss and mentor. The man owned the security firm Torin worked for, as well as this eight-hundred-acre outpost in the remote part of the West. "Think of what? The class?"

Six times a year, recruits new to the VIP protection program cycled through the Aiken Training Facility. It wasn't Torin's job to get them through. It was his job to make sure that everyone, except the very best, washed out.

"That recruit in specific. Going through the bog." Aviator glasses shaded Hawkeye's eyes as well as his thoughts.

"Mira Araceli?" Torin asked.

"That's the one."

Carrying a thirty-pound pack, face smeared with mud, her training uniform soaked, Mira Araceli dashed at full-out speed toward the next obstacle. She grabbed the rope and began to pull herself up the ten-foot wall as if she hadn't just navigated a killer course designed to destroy her energy reserves.

Today, her long-black hair with its deep fiery highlights was not only in a ponytail, it was tucked inside her jacket. She concentrated on the task in front of her, never looking away from her goal.

Torin had been running the training program for several years. During that time, only a few recruits stood out. "She's…" He searched for words to convey his conflict. Brave. Relentless. Driven, by something she'd never talked about during the admission process.

On a couple of occasions, he'd studied her file. Hawkeye's comprehensive background check had turned up nothing out of the ordinary. Youngest of three kids. Her father was a congressman and former military. Both of her brothers had followed his legacy—and expectations?—into the service.

Araceli's academic scores were excellent. She'd graduated in the top of her college class but had opted not to put her skills to use in a safe corporate environment. Instead, she'd applied to be part of Hawkeye Security, even though she knew the scope of their work, from protecting people and things, to operating in some of the most difficult places on the planet. *Why does she want to put her life at risk?*

Fuck. Why did anyone?

Hawkeye cleared his throat.

Torin glanced back at his boss. "She's one of the most determined I've ever seen. Works harder than anyone. Longer hours." Yesterday he'd hit the gym at five a.m. She was already there, wearing a sports bra beneath a sheer gray tank top. Rather than workout pants, she opted for formfitting shorts that showed off her toned legs and well-formed rear. They exchanged polite greetings, and she'd wandered over to be his spotter for his bench presses, then offered a hand up when he was done.

He shouldn't have accepted. But he had. A sensation, dormant for years, had sparked. Raw sexual attraction for Mira Araceli had shot straight to his cock, a violation of his personal ethics.

She hadn't pulled away like she should have. Her palms were callused, and so much smaller than his. Torin was smart enough to recognize her danger, though. He'd honed her strength himself. She would have him flat on his back anytime she wanted.

In the distance, a door slammed, and they moved away from each other. From across the room, he saw her looking at her hand.

No doubt she'd experienced the same electric pulse as he did.

Since that morning, he'd been damn sure she wasn't in the gym before he entered. Relationships among Hawkeye operatives weren't expressly forbidden. Hawkeye was smart enough to know that close quarters, adrenaline, fear, and survival instincts were a powerful cocktail. But the relationship between a recruit and instructors was sacred.

Having sex with Araceli wouldn't just be stupid—it would border on insane.

In addition to the fact that he was responsible for her safety, Araceli was far too young for his carnal demands. And it wasn't just in terms of age. Life had dealt him a vicious blow, leaving parts of him in jagged pieces.

He no longer even pretended to be relationship material.

When he could, he went to a BDSM club. There, he found women who wanted the same things he did. Extreme. Extreme enough to round the edges off the memories, the past.

There was no way he would subject a recruit to the danger that he represented, even if she was tempting as hell.

Hawkeye was still waiting, and Torin settled for a nonanswer. "Her potential is unlimited."

"But?" Hawkeye folded his arms. Despite the thirty-seven-degree temperature, he'd skipped a coat and opted for a sweatshirt to go with his customary black khakis. Combined with his aviator glasses and black ball cap embroidered with the Hawkeye logo, the company owner was incognito.

Torin looked at her again. "She does best in situations where she is by herself." And that wasn't how Hawkeye Security operated. They believed no person was better alone than as part of a team. Certainly there were times when an agent had no backup and was left with no choice but to take individual action. But the ability to work with others was crucial to success.

"What do you think of her chances?"

Torin shrugged. When she first joined Hawkeye a year ago, she'd trained at the Tactical Operations Center. She could pump thirty-seven out of forty shots into a target's heart and was first through the door during hostage rescue exercises. Though she'd excelled, she took unnecessary risks. At times, she calculatingly ignored superiors' commands. So far it had worked well for her, much to the annoyance of her numerous instructors.

On her application to the program that Torin headed, she'd indicated she had too much downtime during her assignments. She wanted something more demanding. VIP protection could provide that. If she made it.

Araceli summited a second wall, then leaped off and kept moving, dropping down to crawl through a tunnel, then back up to navigate the ridiculously tough agility course.

Hawkeye watched her progress. "There's something about her."

At the end of the course, she doubled over to catch her

breath; then she checked her time on a fitness watch. Only then did she shrug off the pack.

"Lots of potential," Torin agreed.

"Either hone it or get her out of here." Hawkeye adjusted his ball cap. "They'd be glad to have her back in tactical. And with her IQ scores, she'd do well in a support role. Strategy."

She was a little young for that.

Then again, age wasn't always a factor. He knew that more than most.

"You doing okay?" Hawkeye asked.

Torin twitched. "It's easier."

In his usual way, Hawkeye remained silent, letting time and tension stretch, waiting.

"I think about it every day." Dreams. Nightmares. Second-guessing himself, his reactions, replaying it and never changing the outcome.

"You've accumulated plenty of time off."

"I'd rather work."

"Understood."

Torin and Hawkeye watched a couple more recruits finish the course. Results were fed through to his high-tech tablet. Not surprisingly, Mira had finished in the top three.

In the distance, an old bus lumbered toward them, spewing a cloud of dirt in its wake.

Turning his head to watch it, Hawkeye asked, "You heading to Aiken Junction?"

"Yeah." Torin grinned. Drills in the mock town were one of his favorite parts of being an instructor. And he fully intended to use the opportunity to be sure Araceli learned a valuable lesson. "Want to join us?"

"If I had time." Hawkeye sighed. "Another damn dinner. Another damn meeting with a multinational company." Hawkeye wasn't just the founder and owner of the security firm—he was their best performing salesperson. "And I'm going to get the account."

"Never doubted you, boss."

Hawkeye clapped Torin on the shoulder. "I've taken enough of your day."

After nodding, Torin descended the steps, then jogged over to the finish line where recruits were talking, drinking water, dreaming about a beer or the hot tub. "Listen up!"

Talking ceased.

"You're responsible for protecting the family of an important diplomat. Their youngest daughter is seventeen and just slipped her security detail. And you're going to get her back."

There were groans and resigned sighs. The group had hit the running track at six a.m., had hours of classroom instruction, missed lunch, and been timed on their run through the mud challenge. And their day was just beginning.

He pointed to the approaching vehicle. "Gear up."

Exhausted recruits picked up the packs they'd just shucked.

"The bus will stop for ninety seconds. If you're not on it, you'll be hiking to Aiken Junction."

Mira grabbed a protein bar from her bag then slung it over one shoulder. She made sure she was first on the bus and moved to a seat farthest in the back.

Torin jumped on as the driver dropped the transmission into gear. While others had doubled up and were chatting, Araceli leaned forward and draped a T-shirt over her head. Smart. She was taking time to recover mentally and physically.

"Here's the drill." He stood at the top of the stairwell, holding on to a pole as the ancient vehicle hit every damn rock and pothole, jarring his jaw. "The tattoo parlor denied her because she's underage, and the artist we interviewed said he saw her move over to Thump, the nightclub next to

Bones." The name of their fictitious high-end steakhouse. "She has a fake ID, so it's possible she got past security. Her daddy wants her home, and wants her safe. This isn't the first time she's slipped her detail. You'll stage at the church. Choose a team leader and make a plan. Any questions?"

Most people lapsed into silence, a few engaged in banter and trash talk, and he took a seat behind the driver.

A mind-numbing thirty minutes later, the bus churned through Hell's Acre, the seedy area of town, then crossed the fake railroad tracks that separated the sleazy area of town from the more respectable suburban setting.

The driver braked to a grinding halt in front of the clapboard All Saints Church.

"Not so fast," Torin said when the recruits began to stand. "This isn't your stop."

He jogged down the steps to the sidewalk, and the driver pulled the lever to shut the door, then hit the accelerator fast enough to cause the occupants some whiplash—good training for real-life evasive driving. The recruits would be taken around the town several times in order to give Torin and the role-players time to set up.

Once the bus disappeared from view, he pulled open the door to the restaurant and entered the dining room where he greeted fellow instructors. "Who's playing our principal?"

"That's me, Commander." Charlotte Bixby—four feet eleven, ninety-two pounds, and ferocious as a man twice her size—waved from the back of the room. She wore a black dress and flats that would give her some maneuverability.

"And your gentlemen friends?"

Two agents raised their hands.

Torin went through the rest of the roles, couples, bartenders, cocktail servers, DJ Asylum, partiers on the dance floor. All in all, over two dozen people were assigned to the scene. "Okay, people! Let's head over."

Twenty minutes later, music blared. Charlotte was seated in a booth attached to the far wall. She was wedged between two solid men, a cocktail in front of her. The dance floor in the center of the room was filled with gyrating couples, servers moved around the room, and a bartender was drawing a beer. The surveillance room was being manned by one of the instructors, and he was wearing a polo shirt that identified him as one of Thump's security team. The bouncer, nicknamed Bear, was dressed similarly, but wearing a jacket that emphasized his broad shoulders and beefy biceps. Arms folded, Torin stood behind Bear.

Since a cold front was moving through and the temperature had dropped to just above freezing, a coat check had been set up near the front door, close to the restrooms.

Everything was in place.

A role player sashayed through the front door and gave Bear a once-over and an inviting smile. That didn't stop him from scrutinizing her ID.

"Enjoy your evening, Miss."

After snatching her ID back, she breezed past them and headed straight for the bar.

Several more people entered, and none of them were Hawkeye recruits. Hopefully that meant they were still strategizing. He preferred that to seeing them head in without a plan...like they had last time they ran a similar drill.

He checked his watch.

Fifteen minutes.

Then thirty.

Charlotte was on her second cocktail.

An hour.

Torin left the door to grab a beer at the bar. Then he carried it to the side of the room and stood at a tall round table.

DJ Asylum turned on pulsing colored strobe lights and cranked up the music. The walls echoed from the bass. People shouted to be heard.

Exactly like an ordinary bar in Anytown, USA.

One of Charlotte's companions signaled for another drink and then draped that arm across her back. She leaned into him.

Within minutes, Araceli strolled in. Her face was clean, and she'd changed into clean clothes—obviously they'd been in her backpack, along with a shiny headband. Nothing could hide her combat boots, though.

Life wasn't a series of perfect opportunities. Blending in mattered, but speed was critical. It did mean that the role players had an advantage, though.

Along with a fellow trainee, Araceli found a table. Instead of waiting for a cocktail waitress, she headed to the bar. She scanned the occupants, saw him, gave no acknowledgment that they'd ever met.

Yeah. Hawkeye was right. She was damn good.

She secured two drinks, then, instead of heading back to the table, walked to the far end of the room and began a search for their principal.

Smart. She wouldn't approach right away, she'd make sweep, assess the situation, all the while looking as if she fit in.

Except for those ridiculous combat boots.

Under the flashing lights, he lost her. Until her headband winked in the light.

He checked out the other recruits and their strategies. Two of them—women—looped arms like besties and pretended to look for men.

DJ Asylum's voice boomed through the room, distorted by some sort of synthesizer. "Get on the floor and show me your moves!"

One of the trainers walked to the table where Charlotte sat and whispered into the ear of the man with his arm draped over her shoulder.

Araceli put down her drink.

The companion nodded and moved his arm to reach into his pocket. Money exchanged hands.

The second guy slid off his seat, effectively blocking the pathway to the booth.

The man Charlotte was cozying up to led her to the dance floor. Araceli stood, looked around for a male agent, grabbed him, then pulled him toward the other couple.

Moments later, fog spilled from machines, clouding the air.

Lights went out, and the music stopped so abruptly that it seemed to thunder off the still-pulsating walls.

It took a few seconds for emergency lighting to kick on. When it did, the fog was thick and surreal, and Charlotte and her dance partner were gone.

Araceli headed toward the exit and shoved her way past Bear and out of the building.

Torin strolled toward the coatroom. He pushed the door most of the way closed, leaving a crack so he could watch the front door.

Moments later, Araceli hurried back in, her winking headband all but a neon sign indicating her position. He eased the door open, then, as she started past, reached out, grabbed her, pulled her in, and caught her in a rear hold, an elbow under her chin, his right arm beneath her breasts.

She was breathing hard, but she grabbed his forearms to try to break free. In response, he tightened the hold to ward off an elbow jab. And he leaned her forward to prevent one of her vicious, calculated stomps. "Knock it off, Araceli," he growled into her ear.

"Commander Carter?" She froze. "It's dark. How did you know it was me?"

"Your headband."

"Shit."

"That's right. You lose." He loosened his grip slightly, but she kept her hands in place. "Your target is gone."

With a deep, frustrated sigh, she tipped her head back, resting it on his chest. And he noticed her. The way she fit with him, and how she trusted him, despite her annoyance at having been bested. And even the way she smelled...wildflowers and innocence, despite the grueling ordeal earlier today. He wanted to reassure her, let her know how proud he was of her efforts.

Jesus. Immediately he released her. He'd held her longer than he need to. Longer than he should have. "Go to Bones. I'll meet you there." Torin took a step back, literal as well as mental.

In the near dark, she faced him. "But I can—"

"Go. I'm one of the bad guys, Araceli." And not just for the role-playing scenario. He was no good for her. "I took you out of the game. You never even noticed me. You didn't make a plan. You rushed forward without assessing the situation. You failed."

After a few seconds of hesitation, she nodded. "It will be the last time, Commander Carter. You underestimate me and my capabilities."

Something he didn't want to name snaked through him.

She had to be talking about the job, nothing more. Araceli couldn't know about his inner turmoil and his dark attraction to her.

Alone in the dark, Torin balled his hand into a fist over and over, opening, closing. Opening. Closing.

By far, Mira Araceli was the most dangerous student he'd ever had.

"You all right, Mira?"

For three years, six months, and twelve days, Torin Carter had haunted Mira Araceli's days and teased her nights.

Jonathan, the personal trainer she worked with when she was staying in New Orleans, snapped his fingers in front of her face. "Mira?"

His proximity, along with the sharp sound, finally broke through her runaway thoughts, and she shook head to clear it of the distraction that was her former Hawkeye instructor.

What the hell was wrong with her? She shouldn't have checked out mentally, even for a fraction of a second. In the wrong circumstances, it could mean the difference between survival and death. "Sorry." With a smile meant to be reassuring, she met his eyes.

For most of her life, she'd practiced yoga. Five years ago, she'd learned to meditate. Yet when it came to Torin, she never remembered to use her skills.

"Something on your mind?"

"Was. There was. I'm good to go now." She was almost done with the final set—squatting over two hundred pounds. She could do this. *Right?* In a couple of minutes, she'd be out of here and headed for the house where she would spend the next nine weeks living with her nemesis.

How the hell had this even happened? Hawkeye required all instructors—even the head of the program—to spend time in the field to keep their skills sharp. But for them to be assigned to the same team...?

"Ready?" Jonathan asked. "You have three more reps."

With single-minded focus, she tucked way thoughts of her demanding and mysterious former instructor.

Jonathan scowled. "You sure everything's okay?"

She got in position, adjusted her grip, then took a breath.

"Hold up." He nudged one of her feet.

"Thanks." After executing the squat, watching her form,

breathing correctly, she racked the bar and stepped away. No matter what she wanted to believe, thoughts of Torin had wormed past her defenses to dominate her thoughts. "I'm calling it."

Jonathan nodded. "Good plan." He checked his clipboard. "See you back the day after tomorrow?"

"Six a.m. I won't miss it." She grabbed her water bottle, took a swig, then headed for the locker room. This was the first time in her adult life that she'd cut a workout short.

Mira showered, then took longer than normal with her makeup. Long enough to piss her off. Frustrated, she shoved the cap back onto her lipstick and dropped it in her bag.

Even though she routinely had male partners, she wasn't in the habit of primping. Of course, she'd never had an all-consuming attraction to one of them before.

Torin Carter wasn't just gorgeous. As her VIP Protective Services instructor, he'd been tougher on her than anyone ever had been, demanding her very best, harshly grading her work. It was his job to make her a stellar agent or cut her from the program. He hadn't known that failure was never a possibility.

During her training, he'd never shown anything beyond a hard-ass, impersonal interaction toward her. Except for that night at Thump.

When he'd caught her in that choke hold, she'd struggled, elbowing him, attempting to stomp on his foot. His commanding voice had subdued her, and when she stopped struggling, she noticed his arms around her.

Even though he loosened his hold, Torin didn't release her right away like other instructors had. And in a reaction that was wholly unlike her, she tipped her head back and relaxed into him, seeking comfort, a brief respite from the relentless and grueling training exercises. For a moment, she forgot about her job, stopped noticing the fog and pandemonium around them.

She thought—maybe—that he experienced an echoing flare, but he pushed her away, with a harsh indictment of her skills.

Drowning in rejection and embarrassment, she squared her shoulders and locked away her ridiculous unrequited emotions and vowed never to examine them again.

Even though she'd graduated years ago and hadn't heard his name since, he was never far away. Frustratingly, she thought of him every time she went out on a date. It was as if her subconscious was weighing and measuring all men against him.

The comparisons even happened when she scened at a BDSM club.

Torin was everything she wanted a Dom to be—uncompromising, strong, intelligent…and, at the right time, reassuring. In his arms, in that coatroom, she'd discovered he was capable of tenderness. Maybe if she'd only seen him be an ass, he would have been easier to forget.

Surviving Torin might be her greatest test ever.

Mira dragged her hair back over her shoulder and stared at herself in the mirror. "You." She pointed at her reflection. "You're smarter this time. Wiser. More in control."

A blonde emerged from one of the shower stalls. "Man problems?"

Embarrassed, Mira lifted a shoulder. She hadn't realized her words would be overheard.

"Isn't it always?" the woman asked.

For other people, not her. "That's the thing. It never has been until now."

"I see you here all the time. You're tough. Whatever it is, you can handle it."

Mira hoped so. She smiled at the other woman. "Thank

you. I needed that pep talk." After blotting her lipstick, she gathered her belongings, exited the gym, then strode across the parking lot to her car.

She and Torin were scheduled to rendezvous at seven p.m. at Hawkeye's mansion in the Garden District. Since it was equipped with modern security both inside and out, he preferred his high-value clients utilize it when they visited NOLA. In addition to eight bedrooms, there was a spacious carriage house apartment for use by security personnel.

The grounds were spectacular, with a large outdoor swimming pool, a concrete courtyard with plenty of lounge chairs, tables, and umbrellas. Potted plants provided splashes of color, while numerous trees offered privacy as well as shade.

She'd stayed on the property several times, including earlier this year for Mardi Gras while she was working the detail for an A-list actor. She planned to arrive before Torin so she could select her bedroom, get settled, have the upper hand. Any advantage, no matter how small, was a necessity.

Since it was still early afternoon, she managed the traffic with only the usual snarls.

After passing the biometric security system at the gate, she drove onto the property.

More confident now, she grabbed her gear, then jogged up the stairs to enter the code on the keypad. A moment later, the lock turned, and she opened the door.

Torin stood in the middle of the main living space, arms folded, damn biceps bulging. His rakishly long black hair was damp, and the atmosphere sizzled with his scent, that of crisp moonlit nights. He swept his gaze over her, and it took all her concentration to remain in place as he assessed her with his shockingly blue eyes.

When he tipped his head to the side, reaction flooded her. Her knees wobbled, and she dropped her duffel bag off her shoulder and lowered her gear to the hardwood floor to disguise her too-real, too-feminine reaction.

"I won't bite." His grin was quick and lethal.

Damn him. Part of her wished he would. It might help get rid of the tension crawling through her so she could move on, forget him. There was no way any man could be as hot as she believed he would be. Was there?

Read more of Meant For Me.

ABOUT THE AUTHOR

I invite you to be the very first to know all the news by subscribing to my very special VIP Reader newsletter! You'll find exclusive excerpts, bonus reads, and insider information.

https://www.sierracartwright.com/subscribe

For tons of fun and to meet other awesome people like you, join my Facebook reader group, Sierra's Super Stars.

https://www.facebook.com/groups/SierrasSuperStars

And for a current booklist, please visit my website.

http://www.sierracartwright.com

USA Today bestselling author Sierra Cartwright was born in England, and she spent her early childhood traipsing through castles and dreaming of happily-ever afters. She has two wonderful kids and four amazing grand-kitties. She now calls Galveston, Texas home and loves to connect with her readers. Please do drop her a note.

facebook.com/SierraCartwrightOfficial
instagram.com/sierracartwrightauthor
bookbub.com/authors/sierra-cartwright

ALSO BY SIERRA CARTWRIGHT

Titans

Sexiest Billionaire

Billionaire's Matchmaker

Billionaire's Christmas

Determined Billionaire

Scandalous Billionaire

Ruthless Billionaire

Titans Quarter

His to Claim

His to Love

His to Cherish

Titans Sin City

Hard Hand

Slow Burn

All-In

Hawkeye

Come to Me

Trust in Me

Meant For Me

Hold On To Me

Believe in Me

Bonds

Crave

Claim

Donovan Dynasty

Bind

Brand

Boss

Mastered

With This Collar

On His Terms

Over The Line

In His Cuffs

For The Sub

In The Den

Printed in Great Britain
by Amazon